Also by Jessi Thind

Lions of the Sea
Saragarhi
The Singer, The Player, The Bard and his Dragon

978-1-927028-05-6

"The beginning, the end: all the world's roads, all the outcries of mankind, lead to this accursed place. Here is the kingdom of night, where God's face is hidden and a flaming sky becomes a graveyard for a vanished people."

Elie Wiesel, "Pilgrimage to the Kingdom of Night"

For those who disappeared
For those who didn't
For those who want to remember
And for those who don't

For those who keep the memory alive
Pursuing justice any way they know how--
Planting trees, singing songs, writing books
Making movies, painting murals, throwing shoes

For those who roar against oppression
Wherever oppression sticks its ugly demon head
And for those who refuse to bow down
And vanish into the 'Kingdom of Night'

CB

The boy surged through the crowded street. The street was narrow and calm in the early morning and only a faint ambrosial light poured down from the clear blue sky and bounced and spread over the flat roofs of the small pucca homes of the Trilokpuri resettlement colony. From inside the huddled homes the morning prayers had begun and the rhythmic hymns rose and swirled and drifted gently out of the barred windows and dusty wooden doors, filling the colony with the words of the last and only Sikh Guru embodied in the Sri Guru Granth Sahib.

In one ear and--

Out the other.

The boy took in the muffled words without thinking about them.

He had heard these words countless times before. He had heard them every day for the last seven years of his young life and this morning was like any other morning; only this morning he was running away from his home, and this morning he would not be joining his parents in Japji, the very first prayer of the Sri Guru Granth Sahib, recited every morning with reverence and devotion by practicing Sikhs.

Jessi Thind

In the ambrosial hour of the morning
Meditate on the True Name and
The Almighty's Greatness
By God's Grace is acquired
The vesture of human life
And by God's Grace
We obtain salvation from egoism

The boy listened to the words and thought:

God. You've taken my brother from me and now
you are taking my mother, too. Why? What have I done
in this life or the last to deserve such a thing?

The boy ran to the end of the narrow street and turned the corner. He leaped out of the way and evaded buckets and trash and crates. Then he turned another corner and another as he navigated his way through a tangle of uneven cement streets, rushing through an endless jungle of growing light and shrinking shadow, his mouth moving with the words coming at him from every angle of the colony as he passed home after home.

The boy bolted by one home as a hoarse male voice--almost as deep as his grandmother's-- began the prayers. The boy repeated:

God is One
Whose Name is Truth

Lips forming the words, he approached another home and a young girl's voice greeted his ears and was a little further in the prayer; the boy recognized the voice, smiled and repeated:

Beyond this earth there are other worlds,
More and more
Which is the power
That sustains their weight?

A Feast for Lambs

And as he rushed down the alley her words faded into morning din and merged with all the other words and sounded to him like the distant humming and churning of the sea. He finished:

The names of living creatures,
Their species and colors
Have all been written
With God's flowing pen

Passing another home, he almost froze in his tracks when he heard his mother's favorite phrases unexpectedly come to him like an omen or message from another realm; and he thought, for a moment, just a moment, it would be wise to return home. He repeated:

By Word we write and utter holy hymns
By Word is recorded our destiny

But the boy didn't return home, and he wasn't so wise. He continued under his breath:

We do not become sinners and saints
Merely by words
It is our actions that are recorded
For hereafter

Somewhere in the distance a cow mooed irritably as working men pleaded with it to move out of the road. He could see the policemen in his mind's eye, working together, employing their intervention and negotiation skills to convince this complacent old cow that the middle of the road wasn't the safest place for nostalgic contemplation.

The boy could hear them shouting out polite commands and desperate suggestions on how to deal with this immovable cow as they attempted to gently and respectfully usher the beast out of harm's way, guiding it to a place of safety and security, a place where it could graze, chew, meditate and sleep under a pomegranate tree in a small garden without fear of being struck by a car, truck, taxi or rickshaw.

The police, the boy knew, were excellent at comforting and helping and rescuing cows in times of tremendous need. He had witnessed several cow rescues in his young life and suddenly he remembered an incident where a cow must have fallen down a well.

Two constables had bravely climbed down the open well. Determined, they squeezed beside the squealing cow and fastened its sweating body with a rope they had taken from their van and a harness they had ingeniously fashioned out of their collective shirts and jackets. When the rope was fastened and the improvised harness secure, they carefully climbed back up into the blistering sunlight and proceeded to hoist the nervous cow up to safety.

It was a long and difficult struggle.

Six or seven constables spent a good part of the afternoon pulling with all their strength and weight. When at last they hoisted the poor, terrified cow to safety, a crowd of villagers cheered and yelled that they were all heroes of the highest order and that they were sure to be rewarded in the hereafter.

To the boy it was an impressive display of teamwork, patience and compassion. That day the constables raised their naked chins high, straightened their backs, returned to their endless paper-

A Feast for Lambs

work and routines and received praise from all. And all day they longed to return to their wives and children to bless them with a wonderful story to enrich, entertain and inspire their hearts. To tell them a story that the whole family could be proud of for generations to come.

Another time, while traveling with his father in Delhi to sell a batch of kites his father had made for an elementary school, the boy remembered the police and bystanders rescuing a poor and unfortunate cow who had somehow fallen in a deep, narrow gully on the side of the road.

Somehow the poor animal had landed on its back so that only its four hooves wiggled and snapped and shook and protruded out of the filthy gully.

The boy remembered how five constables ingeniously wrapped each thigh and leg with a rope. He remembered them working together as they gently and carefully and patiently hoisted it up. One constable, after an hour or so, suddenly lost his focus, felt a little weary under the scorching, unforgiving Indian sun, and, to the horror of all, momentarily lost his grip.

A quarter of the cow fell.

A loud crack like a gunshot shook the boy terribly.

The boy remembered the bone protruding through skin; he remembered an onlooker rushing to the constable's aid, trying his very best to help him hoist the cow to safety. And, after much intense labor, the cow was finally hoisted out of the gully to safety and placed gently on its side where it wheezed and squealed in pain.

The head constable shot the weary constable a look of fire that could have burned him to cinders. The constable lowered his head in shame as dozens of eyes burned right through him. Then, with a great sense of urgency, the head constable had the cow hoisted into his van so that he could personally rush the wounded animal to the local veterinarian, where its fractured leg could be snapped back into place and nursed.

That day, the boy was sure, the weary constable had lowered his head and avoided all his coworkers and wandered aimlessly about wondering if he even deserved to return to his family.

The boy sighed with the memory, felt sorry for the constable and the cow as he continued his mad dash though the alley.

Not too far away from these determined policemen he heard a pack of feral dogs barking and growling, savagely attacking one another as they fought shamelessly over a scrap of rotis the rats and wild pigs had somehow overlooked. Then, over the barking of dogs and the shouts of the policemen, he came upon the sound of gushing water splattering against the cement floor, turning a layer of dust into a layer of grime.

The boy leaped over a box and another as he passed a home with its door wide open. Inwardly, he repeated:

> *Air is the Guru, Water the Father*
> *The Great Earth the mother of all*
> *Day and night are male and female nurses*
> *In whose lap the entire world plays about*

A Feast for Lambs

Aloud, he finished:

Deeds good and bad shall be reviewed
In the presence of the righteous judge

Already the taps on every other street corner sprinkled and splashed against the ground and filled wooden and tin buckets. Already men and women installed themselves with their buckets in the shadows and sluggishly undressed to their underwear as they prepared to cleanse and purify themselves for the day.

Follow the path of purity

Already the boy could smell the masala tea brewing over small kerosene stoves, the cardamom, the anise, and the burnt caraway seeds permeating the crisp, cool morning air as he passed home after home without slowing down.

Let your sect be the family of man

Already some mothers had begun taking down colorful and vibrant laundry that grew brighter and brighter in the growing dawn: kurta pajamas and Punjabi dresses and saris and shawls and chunnis. The laundry dangled and drooped from cords across the alley, from one flat roof to another, like brilliant jewels on a necklace sparkling in the sun.

Conquer your own mind
And be victorious in the world

The boy rounded a corner and quickly evaded a scooter that suddenly blasted past him and honked its feeble horn over the drone of the churning colony.

The boy instantly regained his balance and continued through the dark alley where an old, thin man with frail shoulders and a long white beard and hair down to his thighs squatted in his underwear and ladled water out of a wooden bucket.

The man smiled at the boy and dumped the cool, refreshing water over himself. He then watched with wonder as all the oil, grime and suds gently slipped off his wrinkled body and dripped and filled the cracks and fissures of the cobblestone street. Soapy water pooled and bubbled and streamed down the slanted alley into the side gullies that emptied sewage and scum into a drainage ditch that slithered out of the colony. The filthy stream was like a deadly snake full of puss and venom, ready to sink its toxic fangs in the nearby Yamuna River.

The old man ran his fingers through his soaked beard and wrung it like a wet towel as the boy passed him and quickly disappeared around another corner where he sent a covey of sparrows panicking into the brightening blue sky.

And the boy slowed a bit when he suddenly heard from one home a song that transcended his fear and frustration and sent a wave of euphoria surging through him.

He almost slowed to a stop as he listened to the words, and the words beat in his head and made him want to stop and sing an ode to the world.

The boy loved the words and the words loved him as they danced through every cell of his being. And as he passed this home that would make any child instantly stop to listen with ears wide open, he wished with all his heart that one day he, too, would own a record player or a tape player or a radio; whichever, it didn't matter. He simply longed to hear the song over and over again.

A luxury.

One he didn't have.

For a moment the boy listened to the song and imagined himself a superstar. He imagined himself dressed in a pitch black kurta pajama, wearing a sparkling black turban with one majestic, sparkling white glove that reflected a thousand stars in the night.

One white, glittering glove on his right hand.

One white, glittering glove on his right hand like a musical superhero that could walk on air.

One white, glittering glove where an iron kara bracelet dangled to remind him to do good in the world and for the world.

The boy breathed in deeply with the thought of defeating all his imaginary villains-- villains that his young, quick, discerning mind had carefully culled and crafted from the countless movies he had seen with his father and uncle. All those frightful villains. A lot of them Sikhs. Most of them Sikh. Or so he thought, because they always showed villains wearing a kara along with other articles associated with the Sikh faith.

Those villains…

Those dark, wild-eyed, kara-wearing men with wild, bushy eyebrows and even wilder, unkempt beards.

Perfect villains.

Truly perfect.

Though, strangely enough, these perfect villains, despite the resemblance, were unlike any Sikh man he had ever seen or known in his life.

The boy had often wondered where the directors had found their inspiration for such eerie characters. He had once asked his uncle, but his father instantly stopped his uncle from explaining anything, and then asked his uncle to please not put politics and conspiracy theories about movies into his son's head. He pleaded with his uncle to let him just enjoy the movies and be a child.

The boy's father and uncle argued quite a bit, and generally his uncle never held back his thoughts on the government or Bollywood; not unless the request was made by his father on the boy's behalf to spare him the weight of political thoughts and conspiracies.

But even though his uncle refrained from one of his lectures, the boy still very much wondered where these perfect villains came from.

He often told himself they were probably Sikhs from the South, since he didn't really know Sikhs from the South, and since Sikhs from the South, his mother had told him, were darker and fiercer looking; and so, he guessed, they were probably the inspiration for these perfect villains.

Once, the boy remembered, the director of one movie probably hadn't been able to find a Sikh from the South, so they used a Sikh from the North; and, he surmised, they had painted his face with black paint so that he would seem more authentic.

A Feast for Lambs

More perfect.

All the boy remembered was the painted, pitch black face and the glaring white, bloodshot eyes. He would never forget that villain. That villain gave him nightmares. That villain shook him to the very core and made him wish such people did not exist in the world.

Once, the boy had even scoured the entire colony searching for one villain like the ones in the movies. And he had definitely found one, isolated in his home like a hermit that many in the colony gossiped about.

He was a strange and dangerous-looking man with a missing eye that had been replaced by a sphere of glass. Every day the boy tracked this villain through the colony like the white ninja he had once seen playing on a television in a crammed little video store filled with amazed children, all of them profoundly impressed by this great warrior from America, who the video store owner had called Chuck Norrisji. The video store owner had smuggled the tape from America and was renting it out at a premium, as such movies were hard, if not impossible, to find.

And though the boy would never admit this to his friends, he knew deep down in his heart by what he saw on that television screen that Chuck Norrisji was faster, stronger and a lot more realistic and tougher than Amitabh. Also--

Chuck Norrisji didn't hurt as many Sikhs from the South as Amitabh did, and he seemed to focus all his anger on the black ninjas from the orient.

And so every day the boy tracked the villain of Trilokpuri like a stealthy white ninja, and he would follow him to his uneven, crumbling little home where the black ninja would suddenly disappear without taking off his sandals, without taking tea, without doing the things normal men did.

This man was definitely not normal.

This man was a villain--

No doubt.

At such times the boy would rush up to the villain's home and peer through the small, barred window. He'd grab a bar and hoist himself up. But as he slowly peered into the dark room, he found himself staring at nothing. Nothing but darkness and old furniture and flies circling in and out of shafts of sunlight that barely managed to penetrate the grimy windows.

Where had he disappeared to?

Where had this perfect villain gone to?

This villain was exceptional!

Even Chuck Norrisji probably couldn't track him down. And Amitabh would probably leave him alone because he didn't have a kara or a turban.

For days the boy followed the black ninja through the colony and he even began to question his villainy.

He didn't have a turban. He didn't have thick eyebrows. He didn't have a beard. He was fair-skinned and he didn't try to paint his face with black paint. Maybe he wasn't a villain after all. Maybe he was one of the good guys.

A Feast for Lambs

But he did have other things he had seen in the Chuck Norrisji movies. He had a creepy blue glass eye where a real eye should have been. He had a thick scar from his mouth to his ear like someone had grabbed him by the lips and ripped his mouth apart like a piece of paper. And he walked like a constable or soldier so that the boy had secretly begun calling him 'Major'.

For days he would follow Major around the colony. He thought that maybe, just maybe, he was planning something big, and that he, the white ninja of Trilokpuri, would be the one to foil his dark plans. Then one day, staring through the window, searching for him in his shadowy home, he could take no more.

He needed to know.

He needed to know where the villain was hiding. So he pushed the thick, wooden door that dangled off one broken hinge and entered silently.

Stealthily, he picked his way around a string bed, a table and a chair. Holding his breath, he checked a small pantry where most people kept stacks of cow pies for fuel when they ran out of kerosene, as kerosene was tightly regulated by government officials and was, in general, too great a luxury to use every day.

The boy searched and searched, but there wasn't even a hint of the glass-eyed black ninja. And just when he was about to give up he heard a groan and a creak above his head. He gazed upward at the crumbling chinks in the sagging plaster ceiling. He suddenly realized the ceiling was falling apart. He also noticed it was lower, much lower than other homes in the colony, and this was suspicious.

Had the perfect villain created another floor? Was it possible to do such a thing? If so, what a great idea! He would ask his father to create a secret ninja place in their home.

Silently, the boy stepped back outside in the gathering dusk and scrutinized the pucca's facade near the roof. He noticed that it was slightly higher than the other homes. Then he observed a funny thing, a strange thing, a curious thing.

The facade was crumbling.

Bits and pieces were falling everywhere like the ceiling.

Perhaps the perfect villain wasn't as nifty at construction as he was at disappearing. In the faint light he could see that there were tiny holes, fissures and chinks like cheese in a cartoon. It definitely wasn't as structurally sound as the rest of the little puccas.

His ninja instincts instantly told him that someone had been tinkering with his pucca. With this new information and renewed determination, he returned inside and searched and scrutinized the ceiling.

Carefully, he picked his way around the string cot, the chairs and the portable kerosene stove. He stopped suddenly when heard a creak above. Then he pressed on, making his way to the back of the room, stopping suddenly at a makeshift wooden ladder that seemed to disappear into the darkness above.

A Feast for Lambs

How had he missed this? How had he not seen this ladder hidden in the shadows? Major was good. Real good. Probably the best glass-eyed ninja out there. For a long, suspenseful moment he stood at the base of the ladder, listening--uneasy and unsure.

To climb or not to climb?

After a moment, curiosity overcame fear and he made his decision and proceeded to climb up the ladder. Nearing the hole where the ladder disappeared into a fold of wool blankets he stopped dead in his tracks.

What if he found weapons up there?

What if he found a body, or worse, bodies?

What if he was walking into a trap set by the black ninja of Trilokpuri?

His heart raced as the endless possibilities swirled through his mind. He considered climbing down and running as far away from Major's home as he possibly could. Then, he had a curious thought. The only dead body he had seen was the body of dog that had dragged itself to a nearby gully after being struck by a taxi. He remembered the smell. The smell of flesh rotting in the sun and he remembered the buzzards pecking at the rot. He had almost gagged on the foul air as he watched ants and other vermin slowly reduce the body to bones. The only smell worse, he thought, than decomposing flesh was the smell of burnt hair. He had smelled that once or twice, and never wanted to smell that stench ever again.

Curiosity once again vanquished common sense and the boy continued up and lifted the blanket. Slowly and quietly, his eyes took in a secret room lit by dozens of thick and thin crisscrossing shafts of golden light revealing--not bodies, not swords, not guns...but books.

Hundreds of them.

Books wherever the eye came to rest.

Small books. Big books. Medium-sized books. Clean books. Dusty books. Books and the unmistakable smell of glue and rotting paper. Beyond those books, by the broken wall, he saw Major's silhouette as it stared out into the street.

Major turned mysteriously from the broken wall to regard him. At once the glass-eye seemed to pierce right through the boy like an arrow. The boy gazed back at him, mesmerized, the eye slowly hypnotizing him like the eyes of a snake.

Transfixed, the boy's eyes widened with every second he stared at the eye; then suddenly he forgot himself and lost his footing and nearly fell off the ladder. But with trained reflexes Major lunged out and grabbed the boy's wrist just in time. He held the boy firmly. The boy swallowed as his dangling feet kicked the air.

With ease Major hoisted the motionless boy up and carried him to a small string bed where he placed him gently. Then he did a strange thing. A most unthinkable thing. A thing you wouldn't expect from a villain. The perfect villain, the black ninja of Trilokpuri invited the white ninja to stay with him a while, saying that he was quite curious to know how he had found his secret place.

After the boy had explained himself, Major smiled at the thought of being followed around the

colony as a villain, then his smile melted into a
frown and he seemed to grow somewhat discouraged with the thought of the movies that had given
the boy this image of villainy.

The boy smiled at Major and told him he
was glad that he wasn't the villain he had supposed
him to be. Major smiled and nodded at this. When
he observed the boy's keen interest in his books
strewn over the sagging, busted floor he gave him
permission to peruse them so long as he was careful not to damage them.

The boy remained in Major's secret library
for hours, admiring all the pictures of strange countries and people and customs. Then, when he realized how dark it was outside, he left in a panic,
down the ladder, out the door and into the night.

When at last he reached his home, his
mother admonished him for not telling her where
he had disappeared to, and after hearing where he
had been and with whom he had been with, she
gasped in horror and made him promise to stay
away from Major's home always and forever.

The boy promised, but he didn't pinky
promise, and he personally thought that she was
hard on Major because of his scarred face and his
glass eye. He mentioned his thoughts to her and
she didn't deny them; she said that he wore the face
he was given by God, and that he had earned that
face either in this life or some former life.

The boy had no idea what she meant by
this, but he sensed it had something to do with a
strange word he had heard elders talk about. A
mysterious word he noticed people considered

more and more with each passing birthday. A word his father had described as the currency of God, who pays out or taxes souls according to their good and bad deeds in life.

Karma.

His mother had said Major's face was the way it was because of karma, and the word went in one ear and out the other and did absolutely nothing to the boy. He simply had not made enough karma in his young life to actually care about karma.

In truth the boy refused to believe that Major's face was the way it was because he couldn't afford a better one. He actually thought that Major wasn't such a bad guy for a ninja and that he was, for the most part, misunderstood. Besides, despite his karma and his cryptic glass eye, they had become, over time and many shared stories, good friends.

In truth the boy enjoyed nothing more than to hear Major's stories, which were different from all the religious stories his mother told him before bed. It wasn't that he didn't like his mother's stories. He did. Very much so. It was just that she told him stories of great courage and tremendous acts of martyrdom in the face of religious persecution, stories he could listen to and visualize, but stories, nevertheless, he could not really understand or relate to.

Major, on the other hand, always found a way to make the story about him, or at least include something that had to do with him, and he liked that a lot..

A Feast for Lambs

The boy continued to run down the alley, listening to a song that lifted his spirit with fun words and helped him forget his fears and frustrations of being a whole two months without his mother; and as he ran with the song beating in his head he saw himself with a glove defeating a whole mob of perfect villains.

On the endless screen of his imagination he watched himself defeat those villains with powerful music and ferocious dance moves as he swayed and swiped and swished his gloved hand this way and that, beating through the mob like Chuck Norrisji.

The boy had wanted the glove for many months now.

He had pestered his mother; he had begged his grandmother; and he had pleaded with his uncle, who had grown redder and redder with his every word and who had eventually erupted in a splurge of accusations, charging the boy with idol worshipping and unrestrained ego.

But his religious tirade didn't last very long. Almost instantly his grandmother had come to the boy's defense. In her husky voice she told her only son to shut his big, angry mouth up and to let the boy be a boy.

His parents had remained silent during the eruption and knew better than to interfere with Chachaji. They sat and ate dinner and his mother counted the throbbing, blue veins on her brother's angry forehead.

The boy had taught his mother this trick to pass the time, and she, in turn, had taught her husband. It made uncomfortable and uneasy moments with his bellicose uncle somewhat enjoyable.

And though his parents thought a sparkling white glove was, for the most part, the most ridiculous thing in the world, they saw nothing inherently wrong with it, passed it off as a fad and hoped he would soon forget about it.

But he wouldn't.

And he wouldn't stop asking for a glove, just one glove, a sparkling white glove, to adorn his right hand.

Deftly, the boy leapt over a cow pie as the song continued to beat in his head and pound in his heart. As he glided through the air he sang in a language his mother had been trying to teach him for two years now, a language that he couldn't quite understand and found, for the most part, unnecessarily complicated.

People always told me, be careful what you do...

He hummed a few words he couldn't quite wrap his lips around, then the song faded in the distance and he finished:

Be careful what you do because lies become truth...

And he repeated:

Lies become truth

Lies become truth

The man with the glove was a miracle, a musical hero, a true master of the light, and every child and teenager, even those adults who wanted to impress children and teenagers, tried their very best to dance like the man with the glove and walk on air like he had done so masterfully on television.

A Feast for Lambs

A glove.

A white glove.

A sparkling, white glove.

It meant everything to the boy as he sighed dreamily with the thought of owning one, and for a moment he forgot all his problems. If only he could have a magic glove for his right hand. He'd be the hero of Trilokpuri. Not even Chuck Norrisji would be as envied as he.

And as he dreamed about a white, sparkling glove he heard something that made him instantly forget his problems and the glove and caused him to stop dead in his tracks. Something even more powerful than the song.

Slowly, he turned toward the source of the sound.

He stared at the home curiously.

It was barely audible, but he could hear it; he could definitely hear it, and it was one of those mysterious sounds he knew he would spend the rest of his life trying to figure out why it had such an inexplicable effect on his entire body and soul.

And now he could hear the great mystery over the soft music of an old Hindi song. Then there was a sudden pause. He could only hear the song. He waited for it again. He knew it would come. He had heard these sounds before several times. There was always a strange, random pattern to them.

The boy turned and tilted his head so that his left ear, which he took to be his better ear, was angled just right to catch any sound he might otherwise miss. He angled it toward the pucca. It was taking longer than usual. But it would come again, he was sure; and it did.

And again. Soft. Loud. Soft. Loud. Soft, soft. Loud. Soft, soft, soft. Loud. Real loud. Heavy breathing. Heavy breathing. No breathing. Silence. Heavy breathing. Groaning. Groaning. Heavy breathing. Silence.

It was a sound that enthralled him. A sound that tickled him, paralyzed him from the waist down, stirred every atom of his being to some sort of eternal, cosmic dance.

A sound that involuntarily made his spirit want to burst straight out of his skin and return to the source.

A sound that he had heard once while walking with his mother to the Sikh Temple down the main road. He remembered the night. It sounded like people doing joyful work, but work nevertheless. Almost instantly his mother had turned red as her sulwar Punjabi dress. Almost instantly she lunged at him and covered his ears. Almost instantly she ushered the boy away from the alley and the sound as he laughed joyously for the sound that rattled his mother in such a way.

It was a sound that loosened his heart, lifted his spirit and filled his entire being with an indescribable buzzing energy. A sound that spoke to all ages and colors and religions. A sound that transcended time and space. A sound that celebrated the eternal and unending song of life. And now this sound was in the boy's ears, making him smile with strange warmth, joy and impossible curiosity.

A Feast for Lambs

Grinning, the boy approached the sound with careful steps, listening hard and imagining; he wasn't exactly sure what he was supposed to be imagining or why that sound made him feel the way it made him feel. For a second it sounded like somebody was hurting someone.

First a woman, then a man. Woman. Man. Woman. Man. Woman. Man. No one. Silence. Man. Man. Woman. Man. Man. Man. Woman. Then both, woman and man. Woman and man. Woman and man. Woman and man. Faster. Faster. Even faster. Silence. Silence. Breathing. Heavy breathing. Fast breathing. Breathing and sucking. And then--

The sudden eruption of pure bliss--or agony--he wasn't quite sure. Then everything stopped all at once and there was only the endless churning of the waking colony all around him, and Hindi music interrupted now and then by whispers and heavenly groans.

The boy, his heart pounding madly in his chest, crept under the window to see if he could see something that would aid his understanding and assist his imagination.

Slowly he grabbed the window sill.

Carefully, he began to pull himself up. But just as he glanced into the window, just as he was about to feed his greedy curiosity, he heard a terrible shriek, followed by a deep, sonorous yell. A quick succession of words he had been banned from saying flew out of the pucca. An instant later he was bolting down the alley as a half-naked man ran out of his home and hurled an old, weathered sandal at the boy, nearly knocking his saffron patka turban straight off his head.

The boy ducked and laughed and charged down the alley infused with the great and unknowable song of life as he watched the sun climbing over the colony.

Staring for a moment at the brightening sky, he knew that his mother was already up, his father too, and that they were both probably combing the colony for him. He knew this and yet he still continued to run, holding in his hand a plane ticket bearing his mother's name.

He didn't want her to go. He didn't want her to leave. Not even for a day. He wouldn't let her leave. He would stop her at any cost, even if it meant placing himself in more trouble than he had ever been in during his entire life.

The boy would hide from her and she would miss her plane and that was all there was to it. She would eventually forgive him as she always did. He just couldn't bear losing her for longer than a day, let alone two months. And as he thought this he approached a crumbling old home and heard:

There is no beginning and no end
Through all ages only the One
And he unconsciously repeated:
There is no beginning and no end
Through all ages only the One

＜ვ

At last the boy came to Major's crumbling pucca. He froze at the green door, listening to the drone of the ocean stirring all around him: the sweeping of brooms in doorways, the escalating cry of a hungry newborn baby, the intermittent frantic honks of taxis and scooters rushing through the main road leading out of the colony.

In the homes behind him he could hear his friends preparing for school. He heard their mothers shouting at them, telling them they had better be good and work hard and that they were lucky they could even attend school. He then raised his eyes to a chink in the facade, searching for Major, but only saw sunlight and shadow.

Before he entered Major's home he kicked the dust off his dirty white running shoes that his brother had sent to him by surface mail. Then he patted down and dusted off his weathered kurta pajama that had once been dark blue and green but was now a faded, indescribable color.

He needed new kurta pajamas. This one was the nicest and most comfortable pair he owned and yet it had grown tight and short long ago. His parents knew this, but they were waiting for his grandmother, and the boy wished that they wouldn't.

His grandmother had promised him a new kurta pajama long, long ago. She had even told him she was making him a pair out of the finest white cotton she could find and that she would have her grandson looking like a fancy, educated congress-man in white starched kurta pajamas before the end of the year; but she had been distracted with an order of sheets for a store in West Delhi whose owner had sought her all the way in the East because of her outstanding and far-reaching reputa-tion for price, durability and quality.

His grandmother crafted sheets, bedcovers and blankets, and though her sheets were the pride of the colony, she could not, despite her best efforts, put together a proper kurta pajama. The boy had been pleading with his mother to buy him 'real' kurta pajamas from a 'real' store; but she told him that they could not afford such a purchase and that all their money was going toward her plane ticket to America.

His mother then explained that even if she had the money to buy him a 'real' kurta pajama at a 'real' store, she would not do such a thing to her mother's heart. The boy didn't understand what a 'real' kurta pajama had to do with his grandmoth-er's heart, and she told him that he would eventual-ly understand with time and experience.

He retorted that in the 'meantime' his friends were making jokes and amusing themselves at his expense. He further claimed that his heart was hurting, and that his heart mattered, too. With those words, she shook her head at him and sighed and told him that he should not mistake ego with heart. With time, she assured him again, life would teach him the difference.

Carefully, the boy entered Major's home. As he picked his way through the gloom he could hear the din of a radio above him. He climbed the creaking ladder. He stopped at the blanket and listened. He could hear the anger of the man on the radio. It was fast, furious and palpable.

Like his uncle, the man on the radio was arguing like a red-faced ape over something political, something that had to do with human rights and Sikhs being marginalized and disappeared in Punjab. The man on the radio screamed that these were all lies and no such thing could happen in India and he continued on about how these human rights organizations were attempting to deface his beloved, peaceful, democratic country in the eyes of the international community. No such thing happened to minorities in the most peaceful democracy in the world.

The boy listened to his vitriol but not his words. He ignored his bubbling lies, politics and rhetoric and imagined all the throbbing blue veins raging across his forehead like rivers of molten blue lava ready to erupt.

If only he could count them.

He imagined the man bald, and he thought that if this man on the radio were in fact bald, he could count a lot more than one or two veins and that he could probably even beat his all-time record of five veins; five distinct veins pumping and pushing pure anger into an ugly man's head as he battered a helpless young woman with the heel of his fancy European-style chappals for having worn sandals in his presence.

The boy never quite understood what he had witnessed or why this man had the right to do such a thing in front of so many people, including the police. His mother had tried to explain the situation, telling him that the young woman was allowed to wear sandals but that she was not allowed to wear sandals in his presence.

The boy still didn't quite understand. So his mother explained that she was a Dalit, an untouchable, a lower caste and that the man she had offended was a Brahmin, an upper caste, a politician; she told him that upper caste, Brahmin politicians were above the law and that it was their birthright to do whatever they pleased to lower castes and minorities.

She explained that Brahmin blood was somehow superior to Dalit blood and that those with tainted blood had to adhere to very strict rules when addressing those with pure blood. One of those rules was that they could not wear sandals or shoes in front of those with pure blood.

The boy said that this wasn't fair, and his mother said that fair had nothing to do with it. She said that one of the leaders that had helped free India from British rule had been assassinated because he sought to abolish this idea of grading and sorting people into castes.

Even though this leader had been born into a high caste he preached that all were equal and he permitted the low castes to involve themselves in the political system and the freedom movement.

A Feast for Lambs

And because this leader had preached all were equal and because he didn't believe in grading blood, he had been shot by the Brahmin extremists who had been conspiring to murder him for years before a Brahmin from Poona had actually succeeded. This Brahmin from Poona believed that Brahmins should rule over a massive Brahmin-controlled empire that included Pakistan, and that all those who did not embrace or adhere to Brahminical Society should be erased. This was one of the reasons, she told him, that a great soul had been assassinated when India needed him most.

Then, sensing the boy's concern and unease, she had told him not to worry and that there were other types of justice in this universe and that somehow, someway, 'Truth alone triumphs', even for upper-caste politicians with fancy, custom-designed flip-flop chappals who walk around the country above the law.

She added that times were getting better for untouchables and that the caste system was slowly being abolished in law and mind. In ten years, she believed, it might not even exist. Not too long ago, she added, an untouchable could be put to death for letting her shadow fall upon an upper caste. That couldn't happen anymore. Now it was just a beating. A small humiliation and a reminder of their proper place in India.

With these thoughts swirling through his head, the boy lifted the blanket and clambered into the attic and found Major standing by the broken wall.

A faint golden light washed over his home and penetrated the cracks and chinks. It bounced off a broken mirror on the other side of his secret library and split in multiple directions to create a web of light in the darkness. Major hesitated before he turned to the boy. There was a silence, then he said:

"Shouldn't you be preparing for school?"

The boy looked up nervously. Major's face had always frightened him. He looked like he had been chewed up by a demon and spit out onto the floor; he looked like he had been through war and was the last man in the world and now he longed for the inevitable. He was tall and dark and he looked foreboding in the sunlight and shadow and his khaki kurta pajama made him look mean and militant. His good eye was dark, tired and tormented and it told everyone to stay away.

Everyone except the boy.

And now the boy was silent as he took in the room and searched for any new additions to the library. Finding no new additions, he walked past a broken hurricane lamp and sat on an old string bed and declared:

"I hate my brother!"

Major's eyes widened with the unexpected statement. He peered at the boy, then he shook his head slightly and looked very sad. "You shouldn't say such things," he said. "You should watch what you say, even if you are angry."

The boy grimaced.

"Why?"

A Feast for Lambs

He didn't see anything wrong with hating his brother, who had abandoned him and was now about to rob him of his mother.

Major shuffled. "You may regret it one day, that's why," he said. He approached the boy, turned off the radio, sat down beside him and indicated the ticket in his hand. "What's that?"

"Nothing," the boy answered. He made a conscious effort not to stare at Major's glass eye, but wasn't very successful. The more he tried to look away the more he ended up staring right at it. He still wasn't used to it; perhaps he never would be. And perhaps Major didn't mind. People seemed to stare at his eye, at his face, at his karma all the time. He never said anything or seemed to care.

"Can I see this 'nothing'?" he asked, holding out his hand.

Reluctantly, the boy handed over the ticket. Feeling anxious, he stood and shuffled over to the broken wall to stare out into the street where he could hear a breathless woman admonishing someone.

Below a mother washed her pots, pans, clothes and a little girl while she looked over her shoulder through the open door of her home and commanded someone to stop trying to walk on air and finish their rotis. The whole while the little girl squirmed and wiggled in her mother's hold, struggling and flopping around like a slippery fish, desperately attempting to escape the bucket, screaming that she wasn't dirty and that she had taken a bath just a few days ago.

Major read the ticket in the growing light. "Someone going to America?" he asked as he read the name. He looked up at the boy.

The boy didn't answer right away. The sound of a bucket tipping over and water splashing told him the girl had wiggled her way to freedom and had been triumphant in the great battle of the bath. "She's leaving me," he said at last. "She's going and she's leaving me." He said nothing more.

The boy stared at the mother; she chased her toddler around a colorful mound of laundry in frantic circles; the mother pretended to chase her at full speed, telling the little girl that when she caught her she was definitely going to tickle her. The little girl shouted for the tickle monster to leave her alone, and the mother made strange, unnatural noises with her throat as she slowly lost herself in the boundless secret kingdom of her child's imagination.

"I see," Major said, and rose slowly. "Your brother cannot return, so your mother is going to see him."

The boy nodded solemnly. He stared below as the mother suddenly caught her toddler, tossed her gently into the mound of cloth and colors and commenced to tickle her. For a brief moment the boy forgot his sadness as the excited cries and laughter coming from the vibrant reds, blues, and greens covering the little girl tickled his heart. His face softened a little as the toddler's laugh danced through his ears and lifted his spirit.

Listening to the pure joy and laughter, the boy suddenly thought of his favorite spring holiday--Holi. A time when he and his family wore old, white clothes from head to toe and walked through the dancing streets, hurling colored powders and spraying colored water at complete strangers to celebrate with their Hindu neighbors the triumph of life over death.

They would celebrate well into the night and in the morning his entire being would be numb and vibrating with something powerful and inexpressible as he stared at all the living works of art around him; everyone a walking masterpiece, smiling through the euphoric streets with the same divine feeling, covered head to toe in the random and unpredictable colors of life.

Always the boy felt a powerful and mysterious numbing sensation as he stared at everyone and all the colors. It was like his whole body, even his face, prickled with pins and needles. A sensation he would also experience while praying at the Sikh Temple for a long time and with many people.

His mother had explained that this vibrating sensation was something that could not be explained and that it usually occurred in the presence of something so pure only the soul recognized it. She said that his soul vibrated because he was in the presence of pure love. A love that transcended human thought and understanding. His soul recognized what conscious thought would not and could not, and his body filled with the indescribable and the incontestable mystery, the sublime--God.

Major approached the boy and stood alongside him, squinting in the light. "Your brother probably has exams," he said. "This is probably why he cannot return home."

The boy nodded and looked to Major, then he turned back to the street. "I don't care about his exams. I don't want her to leave."

"I see." Major said. He fell silent and thoughtful. Then he said, "Your brother is a brave man, you know? He's been in a strange new land for a very long time now." He paused to regard the boy. When the boy didn't react, he continued. "I wager he wishes he could come home and see you. I wager he wishes he could return home instead of staying in this strange land all alone studying for exams. That's what I wager. What do you wager?"

"I don't wager," the boy said flatly. "He didn't have to go. He didn't have to leave."

Major breathed in deeply.

"I see. You don't think he had to go."

The boy shook his head in reply.

"One day you'll understand," Major said. "Not today...but one day."

"I don't need to understand!" The boy said. "I don't!"

Major didn't respond to this. He watched the street with the boy in silence. A mother tickled her little girl and a group of teenage boys in blue uniforms kicked and juggled a multicolored ball made out of compacted old cotton and polyester cloth that had probably once been a chunni or a turban or a chunni and a turban or several turbans and several chunnis. They kicked the colorful ball out of the alley and followed after it like a pack of dogs chasing a cat. Major stared at the boys until they disappeared out of view. At last he said:

A Feast for Lambs

"Did I ever tell you the story about the lion?"

The boy looked up at him. Major had told him many stories about lions in the last few weeks. It sometimes made the boy think that Major was a Sikh, talking about Sikhs as lions, though he couldn't be sure as he had none of the articles of the Sikh uniform, not even the kara. "You told me many stories about lions," he answered. "I heard them all."

"This one I'm sure I never told you."

"Which?"

"The story of the lion that lived in a world made of stories."

Passing his hand in and out of a beam of sunlight, the boy looked up at Major with curiosity. He had never heard this story, and he tried to imagine what a world made of stories would be like. He shook his head to let Major know that he had never heard the story. Major grinned down at him, stared outside at the mother and daughter who were now just lying in the heap of colors staring up at the blue sky. After a reflective moment, he began:

"Long, long ago in a world made of stories, there was once a jungle with many animals and many stories. Stories that made each animal interesting and unique and special. Stories that each animal told their children so that they would always remain interesting and unique and special. And this was the way it was for some time until one group of animals discovered something very interesting. They discovered the power of the story in a world made of stories."

The boy listened with sudden interest and wondered when he'd be introduced in this story. After a pause, Major went on:

"Now, these few lambs realized that if they could control the stories they could control the jungle. And so efficiently and cunningly these polite and well-spoken lambs began to change the main story of the jungle and add things that made it so that only they could read, interpret, and discuss the story. They did this so that the story would place them on top of everyone who believed in the main story of the jungle. Patiently and cleverly the lambs seized control of the most popular story in the jungle and had through time and patience made it their story."

Major breathed in the cool morning air, then continued:

"Once the lambs took control of the popular story they knew that they would have to do the exact same thing to the other stories. It was the only way they could stay in control and maintain control. So they began changing the stories of other animals, and doing so only one small detail at a time so that the changes would hardly be noticed. They knew that if they changed things too quickly and too drastically, the lions, who had a very strong story, who did not believe lambs were born to rule, would roar their anger, and the lambs' ambition to tell only one story that kept them in power would be undone."

The boy moved his finger along the edge of a fissure and listened, wondering what this story had to do with him or his mother leaving for

A Feast for Lambs

America. He thought about lambs, about how they seized control of the most popular story of the jungle and made it their own and couldn't see the link. Not yet, anyway. Major continued:

"So the changes came slowly and patiently. No animals, not even the lions, realized the trickery of the lambs. Those who did realize what was happening were strangely and mysteriously disappeared and they were never seen again by those who loved them."

The boy tilted his head and angled his left ear to him. He was still waiting to see how he would fit into this story about a lion in a world made of stories. But now Major was talking about something else he knew about. The disappeared. There were many of those in the Punjab, and lot of people believed more and more Sikhs would disappear in the future as the government was trying to make laws that would help them disappear Sikhs. Major closed his eyes. After a reflective moment, he opened his eyes and continued:

"And so the stories changed and because the stories changed the animals changed and those who didn't change or didn't want to change...disappeared. And soon a very strange and curious thing happened: other animals began to not only bow down to the lambs, but they actually began to act, speak and sound like lambs. As ridiculous as this may seem, elephants began to act, speak, and sound like lambs. Monkeys began to act, speak, and sound like lambs. Lions began to act, speak and sound like lambs."

The boy's eyes smiled with the thought of lions roaming around the jungle acting like lambs. The boy could see this was becoming one of Major's silly stories; but he said nothing and waited to see how he would be weaved into the yarn. With a beam of sunlight cutting the darkness and warming his face, the boy watched the street as it filled with the song of life. After a reflective pause, Major continued:

"It's true. So true that lions, as much as they tried, couldn't even roar anymore. Either they were too scared to roar or they had just plain forgotten how to roar, because they had forgotten their stories and the importance of roaring in the face of oppression and how this very thing--this roaring against the tyrant--had once been a very big part of their story."

Suddenly the boy's eyes grew serious and feral and they no longer smiled. The words entered his ears and the thought of a voiceless lion did something powerful and mysterious to his heart.

"And, sad as this may sound, this particular jungle was no longer an interesting or unique or special place to live. It seemed peaceful to many outsiders, but it was really a very violent and dangerous place to live for anyone who challenged lamb rule or what the lambs were doing to their stories."

Now the boy could feel his heart pounding in his chest; he could feel his blood boiling; his face tightened and his eyes narrowed and at once he remembered all the stories of martyrdom and sacrifice of his ancestors. Major continued:

A Feast for Lambs

"And though you may not believe such a thing could happen, it did; and this jungle became a very difficult and dangerous place to live in for lions who still wanted to be lions. So some lions left their families in search of a new jungle where they could be free to tell their stories and to teach themselves how to roar again without fear of disappearing."

The boy sighed, and he instantly understood where Major was going with this story and he was already beginning to feel a twinge of shame.

"And there was this one lion who was so, so smart and so, so lucky that he was invited to live in one of the freest and most diverse jungles in the world. But there was only one problem: to do so he would have to make the ultimate sacrifice." Major paused. The boy looked up at him, thinking about his brother. He continued: "He would have to leave his family and live alone for many, many years."

The boy's head sagged. His poor brother, in a jungle far, far away from his family, all alone. Major had always found a way to reason with his heart when he couldn't reason with his head. Now all he wanted to do was charge out of his attic and return home and tell his mother to go and stay with his brother for as long as he needed her. Major continued:

"But the lion knew that if he worked hard and if he could bear the loneliness, he would give his entire family an opportunity unlike any other. An opportunity to live in a free jungle where they could be who they were without fear of disappearing. An opportunity to hear and learn their story,

their true story, of how lions had once roared fiercely against lamb oppression."

Major regarded the boy, threw him a severe
look, and finished:

"And in a world made of stories, this is
everything."

The boy lifted his head. He wanted to
know more about the lion. Did he succeed? Was he
able to help his family? Did they learn how to roar
again? And so after a silence the boy asked:

"Then what?"

Major seemed taken aback by the question.

"What do you mean?"

"What happens to the lion in the free jungle? Does he help his family become lions again?"

Major shrugged.

"Not sure yet."

The boy sighed deeply.

"To be continued?"

Major nodded.

"Yes, I suppose so. To be continued."

The boy was silent for a long while and he
wondered if he was one of the lamb-lions in Major's
story. He hoped that he wasn't, and that if he was,
he hoped it wasn't too late and that there was some
way to cure him from his lambness. He finally
asked:

"Major...am I a...lamb?"

Major regarded him with a smile. When he
realized the boy was serious, his smile faded and he
tapped the boy's kara lightly. "Do you believe that
in a world made of stories only one story should be
told?" His good eye peered right into the boy, while

his glass eye seemed to look beyond him into another world.

The boy thought about this question carefully. He believed that in a world made of stories there was only one storyteller, but that this storyteller loved to tell many different stories to many different people who all have different needs and expectations. He most certainly did not believe the Original Storyteller would have wanted to tell just one story or make it so only one people had the divine right to hear, read and interpret the story.

He believed that in the end he'd become tired of just one story, especially if hearing one story meant everyone in the whole world would end up thinking and acting and talking in the same way. He liked differences. He embraced differences. He just couldn't imagine a jungle with one story, where only the lambs were permitted to appreciate and interpret the story. What a bleak, uninspiring, colorless jungle that would be. He wouldn't want to live in such a jungle. Neither, he felt, would the Original Storyteller.

The boy believed that, in the end, at the heart of every original story he had ever heard or read, was a message of love and tolerance and respect for other stories. This was why he would never be able to embrace or accept the idea that some people were born to rule and some people were born into slavery. The idea of living in a world with just one story, undermining the messages of other stories, or preventing others from telling their stories seemed absurd and unnatural and against every belief he held about the Original Storyteller.

With all his heart, the boy liked hearing other stories and saw them all as divine gifts for the heart, soul, and imagination. He liked sharing his lion stories with others without thinking that his story was better or truer than other stories. They were all true. They were all true in that they served their audiences. One Original Storyteller telling a thousand different stories to a thousand different audiences. That felt truer in his heart than one story for one audience, and a few lambs trying to force all the animals in the jungle to stick to their distortion of one of the original stories. He couldn't accept such an absurd idea.

And if it was true that the story was the key to the door to the castle of paradise, he imagined a golden path of love and tolerance leading to a castle with a thousand and one doors and a thousand and one secret entrances with a thousand and one unique locks where souls met to tell stories. A castle he felt many might miss by trying so hard to force everyone to use the same key. Focusing on the key, they would forgo the path and even possibly forget that there was a castle where they could meet the Original Storyteller and tell him or her, or him and her, the stories of their lives.

Getting to the door, the boy mused, was just as important as having the key. Otherwise you were just lost in the woods with a key and no door to open.

But the boy also knew these varying stories often caused audiences to fight with one another over tone, words and punctuation so that they could no longer experience substance, meaning and

A Feast for Lambs

essence. But that, the boy also knew, had nothing to do with the Original Storyteller. It had to do with lesser storytellers, extremists, lambs--lambs who tried to say they were the only audience, the chosen audience, and that their stories had the right number of periods, commas, and exclamation marks and that their stories were the only story the Original Storyteller had ever told.

But this, the boy also knew, had more to do with politics and economics and control than the Original Storyteller. Things his uncle liked to think about and to debate, and things his parents like to stay away from. And so the boy shook his head, letting Major know that he absolutely refused to believe that in world made of stories, only one story should be told, to which Major responded simply:

"You're not a lamb."

The boy sighed in relief.

"I'm still a lion."

"Well, I wouldn't say that. But you're definitely not a lamb."

The boy squished his face.

"What do you mean?"

"I'd say you were a cub."

"A cub?"

"A cub."

A sudden knock at Major's door startled them both. The boy stared down at the street and saw his mother. She wore a blue Punjabi dress and her hair was slick black with oil. She looked up without seeing them. Her eyes were smoke and fire and they promised trouble.

Big trouble.

"And I'd say the lioness has come for her cub."

Below them they could hear the door creak open, then careful footsteps as she made her way toward the ladder.

"I better go. She doesn't want me here."

"I know."

Without another word, the boy turned and picked his way around the scattered books and headed down the ladder, only to turn and face his mother.

She glared down at him. He knew that she was upset, so upset that she was counting in her head, and if she counted past ten it meant she was bordering on furious. If she counted past twenty it meant she was so enraged she wouldn't speak at all for fear of the words that would erupt from her mouth. He counted in his head to gauge how much trouble he was in.

At twenty-two he stopped and realized it was a lot worse than he had anticipated. Before she said anything he handed her the plane ticket. "I'm sorry," he said, and made pitiful eyes, knowing that was all he could say, or should say; then he lowered his gaze to the floor.

With his father he'd say more, much more; he'd even try to explain himself. And then, when he finished explaining he would look at his father and slowly fill his eyes with salty tears and stop just before they spilled. Then somehow his alchemy would slowly take effect; his father's anger would melt into guilt and within seconds he'd somehow manage to believe that he had, in some way, messed up as a parent and believe that the boy's mischief was his fault. But with his mother it was a whole different process.

With his mother this tactic only infuriated her more as she could smell a ploy a thousand yards away. She would only grow angrier with every word he used to try and convince her that she was the ultimate cause of his mischief or misdeed. It had taken him a while to puzzle out the best approach to use on his mother, who he sometimes felt had no emotions and who he had only seen shed a tear once.

And he never wanted to see or hear her cry again.

He never wanted her to experience the pain that had unlocked all that pent-up, uncontrollable grief.

And he remembered the altercation.

His mother had been arguing with her sister over something that had meant something to her at the time but now nobody really remembered or cared to remember. His mother had said things in her anger that she didn't really mean. Hearing these words, her sister had instantly fled from their home, swearing with intense Punjabi passion that she would never return again. The boy thought his aunty must have really meant what she had said, and God must have been listening, because as she charged back home she was struck by a car that didn't even stop to help her.

His mother hadn't reacted or said anything about her sister's death for months. It was as though she had shut it out of her mind so that she could continue on with her life. Then one night she ripped the silence with a cry so full of guilt, so full of anger, so full of anguish it was hard to believe a human had made such a sound; it was like a thousand older sisters crying in the night for their dead sister.

She cried and begged and pleaded to eternity for one more moment with her sister and all she heard was the silence; and the silence only made her cry louder and louder, and she begged harder and harder, pleading with all her heart and soul for just one moment to say three words--just three words.

She stayed in bed for the next few days and said nothing. The silence had beaten her down. But not completely. One morning she rose out of bed, turned on the kerosene stove, began to prepare some daal-rotis, and began to sing a hymn she and her sister used to love to sing together. And now before any angry words slipped out of her mouth she counted.

The boy waited and he slouched a bit to distract his mother. She didn't permit him to slouch. It was a technique he used to direct and divert her attention away from her anger. Any moment now she would tell him to keep his head up and straighten his back.

He could feel her observing his posture. With a sigh she placed her finger under his chin and lifted his head to meet her dark, piercing eyes. "Head up," she said. "Back straight."

A Feast for Lambs

The boy straightened his back and told her he was sorry again. She said nothing. She just stared at him, letting herself cool down. He could see she was still counting despite his divertive tactic. "Wait here," she said at last; then she ascended the ladder and stopped when her head disappeared in the attic. The boy angled his left ear and listened. He heard her say:

"Please...I don't want my son coming here anymore."

The boy barely made out Major's muffled response.

"Then you should tell him so."

"I have told him."

"You should tell him again."

"I have told him again."

"Then you should tell him to listen to his mother."

The boy felt a pang of guilt. His mother pointed out:

"You could send him away."

"Why would I do that? I enjoy the boy's company."

The mother was silent for a long moment. It seemed as though she had nothing more to say to Major. Maybe there was nothing she could say. Then she said something that seemed to upset him. "You'd understand if you were a parent."

The boy could hear Major start at this. He could hear him march toward his mother as dust crumbled from the ceiling. He could even see him in his mind's eye staring at his mother with his glass eye.

"I'd never hurt him! I'd never hurt him!"

"It's not common for someone to live like this," his mother said. Then, after a silence, she added:

"Here…take it…"

There was an awkward silence then Major said:

"I don't want your charity."

His mother had probably thrown him money as she believed him to be a beggar who had somehow drifted into Trilokpuri and taken over an abandoned pucca whose owner had disappeared in the early summer months. Then after a silence he heard Major grumble that he would send the boy home if he ever returned. "I will send him away if he comes again," he said. "But not because I want to."

"You would understand if you had children."

A profound sadness crept into Major's voice.

"Please go…please…"

The boy's mother climbed down the ladder and took the boy's hand. "Listen to me," she said. "I never want you coming here again--"

"But--"

His mother's eyes widened. He sighed. Her eyes widened more and dared him to continue to protest against her. When she saw he wouldn't, her face softened and she whispered:

"He isn't married. He doesn't have a family. We don't know where he comes from or what he's doing here. He's hiding from something or someone and I don't want you coming here anymore. Understand?"

The boy's head fell. She lifted his chin. "Understand?"

"Understand," he said.

She looked at him uneasily then shook her head. "Not good enough," she said. She extended her arm, opened her hand and gave him her pinky. "Pinky promise."

The boy looked up at her incredulously. He hesitated. He couldn't believe it. This was something he did with his brother and now she was using it to her own practical, parental end like the lambs had done with the story.

Somehow she had discovered that he could convince himself to break normal promises, but he had a hard time breaking pinky promises. Pinky promises were almost impossible to break. They were sacred. The only thing more powerful than a 'Pinky Promise' was a 'By God'.

She was sharp, his mother.

Nothing went by her.

He let out a deep sigh of utter and total defeat. Reluctantly, he held out his pinky, curled it around hers and shook. This seemed to close the deal and satisfy her. She smiled, took his hand, told him they had to find his father and proceeded to lead him outside into the golden day.

With his mother conducting him through the colony, the boy searched for his father for a long while before they spotted his yellow turban in a sea of colorful turbans on the crammed and bustling main road. They called out his name but he couldn't hear them over the din of morning traffic.

At last he heard his name and turned to face them. He was a quiet, soft-spoken man in a beige kurta pajama who spent most of his days crafting kites out of colorful, transparent paper, wax, glue, butcher cord and slivers of bamboo.

The boy's father marched up to his youngest, kneeled before him and looked him in his eyes. The boy's eyes instantly brimmed with tears and his mother shook her head at the kitten she had married. "Where were you?" he asked softly, not wanting to stir any more tears.

The boy's eyes filled a little more in answer, and his father tried not to look at him and began to stare at the boy's nose. His father was using his own countermeasures. Seeing this, the boy took a small step forward and angled his head so his father could see the despair in his eyes and realize that he, and not the boy, was at fault. The father stared at the boy's wet eyes and a after a silence he admitted:

"I should have explained things to you--"

But the boy's mother interrupted the kitten with a deep, disbelieving sigh and quickly put her hand on the back of the boy's neck. "He's okay," she said, sparing her husband from the boy's act. His father held the boy's shoulders, trying to understand.

"Why did you take the ticket, bete?"

The boy wiped a tear and his father wiped another one for him.

"I don't want Mum to go...but now I think she should go."

A Feast for Lambs

His eyes filled even more and the kitten melted. A moment later he embraced his son tightly and told him he would take good care of him and that he would teach him how to craft a solid kite. His father, unlike his grandfather who had traded salt, made kites for a living and sold them in the city and nearby villages.

As he held the boy, a middle-aged woman in a black, weathered Punjabi dress trudged by them, stepping over and crushing a fresh mango that had fallen off a truck or out of a basket. The boy saw her from the corner of his eye. He turned to her and stared. For some inexplicable reason he couldn't take his eyes off her.

Sensing the boy was distracted, his father released him.

The boy's eyes followed the pale and expressionless woman. His father and mother looked at his eyes, then followed his gaze and began to watch the woman, too.

They watched her as she lumbered down the road like a ghost in a graveyard, slowly moving toward two constables who were leaning against a police van watching the people in their plain khaki uniforms as they listened to the radio. They looked to the boy like alligators keeping an eye on the pond for the lambs.

The ghost woman edged right up to the alligators and stopped and stared at them with her empty eyes. At first they looked at her and laughed and asked her what she wanted. When she didn't answer, they told her to scram before they made her scram. But she didn't scram. She didn't move.

She just stared at them with her blank eyes.

The boy looked to his father, but he didn't take his eyes off the woman; neither did his mother and then a few a passersby began to stare at the ghost and the alligators. It was rare for someone to approach the police in such a bold, silent, fearless manner.

The alligators looked at her like she was mad. They laughed at her, dismissed her, made jokes at her expense, then ordered her to quickly move along.

But she didn't move along. She just stared at them, and her eyes seemed to bore holes right through their souls. They shifted uneasily and then shooed her away with their lathi sticks.

But she didn't move.

Not an inch.

On the contrary, she took a small step closer and opened her mouth slightly.

But still no words came out.

With rising anger, the alligators demanded that she move along. But she just inched closer and closer to them like a decrepit old corpse that had been walking the earth for centuries searching for answers. She whispered soundlessly to the alligators. They yelled for her to speak up or leave.

But still nothing issued forth from her open, trembling mouth.

The boy gazed at her but didn't recognize her.

Her clothes looked like she had walked for weeks and that she would not stop walking until she collapsed and was released from her inner

A Feast for Lambs

prison. The boy thought that maybe she had walked all the way from Amritsar. All the way from the Golden Temple.

One alligator smiled and told her that she was more stubborn than the cow they had conducted to safety in the early morning.

But the ghost said nothing, even though it seemed as though she would speak at any moment. It was like she wanted to say something but couldn't push the words through the sadness in her throat. Her mouth began to close again.

And the boy could see these alligators growing uncomfortable. The woman then mumbled something through her closed, quivering lips.

But no one heard a word.

Frustrated, aware that many eyes were watching them, the alligators continued their jokes, calling her mad, delirious, and demanding for her to speak up, to speak to be heard, or to go back to whatever village she had crawled out from.

The ghost woman mumbled a little louder, but still through a mouth that seemed glued tight at the lips. But the boy could see something dark growing in her. Something dark that she had carried with her for a great distance and was preparing to unleash on these poor, unsuspecting alligators.

They laughed at her more.

And she opened her mouth slightly and said a single word that silenced and angered them at once.

This time they didn't laugh.

This time they made no jokes.

One alligator asked her to repeat what she had just called them, raising a stick at her, letting her know that he would make her pay for any insolence or civil disobedience and that she had better watch what came out of her quivering mouth.

She didn't say anything. She just stared at the stick, then at the man staring at her as if she had slapped him in the face.

Suddenly something urgent sounded on the radio.

One alligator immediately slipped into the van to find out what was happening. The ghost watched him as he listened intently to what was being announced on the radio. Then she returned her gaze to the other alligator holding a stick high above her head. After a moment he lowered it and shouted for her to leave or be arrested.

But she still wouldn't leave. At last her mouth opened slightly and she whispered:

"Murderers."

The constable's first reaction was to swipe her down, but he suddenly restrained himself, remembering the dozen or so pedestrians now watching what was transpiring with the ghost woman. Lowering his stick, he ordered her to shut up.

But she would not shut up.

She would not be silenced.

"Murderers!"

All who heard this fell silent and gazed at the scene incredulously. Everyone knew better than to challenge those who protected the lambs.

A Feast for Lambs

The woman glared at the alligator. Then, after a silence, with all the air and power in her lungs, the ghost woman yelled:

"Murderers!"

The boy asked his parents what she meant and why this woman had accused these constables of murder and they told him when he was older they would explain. The boy repeated the word, again and again and could not believe a woman would call the police such a thing. He didn't understand, but his parents did, and they told him to start walking away and fast.

But the boy refused to walk away.

He wanted to see. He wanted to know why this woman would do such a thing.

And just as the alligator went to strike her, the other alligator screamed from inside the van that something terrible had happened and they had to leave fast.

His mother tugged the boy against his will and ushered him through the strangely emptying street as pedestrians gathered around any home or car or stall with a radio to listen to some breaking news.

The boy repeated the word inwardly and had no idea why she would do such a thing to these constables. He watched the police van screech away, leaving the woman in a cloud of dust. Suddenly, the boy heard someone cry out the prime minister's name in the distance and the boy repeated the word:

Murderer.

He didn't know what the ghost woman meant by this. He didn't know what was in her heart to inspire her to say such a terrible thing to the police. But if the boy could know--

He would know--

That she meant the word in the most sincere and most explicit possible way the word could ever be used. That she meant the word in both the material and spiritual sense and that these constables belonged to a system that sought to destroy and humiliate her people's spirit so that they could no longer speak their truth or walk with dignity. She meant that through their silence and their indifference they supported a system that openly used torture to torment and humiliate minorities. A system that used torture not to obtain information, not to punish a criminal, not even to secure justice--if justice could ever be secured in such a manner--but to silence anyone who would dare challenge upper-caste rule; to silence and to humiliate and to terrorize her people. And then to humiliate them again. And again by showing them they could disappear anyone they wanted to in a world that had established laws and conventions to protect minority communities against systemic torture and widespread disappearances. And to humiliate them again by showing them the world didn't care.

Murderer! Where were those laws and conventions now? Where were those laws and conventions for her people? Murderer! How long would her people continue to disappear? How long before the world did something? How long would those who had built the disappearing machine evade justice?

Murderer!

More and more of her people will be erased from the face of the earth if all the machine meets on its dark path is silence.

Murderer!

All her hopes! All her dreams! All my memories! Gone!

Murderer!

The boy could not even begin to understand what she had meant by the word or what it was like to have someone disappear from his life. And because he didn't know, he could not know what it was like to want to split open your own skull and rip out your mind so that you could stop your imagination from telling stories of hope and despair so that you could forget.

Simply forget.

Murderer!

But she cannot forget and her imagination robs her of sleep and the lack of sleep drains her of joy and when joy goes the world goes and peace becomes torment, heaven becomes hell, and she finds herself walking and walking with nowhere to go and no one to talk to and nothing to do.

And she just wants to know.

She just wants to know and she just wants to stop imagining because imagining what happened is worse. And she knows that this inner torment is part of the machine created to silence a people.

And she can't stop imagining and this needing to know is her own personal hell. And no matter where she goes there it is in her, in her head, playing with her, toying with her, torturing her, tormenting her, compounding the humiliation the way it was meant to.

Her own personal hell.

Your own personal hell.

Murderer!

One moment your mind is telling you your husband is okay, telling you he went on a secret vacation and just forgot to tell you, the next moment he's being boiled to death in the land that had invented torture for no other reason than to cripple and humble and instill fear in minority communities that had forgotten themselves.

Murderer!

Where is my husband? Where is my husband? Where is he?

Murderer!

What have you done with him? I can't tell myself any more stories. I just need to know. I just want to know. Please…just tell me….just tell me he's dead and be done with it. Just tell me you killed him and be done with it. Please…where is he…murderer…

Your silence is your crime.

Murderer….

But the boy couldn't possibly know what the woman meant by the word. He couldn't possibly know what was in her heart to compel her to say such a terrible thing to the police. But if he could know--

He would know that she was not even a fraction of the woman she had once been before her

A Feast for Lambs

husband had disappeared.
     He would know the silence, the indiffer-
ence and the cruelty of the police, the government--
     The world.
     Better he didn't know.
     Murderer.

ᘓ

Outside the boy's small home he could hear the whispers rising and slithering and hissing like a deadly cobra as it made its way through the colony. From bits and pieces of gossip he had gathered from his parents, he had learned that the prime minister had been shot by her Sikh bodyguards and now she lay in the hospital thinking about her life and counting her karma. The boy didn't really know how to feel about this. He didn't really care or think much about politics. Not that he was too young to concern himself with such issues. Not that he was indifferent to political issues concerning his country. It was more that the Labana Sikhs of Trilokpuri as a whole--with the exception of his uncle, who always needed to be right and who was probably the most political man in Punjab--were not very political; they rarely discussed political issues, or they at least tried their very best to stay away from those issues that seemed to be vanishing Sikhs from the very face of the earth like magic.

The boy had heard about the disappearances for some time now. Everyone seemed to have heard of someone who had disappeared for having protested against the government. For having protested against the government attempts to shrink and disappear the border of the Punjab; for having protested against the government attempts to shrink and disappear Sikh identity; for having tried to teach Sikh children in public school that they were Hindus and not a separate and distinct religion; for having tried through media and favoritism to erase the Punjabi language in Punjab in favor of Hindi so that in twenty years Punjabi would disappear and Sikhs would be unable to read or understand or interpret their own scripture or know if that scripture was slowly beginning to change or evolve to embrace lies.

Disappearances had been going on long before the boy had been born. Now they were becoming more frequent and he was hearing about how more and more Sikhs were being arrested without warrant or cause and being disappeared from the very face of the world never to be seen again or heard from again by their loved ones. He had even heard about how the police never even bothered to investigate the disappeared, as minority communities weren't much of a concern as a whole and were generally looked upon as lower than the low castes by the ruling caste government, which controlled the police, who controlled the military, who controlled the media, and who parceled out promotions and bonuses for silent obedience or demoted and banished and stigmatized for disobedience.

The police would often swear to agonizing families that their son or father or husband had been released from custody and that the matter was out of their hands. Some inspectors even suggested that perhaps their loved ones had run away, or per-

haps they had sought out a new beginning somewhere else.

Even when the families pressured the
police they would receive the same cold indifference. Political minions of the great draconian wiz-
ards--Brahmin extremists who could conjure perfect
magic to make anyone disappear--would often
claim that since the bodies couldn't be found no
crime had been committed; if no crime had been
committed then, really, there was no need for an
investigation. And those Sikhs who took it upon
themselves to investigate the disappeared...disap-
peared. And now the government was trying to
make this draconian disappearing magic legal.

And so the boy rarely overheard political
discussions in Trilokpuri, and the Sikhs of the
colony who were generally quiet and relatively
well-behaved rarely if ever incurred the wrath of
the wizards or their draconian magic.

In truth the boy had thought more about
politics in the short time that he knew Major and
his stories than in his entire life with his family and
neighbors. In truth the only time he remembered
that Trilokpuri had ever been stirred up in a political way was when the Sikh community had been
terrorized in a spiritual way.

When the government had attacked their
most sacred temple and slaughtered thousands of
Sikh pilgrims with tanks and grenades and
machine guns to arrest one man who, according to
his uncle, had never committed any crime other
than speaking out against the government for trying to erase an entire Sikh generation along with

their history, their books and their beliefs.

Of course there were accusations hurled at the man by the great draconian wizards, but those accusations were never proven in a court of law, and the man had boldly turned himself in so that they could be.

But even with all the magic in the world they could not prove him to be what they said he was. And so, the wizards had to release him, and they did, but only after burning all his sermons and his speeches against the wizards ruling and controlling his country's story.

His father and uncle argued over this man for days and the boy had never seen his father roused to anger before. His father swore that the man had no business seeking refuge in the Golden Temple to hide from the wizards.

His uncle, his veins beginning to bulge at these words, kept himself calm as he tried to explain to the boy's father that the man had not been hiding and that he had nothing to hide from or to be scared of because he had committed no crime.

His innocence had been proven in a court of law.

And this could not be denied or erased, only ignored by those who didn't want to see or accept truth.

The man was at the Golden Temple to protect Sikh identity, to protect the Sikh library and scriptures, which he claimed the wizards were trying to disappear in order to hide years of ruling caste tyranny. His uncle said that he didn't know how it happened, but the man had somehow secured documents and letters from the head wizard proving this need to destroy Sikh history. And the man--his uncle swore passionately--didn't want what had happened to the Buddhists and the Muslims to happen to the Sikhs; he strongly believed the Sikhs should protect their most sacred temple rather than let it be destroyed or desecrated.

If the man made any grave error it was that he used this letter written by the great wizard to perhaps blackmail the wizard into installing laws that would protect his religion from draconian, disappearing magic.

His uncle had said that if the man feared anything it was that the community would not heed his message to protect themselves against a government that sought to divide, cripple and humiliate them, and that if he feared anything it was that a generation of Sikhs would be erased so that future generations would be lost. That was the man and his message. He saw that the ruling castes would do anything to protect their birthright to enslave the lower castes and control the majority and that any philosophy or religion that spoke against this system of oppression would need to be erased.

Completely.

Erased and forgotten.

His uncle added that in democratic countries like England and the United States leaders representing minority communities were allowed to demonstrate and speak up for the protection of their language and identity or against human rights violations. But in the case of oppressive regimes like China, North Korea and India, minorities were expendable, minorities saw no justice, minorities were humiliated to be broken and broken to be silenced; and when a minority leader demonstrated or tried to point out some systemic flaw or injustice, they were very soon stigmatized by the nation's story, trampled upon, and stomped into the ground.

Forgotten like yesterday's news.

The boy's father laughed outrageously at these ridiculous statements and said he was taking his opinions a measure too far. His father was even insulted that his uncle should compare his country to North Korea, but his uncle made no apology. Not one. And as the boy's father defended India, the boy could see a new vein beginning to bulge and push up his uncle's forehead. The boy counted, 'two' and knew there would be many more to come before this discussion was over.

With unrestrained anger, his uncle stood and started calling the boy's father an ignorant peasant for trying to justify the government's actions. He swore that they were stealing water from Punjab and in twenty years Sikhs would lose everything because the land would be dry, dead, barren. In May Sikhs announced they would not pay water taxes, in June the government sent in the Indian army. Then with great passion and conviction he said that if the government wasn't as the man had said it was--dominated by wizards who sought the disappearance of the Sikh--then why had they attacked their holiest shrine on the

A Feast for Lambs

anniversary of the Guru's martyrdom, and done so knowing full well that it would be crammed with pilgrims who would travel from all parts of India and the world to honor the day.

Why?

Why had they not waited just one or two days to save their lives?

His uncle pounded the table fiercely. No one said a word, not even the boy's grandmother, who was inward and praying for all those unfortunate and unsuspecting pilgrims who had died at the Golden Temple massacre.

Because, his uncle answered after a pause, those lives belonged to Sikhs--devoted Sikhs who knew their history and who would make the pilgrimage to honor the Guru's martyrdom--and whether he wanted to believe it or not the man was right and the draconian wizards and their police and military minions sought to openly humiliate the Sikhs as a message to any minority that would stand up for their religious and language rights. Some of the most devout and religious Sikhs and their children were killed in the Golden Temple massacre. Had they chosen any other day there would have been half the pilgrims, half the casualties, half the murders. But they wanted to murder those who could and would pass on history even after the library was incinerated.

But they had set up a perimeter, shut out the media, and they had strategically calculated the attack to the day, to the minute, to the second so as to show their power and impunity to the Sikhs and to maximize the community's humiliation for one

simple reason--to break Sikhs. To break their spirit--
the spirit of rebellion and protest so that they could
restructure and redefine Sikh identity to embrace
Brahministic rituals and attitudes. To ward off any
future would-be leaders who would dare use their
voice against the government that was trying to
crush and disappear what the Sikh represented or
the message of their Guru.

More than this, he argued that he had
already been hearing from soldiers that the government had been preparing and premeditating this
attack on their temple for more than a year. He had
heard about one general who had boldly refused to
attack the Golden Temple with weapons a year
before the actual attack. He just would not do it. He
had even told the wizards that an attack was not
necessary, that there were several alternate solu-
tions and he even suggested that the government
simply surround the temple and cut provisions to
starve the militants out. A strategy they used before
with success and no casualties.

But this suggestion was ignored and another general who proposed a full frontal assault was
promoted and his plan--his operation--accepted.
And when this general who had said 'no' to the
wizards saw that a direct attack on the Golden
Temple was accepted and now inevitable, he
retired, refusing to do what his conscience wouldn't
allow him to do. Already there were rumors by
esteemed journalists that the government had been
practicing the assault for a year on a mock temple
in the Chakrata Hills. Anyone who said it was a
last-minute operation was with his first word a liar

and not to be trusted with subsequent words. One day, his uncle was sure, this would become fact and not rumor.

Whether the man they were after was in the temple or not they would have attacked to show what they could do without consequence. Whether the man they were after was in the temple or not, they would have attacked to make sure that Sikhs in the future could be assimilated into the fold that was not Hinduism--as many believed--but Brahminical Society. A society that thrived on social inequality and oppression. A society that was in direct opposition to everything the Sikh stood for.

The boy's father was silent. He didn't seem sure about anything anymore. Then his uncle, pacing around the table, added that even if the man had committed a crime, even if the man had hurt someone, even if the man had murdered someone, even if the man had murdered innocent civilians for his cause like the Brahmin extremists did on a daily basis but were left alone by the police and military, the government still had no right by international laws to attack, desecrate, and almost destroy their Vatican on Christmas Day.

His uncle then closed his final argument saying that the government's callous and calculated indifference to their Vatican and their pilgrims was a crowning testament to the man's message. The dark, draconian wizards of India, he swore, made the man's message true. He shouted with three veins pounding and pulsating and surging across his forehead that Brahmin extremist groups had done to minorities far worse than any Sikh had ever allegedly done to any citizen in the history of India; and yet, not a single ruling caste extremist was ever called a terrorist or ever put to justice or ever attacked in his temple.

His father shook his head broodingly. He didn't know much about what was going on or the man's message. So much had been obscured by the media. He said he would have to read more about the man who had challenged the wizards and that he would see for himself if there was any truth to all this. He added that if the man was trying to protect the temple and documents he had secured from the wizards then maybe he knew things about the government others didn't. Then his father tried to throw in a joke for a moment of levity, saying that the man would probably end up on a t-shirt like that fellow from South America and that everyone would remember his face but not his message. And that these t-shirts would be sold by the Brahmin extremists to fund their terrorism.

His father smiled at his own joke; no one except his uncle knew who he was talking about. His uncle forced a thin smile to be nice, but the boy distinctly counted another vein. Sighing and shaking his head in defeat, as though his father's words had delivered him a deathblow, his uncle just said that disgracing, damaging, rewriting and erasing Sikh memory was a serious matter and that ignorance and silence was precisely why their religion was being crushed by the extremists without opposition. Then he sighed sadly and added that they had burned to ashes irreplaceable books and scriptures and artefacts. And this, he assured the boy's

father, was everything. Whispering to himself, he
said:

"Burn our history and kill the most devout
in one assault...perfectly planned...in fifty years no
one will even remember what it was they were supposed to remember, and once again Sikhs will
embrace idols and caste as if it were truly a part of
their religion and not the very thing they stood
against."

When at last they left his uncle's home after
dinner, his father made the boy promise him that
he would stay out of politics as much as he human-
ly could and that he would understand why as he
grew older. Not wanting to upset his father, the boy
promised him that he would.

Now the afternoon sun rose and poured
through his pucca's tiny window and lit stacks of
kites his father had been working on so that their
small home bounced with the colors of the rainbow.
The boy drew and colored on the floor while his
mother prepared a small suitcase she had borrowed
from her mother. In whispers they were discussing
the prime minister and what had happened. Now
and then the boy would angle his ear and catch
snippets of conversation here and there. He knew
that his mother didn't want to leave anymore and
that she was worried for the both of them.

But his father continually reassured her
that there was nothing to worry about. He said that
they had been through far worse as a country and
that there would be peace. He discussed the assas-
sination of Gandhi and how the police and the military were in the streets way before Gandhi's death

was even announced on the radio. He reminded her how there was total media censorship so as not to fuel the fires of hate between Dalits and Brahmins. Even without all these quick and impressive measures taken by the government he still didn't believe low castes would have suddenly murdered upper castes just because a Brahmin terrorist assassinated Gandhi for questioning the Brahmin takeover of government and industry when the British quit India. There had been protests against the Brahmin government but they had been quickly suppressed by the police and army. If the prime minister died in the hospital, he assured her, it would be the exact same for Sikhs. The police and the military would be out in the streets and ready to put out flames of communal violence before they got out of hand. Unless of course she actually believed the life of a Brahmin was worth more than the life of a Sikh. She shrugged, reminding him that historically the Brahmin terrorists had always persecuted the Sikhs for their refusal to embrace the Brahmin caste system or to acknowledge their superior position at the top of the pyramid. Historically they would do all they could to protect their stranglehold on society smothering and assimilating rebellions as they rose. He told her to stop thinking like her brother and that the times have changed. Even though this was a Brahmin government, he was sure they would still do whatever they could do to help Sikhs if anything should happen. They had been able to help the Brahmins when one Gandhi was assassinated they would be able to help Sikhs if this Gandhi was assassinated.

A Feast for Lambs

For a moment his father was sad and ashamed as an Indian that such a thing could happen to one of the leaders who had been a voice for freedom and independence and, at the end of his life, the abolishment of caste. His mother looked at his father with her unflinching eyes; she considered his words.

After a reflective silence, she nodded and said that he was probably right and that her brother's strong opinion against the government was clouding her better judgment. His father agreed and was grateful that she saw things his way and not her brother's--that her brother's delusions weren't hers.

If violence did erupt, it would be quick like a match and would be smothered faster than it started. If there was violence it would be some random mob that would be dispersed just as soon as a constable fired the first warning shot.

Nothing would happen. He promised. Especially, he added, in the nation's capital. They had the whole Indian army in their backyard to protect them. She seemed to look up at him when he said the Indian army. She seemed to want to ask him if he was talking about the same Indian army that attacked the Vatican on Christmas Day.

But she said nothing. She had nothing to worry about and the boy could see she wouldn't let fear dominate her thoughts or actions. He added that they were also in the most apolitical colony in India. Everything, even if her brother was right, would be okay. Trusting his words, she nodded and continued packing, stopping only once to ask why a relative of Gandhi would ever attack innocent Sikh pilgrims to destroy the Sikh library. That's when the boy discovered something he never knew.

As he angled his ear, he heard his father tell his mother that the prime minister had no relation to the real Gandhi and that she had changed the spelling of her last name in such a way as to make the masses believe that there was. He discovered her last name had been distinctly Persian and that she had changed it to a Hindu last name.

But his father assured his mother that the Persian and the Hindu were as related as a mongoose and a cobra. On top of which, the real Gandhi was not a Brahmin, did not believe in the Brahmin birthright to rule and began to campaign against caste oppression before he was assassinated by a Brahmin. The prime minister was a Brahmin and seemed to quite enjoy her birthright to rule and saw an opportunity to rule with even greater ease with a slight tweak of her surname.

When the boy's mother finished packing she zipped up her suitcase and stood from her bed and walked behind the boy. She towered over him and watched him color a yellow and brown lion with something strange and white on its right paw. When she realized what it was she sighed affectionately and lay down on her stomach beside him. After a short silence she asked:

"Who is it?"

"Me."

The boy answered without taking his crayon off his sketch.

A Feast for Lambs

She gazed down at the drawing. A lion
with a white glove on its right paw. She smiled.
"What's that?" She indicated the white glove.

"Me."

"I know it's you." She pointed a finger at
the glove. "But what's that?"

He stopped coloring. He regarded her finger, then her smile, then her finger again. Could it
be that she really didn't know? He looked up at her,
a little disappointed. "A glove," he said and
returned to his coloring.

"A glove?"

"A glove."

"I didn't know lions wore gloves."

"This one does."

"Why?"

With a sigh, the boy stopped to look up at
her and wasn't sure how to answer the question.
"Because he can," he said at last, raising his eyebrows matter-of-factly. It was his sketch. His imagination. He wasn't interested in rules or constraints.
He didn't want to hear what a lion could or could-
n't wear. If he wanted to color a lion wearing a
white glove that was his choice as a young artist.
His mother merely nodded without saying anything. He returned to his masterpiece and she
watched and admired him. Then she stared up at a
few smuggled posters of the pop singer covering
one wall. She turned back to the picture. At last she
asked:

"Why the right paw?" She pointed at a picture of the singer with the white glove on his left
hand. The boy looked up, sighed, then pointed at

two other posters that showed the singer with the white glove on his right hand. "Oh," she said. "I guess if I had the choice I'd put it on the right paw, too."

The boy nodded.

"Who's the picture for?" She asked.

"You."

"So I don't forget you?"

"So you don't forget to buy a glove."

At these words she gasped incredulously. He smirked mischievously and paused in his coloring to look at his mother from the corner of his eye. He had been asking for a sparkling white glove for some time now and he wasn't about to give up just yet. Not on himself. Not on his dream. Not on his right hand. "Just one, not two," he explained. "For the right hand."

She shook her head incredulously and tapped the picture with her index finger. "Where's your family? How come just you and a glove?" she asked, accusing him of something he wasn't quite sure of yet.

The boy smirked, thought about the question, thought about why it had been asked and suddenly realized that there might be a lecture about ego cooking up in his mother's head. He needed a clever answer to subvert and evade the lecture to come. He thought about it a moment, then he said:

"They're in another picture."

And he watched her eyes carefully to see if she was buying into the idea that he had drawn them in another picture.

A Feast for Lambs

"In another picture?

He nodded reassuringly.

"Where?"

He could clearly see she was suspicious. "Haven't made it yet," he said. "When you come back it will be right there." And he pointed at an empty space on the wall.

She followed his finger, stared at the empty space on the wall. Nodding, she smiled at him and extended her pinky. A moment later he shook and sealed the deal. Then, as she withdrew her hand, he said:

"Promise you won't forget the glove."

And he extended his pinky.

She smiled and shook it and sealed the deal. His eyes lit up and in his mind's eye he could already see himself in his black kurta pajama and his sparkling black turban with his sparkling white glove as he walked on air to the amazement of all his envious friends in the colony.

Suddenly his mother interrupted his musical daydream.

"Shall we get some burfee for your brother?"

His eyes widened with his most favorite word in the world.

"And me, too."

He couldn't help himself. His mother's dark eyes widened at his words, and he already sensed his error and the lecture that would follow. He knew he had to throw in a few words to distract and sabotage her train of thought:

"Can he buy burfee over there? Can he make it? I wonder if they have good burfee over there? Do you think they have good burfee over there? I wonder."

She shook her head suspiciously. "Yes, I wonder indeed."

The boy saw in her eyes that she knew exactly what he had just done. He could see that she was just trying to figure out if she should say something or if she should spare him the lesson of ego before her trip. After a reflective moment she said:

"No, he can't buy burfee. They don't have the right milk there either. They do things to their milk and take away all the good stuff."

The boy scrunched his face. He wondered what milk without the good stuff tasted like, if it tasted like anything at all. His mother added:

"We should go to his favorite store. But first we'll go see Bigi. I think she has something for you."

She stood slowly, then looked over his tight kurta pajama, and he knew right away.

A kurta pajama.

This time he hoped his grandmother had made him a black kurta pajama as he had asked for a while back; and this time he hoped the sleeves matched up. His mother continued:

"Something I think you need."

The boy sighed. He'd rather splurge on burfee first. His mother didn't seem to appreciate this reaction in the least. "What's this?" And she mimicked his sigh.

A Feast for Lambs

"I just thought..." He paused and thought about his words carefully. "We could buy burfee before there isn't any more left. People like burfee and it would be a shame if there was none left when we got there."

"You think that could happen?"

"You never know."

"You never know?"

The boy nodded with a hint of concern for his brother.

"You never know."

She smiled.

"Okay. I accept that. We go buy burfee first because," she shrugged, "you never know."

"You never know."

The boy emulated her, shrugging and smiling.

Leaving his father to organize his kites, the boy marched out of their little pucca following his mother into the narrow streets as he passed a little boy in baggy underwear chasing scrawny little flies with a strainer.

Watching him, the boy wondered what fly boy was up to and what he wanted to do with the buzzing harvest that he contained in a small tin can.

Maybe, he too, could catch flies with a strainer and do something creative and unique with them. What? He wasn't exactly sure yet. But he could tell fly boy was on to something. Something big. Something big and fun.

Maybe he would just keep them in a tin can and collect as many flies as he possibly could until he had the most flies in the colony. Then he could release them inside a sweet store or a butcher shop and watch them feast. That could be fun. Definitely. But it could also land him in a whole mess of trouble. What he needed to do was weigh the anticipated fun against the anticipated trouble and see if it would be worth the effort.

As he thought about this, his mother regarded fly boy as he lunged for a fly and missed, then she instantly flicked her gaze down at the boy and her eyes said:

Don't you even think about it!

The boy and his mother soon marched past a cluster of sparrows running around a tea stall picking up scraps of rotis and biscuits here and there while a group of clean-cut men huddled around a radio and glared at them until they disappeared around a corner. The boy thought their looks were strange and somewhat chilling, then he forgot about their eyes as they passed a cluster of children running unsupervised under a tap of water. A woman shouted into the alley asking whose spoiled little brats were wasting water in such a foolish way.

Foolish for her.

Then as they rounded another corner the boy suddenly stopped in his tracks when he spotted a group of teenagers dancing in the street, each one trying to walk backward on air while making heart-pounding music with their mouths. With smiling eyes he observed that they didn't have a radio and that they didn't seem to really care. They would improvise and do just fine with what they

A Feast for Lambs

had. And what they had was life, energy and boundless passion for the song that had taken the whole world by storm.

Now the boy watched one teenager dance as the others made a circle around him, cheering him on. The front of his foot was flat on the ground. He suddenly slid it backward and just as his gliding foot reached the tip of the other foot he snapped it downward and the other foot took off in the same way. He repeated this over and over again until he created an illusion of gliding on air.

His chest pounding with the song, the boy wanted to run up to the teenager and ask him if he could teach him the dance. Suddenly he trembled with excitement thinking about the day he, too, would walk on air. His legs were jerking involuntarily and his feet just wanted to take off and dance and walk on air. His hips jerked to the beat of the music that came from the circle and his mother gave him a look that told him she was impressed with these young fellows and the dance and that maybe he wasn't so crazy for wanting a sparkling white glove.

The boy looked up at his mother and saw that she was impressed, and she was rarely impressed. He smiled and his eyes promised that one day he, too, would be dancing like that in the street. Then he turned to the music and his smile grew from mouth to ear as he watched them and believed with all his heart that he was part of a special generation, an amazing generation, a generation that could walk on air, a generation that would one day do great things in the world.

And just as he thought this, one teenager did a miraculous thing.

No.

An impossible thing.

A thing he had never seen before. A thing the boy would have never believed possible had he not seen it with his own two eyes. The teenager walked on air--

Going forward!

The boy had never seen the dance done in this way before, didn't think it could be done, and he looked up at his mother in complete disbelief. She recognized the look, widened her eyes and raised her eyebrows to acknowledge that she, too, was witnessing the feat as well and that she was definitely in the presence of magic. Then he quickly lowered his eyes to the teenager's feet to pick apart the technique move by move to determine how the boy could do such a thing.

His eyes were glued to the old, torn, raggedy sandals as they glided forward on air. Another boy then pushed the dancer out of the center of the circle with a friendly laugh and commenced to walk on air--

Sideways!

God. Please make it so I can one day dance like these boys! Please!

And just when the boy thought he had seen it all another teenager pushed the dancer out of the circle and motioned with his hands to raise the intensity of the booming beats issuing from their lungs and lips. The strength and bass of the music intensified and the boy's heart trembled with impossible magic as he heard the lyrics in his head and mumbled:

> *Lies become truth*
> *Lies become truth*
> *Tell the girl I am one*
> And the dancer began to walk on air--
> In circles!

These were masters! Genuine masters. Gurus of walking on air. And goodness, when he had his glove, he would use it as a key into their secret kingdom and he would learn from these masters the art of walking on air.

Yes, they would be his teachers. And yes, he would learn. It would take time, but time he had, unlike his parents who were just old, but not as old as his uncle and his grandmother.

At that instant the boy had a sudden epiphany. He looked up at his mother, tugged on her arm to get her attention and told her he had finally decided what he wanted to do with his life. He had been thinking it over for some time now and today at this moment without exception he had decided. For a while it had been between white ninja and moonwalker. And though he was pretty sure he could do both at the same time he had made his decision.

Watching these untouchable souls lost in their music, empowered by the song, transformed by the song, he suddenly realized that he definitely wanted to be a moonwalker.

And not just any old moonwalker.

A singing moonwalker.

A singer.

And he wanted his songs to be like pure alchemy so that they too would swirl, rise and float across distant lands and oceans and find their way into the hearts and minds of children everywhere to transform villages and slums and colonies into kingdoms of pure joy, laughter and happiness, even if only for a short while.

If music wasn't magic, he didn't know what was.

His mother smiled and laughed at this and she asked that his first album be dedicated to her. He made a face and said that he was a long way from an album and that first he would start with a song.

He knew that his mother and his grand-mother had always dreamed of traveling across India like the Guru who had used hymns and songs to open the people's eyes to the injustices of those who used religion to subjugate and oppress women; those who used religion to justify slavery and abuse; those who used religion to their own economic and political ends.

He knew that his mother and grandmother had once dreamed of singing for the movies and maybe, just maybe they had unknowingly passed down the dream to him. And he wondered if that was even possible.

As he watched these teenagers in their kingdom he wondered if the color of dreams could be passed on at birth like the color of eyes. If they could, he was sure he had inherited his mother's and not his father's dream.

A Feast for Lambs

At this thought he scrunched his face. He suddenly realized he wasn't sure if his father even had a dream. He certainly didn't talk about it, and he wondered if making kites was his dream.

His mother, he suspected, had a very real chance of making something of her dream. His grandmother, not at all; though he was careful to keep his opinions to himself. Partly because his mother made him keep his thoughts to himself. Partly because he understood how much his words could hurt her.

But the boy figured she must have known. She had to have known. She had always managed-- without fail--to contort and wrinkle and crack faces in two with every word she sang. People could hide their words, but not their reactions, and their reactions often spoke more than words ever could.

Suddenly the boy's mother tugged on his kurta and yanked him away. He yanked back, not wanting to leave. And she yanked harder and with authority and he reluctantly tore his eyes from this secret kingdom and followed her to the sweetshop.

As they journeyed through the maze she began to remind him that she, too, had once wanted to sing when she was younger. He responded that he knew this and that she had told him this many times before.

As they passed a row of rickshaw cycles she recounted the story about the Guru and his travels. The boy interrupted her and told her he had heard the story many times before, but she could tell it again if she wanted to, as he liked the story and she always seemed to tell it in a different way.

But his mother didn't seem to see the point, and she probably hadn't realized how many times she had repeated the story to the boy ever since he could speak.

They walked on in silence. As they passed a small spice store, she suddenly broke the silence and asked the boy if he understood the meaning of the story. He suspected her question to be a trap. All questions about his people's stories generally were, and he sometimes wished the story could just be a story without all the questions, discussions and parental lessons and interpretations.

His mother was clever and she knew how to smoothly trick him into lessons about life. But he was clever too, and he knew how to ditch school, even when school was cleverly disguised as a walk to the sweetshop; unknowingly, she had passed down her cleverness to the boy, and with every year he was proving to be her equal.

The boy thought carefully and realized saying nothing would be safer than committing to words. He nodded that he did understand the meaning of the story and watched her cautiously to see if school was in or out, watched to see if she would be satisfied with his silent nod.

Not this time.

This time she didn't seem to trust his silent, non-committal nod of understanding. He had probably waited a second too long. It was all in the timing. Next time he'd be quicker, and a lot more confident.

A Feast for Lambs

So his mother began to lecture him on the power of voice and how, if God should ever grant him the power of voice and the opportunity of audience, he should use it not only for monetary gain but to also champion the oppressed; she reminded him that facing tyranny and not turning one's back was a big part of his identity as a Sikh.

She reminded him that the ceremonial kirpan he wore under his kurta was there for a very specific reason, and that it was symbolic of speaking up and defending the religious rights and freedoms of others; that it was there to remind him and future generations that the greatest and most unforgiveable sin in times of tyranny was silence and indifference; that it existed to remind him that oppression required action from the Sikh, not silence--despicable and unforgiveable silence.

She then told him that the same tyranny that the Guru stood against when he dropped his last name still existed today and--she assured him--was stronger than ever. And she said that she would very much look forward to hearing a song against the evils of the caste system, one that would make his Guru proud of the lions he had created out of persecuted men and women that were being exterminated for boldly rejecting caste oppression and religious tyranny.

Lions that would not be persecuted or exterminated anymore.

Lions that would not be silent or indifferent anymore.

Lions that would face the tyrant.

And roar.

She then told him that he should never per-mit fear into his heart and that fear was the great corrupter--fear of poverty and fear of death--and that he should always sing from the heart and that if he sang from the heart he would always sing with God and that his song would be a kirpan in the heart of the tyrant. Having heard this lecture many times before, the boy waited for her expres-sion and he thought:

Let each word be a small punch in the belly of the tyrant, and let every tyrant die the thousand-word death.

But today it didn't come. For some reason his mother didn't say one of her favorite expres-sions, which she had heard somewhere or read somewhere and had tweaked for her own purpos-es. She merely said:

"Many believe that there are no tyrants anymore because there are no more kings. But there are. Only now instead of conquering with flags and swords they conquer with logos and laws, laws that only benefit the spoiled upper caste men who poi-son our water and air here because other abusers cannot do so in other countries."

The boy gave her a confused look. All this he didn't quite understand. This was something else, something new she was adding to the lecture.

A new tyrant for a new generation.

Logo kings.

Laws and contracts and environmental atrocities. She patted him on the back and said he would understand later on with time. Then she made him promise that if he was ever given the gift of voice he wouldn't waste it on fluff.

When the boy asked what she meant by fluff, she said songs that do nothing but distract people from the oppression of caste and the great abuses of the logo kings.

The boy made a face. He had absolutely no idea what she was talking about and he thought that maybe his uncle was rubbing off on her. All he could do was counter that he actually liked the fluff and that he thought fluff made him feel good so long as it had a fun and addictive beat.

His mother laughed out loud. There was definitely truth to his words.

Then he concluded that it was a promise he just couldn't make or keep because he assured his mother that fluff did have its place in the grand scheme of things. Not every word had to be a punch in the belly of the caste oppressor or the logo king. His mother laughed at his comeback and settled for a compromise.

A fine balance between fluff and truth.

This he could agree to, and he did so without hesitation.

The boy agreed that his future albums would be a fine balance between fluff and truth, and he also promised that if a logo king was paying for his music that the king would not own or control his voice and that he would still expose that logo king to the world if that logo king was hurting people somewhere, somehow in the world.

They pinky shook on it and he felt a strange tingling sensation. Somewhere deep down inside him the dream began to take shape and his heart began to devise a plan that included music lessons and dance lessons. And he felt strangely euphoric.

Somehow just talking about his dream made it feel real. Made it feel like it could really happen. Talking about his dream and making deals on his dream lifted his spirit in a way that made every step he took feel like he was walking on air. He cherished the feeling and wanted to make more deals and promises about his dreams.

The boy smiled inwardly and in his mind's eye he saw himself on stage in front of thousands of screaming people searching for him through the smoke and fog of the dry ice. The fog cleared up and there he was. All decked out in black, from turban to shoes, except for one sparkling, white glove on his right hand--homage to the superstar who had ignited the dream in his heart.

After a short silence he shook himself from his daydream and made his mother another promise. He promised her that he would dedicate his first album to his grandmother and his second album to her. She laughed aloud and before they knew it they were standing in front of the sweetshop.

Only the sweetshop was closed.

The boy grabbed the handle and attempted to slide the corrugated iron door open. Didn't budge. He tried again. Didn't budge. Refusing to give up, he tried again. Again, it didn't budge.

The boy swallowed hard and had a really awful feeling inside. He moved toward a small, oily

A Feast for Lambs

window and looked through the greasy handprints covering the glass and appraised the sweets in the refrigerated display-stacks of burfee, bason, glubja-mans--and the flies, circling, diving, sucking, licking and feasting as if they were the logo kings and queens of the world.

The boy looked up at his mother as if it were the end of the world. The kings and queens soiled and desecrated what should have been his to savor and enjoy and he couldn't understand why the sweet merchant would close his shop in the middle of the afternoon.

Didn't they know he was coming?

Didn't they realize he needed his burfee?

Him--

The future star of Trilokpuri.

For a long minute he watched the flies destroy and devour with complete abandon and impunity; for a moment, just a moment, he wished he were a fly.

"Maybe if we wait," he suggested.

His mother shook her head. "No. It's closed." She looked at the other stores, at the doors and the ripped and faded posters of congressmen and movies plastered over them. They were closed as well. None of it made sense. She turned back to the grimy window. The boy kicked the dusty cement ground and mumbled and cursed words he knew he wasn't allowed to use.

But his mother was too distracted to notice.

She seemed to be lost in thought as she stared at a picture of a blue god inside the shop. A serious and somber expression came over her. A moment later she pulled the boy away from this kingdom of butter, spices, sugar and logo kings and queens, and she promised she would make some burfee at home.

ᘓ

Within minutes they were at his grandmother's
home, his mother knocking on the thick, wooden,
freshly painted turquoise door. Standing beside her,
the boy shifted nervously on his feet and was visi-
bly concerned for his cheeks. For one day, just one
day, he hoped his grandmother would leave them
alone; his mother knocked again and the boy
looked up at her and asked:

"Can you ask Bigi to stop?"

"Stop what, bete?"

"You know."

"I don't know."

He made a face, then imitated his grandmother, saying:

"Raj Kumar!"

And he pretended to pinch an invisible
boy's cheeks. Restraining a laugh, his mother's eyes
instantly nudged him and commanded him to stop
before the front door opened. The boy stopped, and
his mother said:

"She loves you, okay? Don't make jokes like
that."

"She pinches me."

"She loves you."

"She pinches me."

"She loves you."

"Pinching is not loving."

"Maybe it is. How do you know? Not everyone says 'I love you' in the same way."

The boy thought about this for a moment and wasn't so convinced. In the movies they always seemed to say it in the same way. In the movies they seemed to just say it. They'd say it with cheesy music, then everyone, including the villains, would suddenly break out into a perfectly choreographed dance.

No one pinched anyone.

Pinching didn't make any sense.

Not to the boy.

"Doesn't feel like love," he said evenly. Then a sudden thought came to him, and he realized he had never really heard his father and mother say the words or dance like in the movies.

Despite this, somehow, deep inside, the boy knew that they did love each other.

Not by songs and dances and poems, but by looks and smiles and gestures that could have very easily been a song, a dance, and a poem all in one; and, if they used words at all, then they were words camouflaged in such a way that they seemed to be about something else. But the boy knew exactly what they meant. He always did, even if they thought he didn't.

The boy didn't understand why his parents did this. He didn't understand why they had to be so complicated and he sometimes wished they could be more like the movies. Then he wouldn't have to observe and dissect and interpret so much. His parents very often made his life a lot more

A Feast for Lambs

complicated than it ever needed to be.

Now he was actually supposed to believe that stretching and pulling and abusing a person's cheeks was an expression of those hard-to-say words.

The boy sighed.

He definitely preferred the movies to real life.

Life seemed so simple in the movies.

The words. A perfect villain. A dance. A fight. Another dance. The words. A dance. A fight. A dance. The words. A dance. Perfect hero defeats perfect villain and everyone lives happily ever after. The end.

"Can't she find another way?"

"I think she has many ways."

"This one hurts! Really hurts!"

"That's love."

"That's love!" the boy mocked, then queried, "Can't she just pinch my arms? At least then I won't have red cheeks all day."

His mother looked down at him and shrugged; she didn't know what to tell him anymore.

Suddenly he heard footsteps approaching the door. He took a deep breath and held it. An instant later the thick door creaked open to reveal a short, hefty, sun-wizened old woman in a bright yellow and green Punjabi dress and a long pink chunni. The hoarsest and happiest voice in the world greeted him.

"Raj Kumar!"

His grandmother beamed down at him as if

103

he were the whole reason for her existence. Behind her, in the shadows, his uncle forced a grin and his lips trembled slightly under the strain. His shoulders were broad and his bearded face was square and serious. Two eyes that never smiled peered down at the boy. His hair was uncovered and it fell past his waist and the boy thought that his uncle looked like one of those big, angry gorillas he had seen in the nature magazines. An aura of concern and discontent seemed to surround him.

The last time he had seen his uncle he had nearly thrown his father out of his home for not agreeing with him on an issue of last names. The boy had counted four distinct veins, maybe five, creeping up his forehead so he knew his uncle was adamant about his position. His uncle had said it was deplorable to see baptized Sikhs adopting an antiquated practice that had been banished by the Guru centuries ago.

According to his uncle, last names had been removed to overcome ego and to undermine the oppressive and segregating caste system of the cruel rajas who used last names to classify, organize, and value people like beans.

By forgoing their last names, Sikhs would show the powers-that-be that they could not and would not be labeled and controlled and counted like beans; by forgoing their last names they would remind themselves that they all belonged to one family, a much bigger family than the one they had been born to. Men to the family of Singhs. Women to the family of Kaurs. Both Singh and Kaur are different, necessarily different, different like Yin and

A Feast for Lambs

Yang; yet both are powerful, strong, equal--both completing each other in a perfect circle of life.

The boy's father said reassuming a last name was fine and that he happened to really like last names and that he didn't think himself less or more of a Sikh for having one. At which point his uncle said he may as well forgo the uniform than live the life of a Sikh who picked and chose what he liked at what he called the baptismal buffet. It wasn't a buffet. A baptized Sikh should not have a last name period, end of story. At which point his grandmother told them to both shut up and eat their daal-rotis.

But his uncle didn't stop. He continued on and on about how this sudden and current fad of keeping the last name would soon become commonplace, and that most Sikhs would forget that the baptismal act of forgoing the last name was as important, if not more important, than the uniform. It was everything the uniform stood for. The rejection of segregation, the rejection of inequality. The rejection of oppression and tyranny. The need to see all as One. A bold denial of caste cruelty.

His uncle swore that Sikhs who kept their last names were not real Sikhs and that most Sikhs would, in due time, forget this requirement because the government would make it so, and that if they ever really did need a quick refresher on the name of a true, baptized Sikh, all they would need to do is peruse the list of the Sikh soldiers that had fought in World War One and World War Two in both Europe and Asia. Not one, he challenged, had a last name other than Singh. Not one. But this, too, he swore, the government would change in their attempt to make Sikhs embrace caste once again.

Most Sikhs, he said proudly, outright refused to return to the old way of being branded like a bean. There were no farmer castes, no warrior castes, no merchant castes with Sikhs. The idea of taking on a name that even suggested a caste undermined the very core of the religion. Sikhs with a last name, he swore with great passion, were not true Sikhs. Maybe, he said, they were half Sikhs. Maybe...

Something deep inside the boy told him that this time it was not his father but his uncle who had somehow missed the whole point of forgoing the last name that sought to grade a person by the contingency of their birth.

But the boy wasn't sure what that something was.

At last his father shook his head and said in a calm tone that it was all a matter of opinion and interpretation and that the baptismal uniform and name was symbolic.

His uncle, chunks of rotis flying out of his mouth, yelled that retaining your last name simply undermined the whole point of baptism and that he was sorry and profoundly disappointed that his nephews had a last name. His uncle then unapologetically accused them of only being half Sikh. At which point his father instantly took offense to this and things grew ugly fast; words were exchanged so viciously that the boy hadn't understood a word.

But his angry gorilla of an uncle never budged on his position. He shook his thick, stubborn head and said that his nephews may as well have been unbaptized Sikhs, who, he said, were only quarter Sikhs, adding that they didn't even deserve the Sikh family name in the first place. Then, with the rage of a silverback, he said worse than the quarter Sikhs were the baptized Sikhs with last names who had the audacity to disrespect the baptismal uniform and everything it stood for by drinking alcohol or using drugs or proudly announcing their caste.

These he called the anti-Sikhs.

And his uncle much preferred the half Sikhs and quarter Sikhs to the anti-Sikhs. At least the quarter Sikhs were not cowards hiding in uniforms pretending to be what they were not. At least the quarter Sikhs had the potential of becoming full-Sikhs one day without disgracing the uniform. The anti-Sikhs had no hope. No hope whatsoever. They were cowards to the marrow and proved it every time they put whiskey or any other mind-altering substance to their lips.

His father stood upright with a deep sigh and said that he didn't want his son to listen to all this angst, anger and misinterpretation he was trying to pass off as truth; he said it would only pollute his mind and make him look at people differently. Besides, it was too much of a beautiful day to have someone call him or his sons a half Sikh for wanting to keep his last name.

The boy thought about his uncle's words for a long time after that and his heart was telling him that his uncle had missed the whole point of the baptismal ceremony. For a long time he didn't know what it was that was bothering him so much about his uncle's attitude, but he knew there was something deeply wrong with his classifications of Sikhs. He thought about it for many nights, then one morning he woke up with the answer: he knew what was bothering him so much.

It was simple.

It was everything the Guru had taught Sikhs to be wary of.

Anger. Pride. Ego.

Even if his uncle had made strong points about his religion and how Sikhs were supposed to drop their last names as a protest to caste, he had somehow, in some strange egotistical way, found a way to create his own caste system for Sikhs. He would take an unbaptized Sikh with kindness on his lips and in his heart rather than his uncle's ego and anger and his need to be right.

In his own egotistical way, in his own egotistical need to be better than others, in his need to be looked upon as higher than others, more complete than others, more worthy of God's praise than others, he had found a way to classify, organize, and value Sikhs like beans.

It wasn't about last names.

It was about being part of a family that appreciated differences and saw others as equals, despite their beliefs or way of life.

It was about being One, and seeing yourself as One with All, which his uncle, despite the baptismal uniform, did not see or could not see or would not see in his need to see himself as superior to other Sikhs. His words were just as despicable as the whiskey or all those intoxicants he jabbered on about. And his baptismal uniform--

Undermined by his anger, vanity and the personal caste system.

Now, standing in a pool of sunlight, the boy squinted at his uncle's forehead but couldn't make out any veins. He really hoped that today he could keep his anger and his ego to himself and, as he thought this, his grandmother approached him and said the boy's name with great pride.

The boy sighed softly. "Bigi," he said as he kept watch of her chubby, wrinkled hands and waited for the assault. He couldn't wait until he was older and the manhandling of his cheeks would stop.

She leaned toward him.

Instinctively, he took a small step back.

Instinctively, she countered his small step back with two quick steps forward. He was no match for the veteran cheek squisher. Two heavy arms reached out and caught hold of his puffy cheeks and pinched them black and blue with what his mother had once described as love and what he had described as torture. To this his mother had responded that as the boy grew older he would soon discover that these words would slowly become one and the same.

The boy looked up at his mother as his grandmother shook his tiny head side to side and back and forth by his cheeks; his mother gave him the eyes and he said nothing.

A second later she kneeled to embrace him tight. He closed his eyes and thought that if by fifteen she was still doing this he would run far, far away and maybe join his brother in America where he knew children with puffy cheeks had rights.

At last his grandmother released him and stood with difficulty. She then told him she had a big surprise for him and ushered them both inside.

In the doorway the boy embraced his uncle, and could now see two veins and wondered what he had been arguing about; then he trudged inside, knowing what to expect as a 'surprise' and hoping his grandmother had at least remembered that he had specifically asked for black and that only a black kurta pajama would go with his sparkling white glove, which would very soon be covering and protecting and empowering his right hand.

His grandmother's pucca was one large room where she slept and one small room where his uncle and his aunty slept. In both rooms there were string beds covered in wool blankets. Both rooms were lit by one flickering light bulb attached to an exposed wire that dangled dangerously from the ceiling.

Humming, his grandmother searched for something under her bed. His uncle slowly made his way to his room. He lay down on the bed and seemed lost in another world as he stared at a single chappal he had high up on a wooden shelf to remind him of the last dinner they had all enjoyed as a family before his brother left for America.

It was a chappal that had been thrown at him by a young Hindu man who had been deeply offended by something his uncle had announced to a table of politicians. For some odd reason his uncle

A Feast for Lambs

had kept the chappal to remind him that there was hope for Sikhs in India and that he absolutely respected and admired the man who had hurled this chappal at him.

The boy didn't want to think about the chappal or the man who had hurled it.

That was a very strange evening he didn't think he'd ever understand. One that would boggle his mind for years to come.

Staring at his uncle, he very quickly understood not to disturb him. He sensed that he and his grandmother had been arguing over something he didn't really care to know about and that they were now trying very hard not to talk about. The tension in the air was palpable, yet there was something about his uncle that was bothering him. He narrowed his gaze on the chappal and his uncle and then realized what it was.

His uncle wasn't angry.

He didn't sense anger at all.

He sensed something else.

He sensed fear. And he had never observed or sensed such worry and anxiety in him. It wasn't like his uncle to radiate fear. Not in the least. It was usually quite the opposite.

When his grandmother returned, she was carrying the folded garments in her hand, and on top of the garments he noticed something glitter in a shaft of sunlight that poured into the house through the small window.

His heart skipped a beat.

Could it be?

No.

Could it?

She stood before him. He stared at the sparkling white glove on top of the white garments, then his grandmother, then his mother, then his grandmother.

He stopped breathing, his mouth opened slightly. His whole body tensed as he touched the glove and felt the granular sparkles. It really looked like the glove of the original moonwalker.

It really did.

Really, really did!

She may have done it.

He lifted the glove slowly and appraised it as if it were the Kohinoor Diamond before it had been split in two.

Now even his grandmother stopped breathing as the boy appraised her work.

"I made it myself. To wear with your kurta."

And with these words her mouth opened slightly, waiting. Her whole wrinkled body tensed. She looked at the boy for a reaction and said softly:

"Hard to find this shiny material…"

His grandmother watched his every move, his every twitch, his every expression, and she smiled nervously, waiting to see if she had given him something he could be proud of, something he could show off to other children, telling them that his grandmother had made so-and-so for him and that she could make anything she put her heart to with her ancient, yet magical sewing machine.

Outside, a sudden swarm of bright colors and children surged by the small, dusty window like a river of bubbling excitement. Dozens of children chased a poor, mangy dog that barked and growled and pleaded to be left in peace. Then the excitement gradually faded as they ran down the street and disappeared in the colony. A quiet settled in the room as everyone, even his uncle, looked to the boy to see how the glove fit.

The boy slipped the glove on and froze midway. Suddenly he realized the glove had five fingers but no real place for his thumb. He swallowed and tried again. But there was no use. The sleeve for his thumb was too thin and too high. He panicked without showing it. He looked at his grandmother and was about to say something. Without realizing it, he was about to break her heart in two. But seeing this, his mother quickly intercepted and put in:

"Bigi traveled far to find the material. She spent weeks to make it just right for you."

Each word was a clear warning punctuated by unflinching and dangerous eyes. There would be consequences to his words if he didn't choose them properly. He knew he could only say one thing and inside he hoped his mother would still buy him a glove--a real glove--in America.

And so the boy proceeded to hug his grandmother and he thanked her a million times and said the glove fit perfect. His grandmother breathed again, and her heart filled with heaven as she unfolded the crisp new kurta pajama and dangled it before his disappointed eyes. "Let's see it with this," she said, her voice filled with renewed confidence.

Jessi Thind

As he forced his chubby thumb into the thin sleeve of his five-finger glove, he looked at the white kurta pajama and asked:

"Didn't you find black?"

He didn't understand how she could mistake white for black. He had been clear. He knew he had been clear. He absolutely needed a black kurta pajama to go with his white glove. But, deep down inside, he already knew the answer. Deep down he knew that she hoped that her grandson would one day be a politician and do good things for the community and country, and that she, more than anything else, wanted him looking like a fancy politician with an unblemished, perfectly starched 'neta' pajama.

"No grandson of mine will wear black," she said, and helped him slip into the pajama, then the kurta. "Boys and girls shouldn't wear black. It doesn't make sense."

It wasn't the answer the boy had expected, nor was it one he understood. Why shouldn't children wear black? What didn't make sense to her about a child in a black kurta pajama?

He looked up at his mother as his grandmother folded the hems of his pajama once so they fell just below the ankles. His mother smiled at him. He indicated that one sleeve of his kurta was longer than the other and was instantly silenced by eyes that promised consequences. He sighed and wished for just one perfect kurta pajama--black-- and one real, sparkling white glove.

"You'll grow," his grandmother said, glancing up at the forced grin on the boy's face. "Boys your age grow fast--too fast." Then she regarded him a moment and she looked concerned. After a moment she asked:

"Are you still having bad dreams?"

The dreams of the fog and the decimated jungle still came--

Every night.

But the boy shook his head, knowing that his grandmother would attempt to teach him some hymn she would insist on singing to help him clear his mind. Even his mother gave him a look. Not an admonishing look. Not a commanding look. A pleading look.

"No--no more bad dreams."

"Good. Boys your age shouldn't have bad dreams."

"No more bad dreams."

"Very good."

Despite his answer she began to hum gently and he knew it was coming. She glanced at him and nodded, seeing if he could guess what she was about to sing. He looked to his mother, and she looked at him and they were both concerned.

Deeply concerned.

Then she stopped suddenly, and relief washed over the whole room. The boy sighed silently; his mother, too. His grandmother grabbed the old kurta pajama and held them and stared deeply at them, looking lost and pensive.

A silence.

A short silence.

Then, all of a sudden, without warning, she began to sing her favorite hymn and all who heard, including his uncle, cringed inwardly and smiled outwardly and waited for the relief that would come with silence. At last his grandmother sang the last two verses of the hymn and--

It was all over.

Then she shook the dust off the old rags she still held in her hands and told the boy he should hum and sing a protection hymn before bed or whenever he felt scared.

The boy agreed with a slight nod and his grandmother folded the old kurta pajama so that maybe he could use it for Holi. As she did, his mother explained to his grandmother how they had journeyed to the sweetshop to buy burfee to take to America only to discover the shop was closed.

At this his grandmother seemed deeply shocked and offended. "You like that burfee over my burfee?" She regarded the boy with her unflinching, demanding eyes.

For the boy it was like looking into his mother's eyes--more seasoned, stronger even--and now he could sense a trap. She wanted him to say she made the best burfee in all of India. And he knew with his grandmother he would have to say something and that silence wasn't even an option. Cautiously, he answered:

"It's very sweet."

"Is very sweet good?"

"For those who like very sweet burfee it is very good."

She paused to consider this.

"Do you like very sweet burfee?"

He thought his answer through.

A Feast for Lambs

"Sometimes yes," he answered. "Sometimes no."

She nodded pensively. "Sometimes yes. Sometimes no." She chewed the answer over, looking at the boy; then she interpreted, "Sometimes you like the sweetshop burfee best...and sometimes you like my burfee best."

The boy nodded and prayed this was the last question he would have to endure about burfee. He knew his grandmother had to be the best at everything almost as much as his uncle always needed to be right. Though his mother had once explained that this observation wasn't entirely accurate. His grandmother didn't need to be the best at everything to everyone in the world. She only needed to be the best at everything to her grandchildren, who were everyone and the world at the same time.

His mother had said that one word from his lips, whether he believed it or not, could fill her with heaven for the entire day, week, month, perhaps even year.

The boy thought about this and suddenly realized he didn't need to be so careful with his words. He didn't need to evade the trap. This trap he would spring. This trap he'd step right into, gladly. "Actually," the boy said after a moment. "I like very sweet the best." And he watched her carefully and he could see her eyes slowly filling with heaven. "Your burfee is the best and we all say so because it's very sweet."

His grandmother regarded his mother with wet eyes. She nodded and grinned at her. "You have a good boy," she said, then added, "two good boys." She then looked at the boy and promised to give him a little taste of heaven later on in the week.

"I will make you the best burfee ever. Not now. Later. Don't think I can make it now. I must feel like making burfee. Takes time to make the best burfee, but I will make it soon, this week, and I will come over to see how Bapu is doing, and we'll eat it together and it will be just for us."

The boy nodded. He suddenly realized that getting himself caught in his grandmother's traps wasn't such a bad thing after all. He might just stumble into more in the future. "Can I lick the spoon?" he asked. Licking the wooden spoon that had mixed the steaming hot, sugary milk fudge was his most favorite thing to do in the world. He even enjoyed the spoon more than the actual cooled-down, square morsels of burfee.

His grandmother peered at him and stuck out her index finger and winked. The boy made a face, not quite understanding what she wanted. At last she said:

"Promise."

The boy was about to correct her when he realized it didn't even matter. Finger. Pinky. Close enough. He stuck out his finger, wrapped it around hers, and they shook. His grandmother looked up at his mother and beamed proudly and felt seventy years younger for knowing the secret finger shake. Then the boy went to the other room and hugged his uncle--who was now holding and admiring the chappal--goodbye.

When he returned he hugged his grand-mother; a moment later she broke away and gave his cheeks another good twist and tug.

God. Please...I'm begging...another way to say 'I love you'. Please inspire her with another way. I'm begging. Please...

His grandmother walked them out into the steadily darkening street. She held his mother by the shoulders, took in a deep breath, and just looked at her for a long moment that seemed like forever. Then she embraced her like she never wanted to let go.

The boy tilted his head curiously. He had never seen his grandmother embrace his mother in this way before. It felt strange, very strange, and yet, very pure at the same time. As he thought this his mother pulled away and stared at her as though she had been slapped in the face. After a pause, she asked why she was embracing her like she was going away forever. His grandmother's eyes filled, but she didn't cry. At once his mother asked:

"What's wrong?"

"You're going away."

"Only for a short time. I'll be back."

"I know."

"I'll be back."

"I know."

With these words, his grandmother embraced her again, harder. Now his mother seemed frightened, like his grandmother wasn't telling her something about her health. She tried to pull away, but with every attempt his grandmother squeezed tighter. "I've never seen you like this," she said, and waited for an explanation. "Is there something you need to tell me?"

His grandmother shook her head and swallowed a lump. "My heart is sad," she said, and she cleared her throat. "My heart feels strange, that's all. I don't know why. Don't ask me why. I have no explanation…I don't know…I just feel like hugging you strong. Is that such a crime?"

"No."

"Don't worry."

"I'm worried."

"Don't."

"I am."

"I've never felt like this, that's all…"

"Like what?"

"I told you…I can't explain…"

At last she released her daughter. Doing so, she opened her daughter's hand and slapped a bundle of rupees in it. Then she took her hand and closed her fist over the money. His mother shook her head, and his grandmother gave his mother a bold, uncompromising look that instantly silenced any objection and told his mother that she could spoil her grandchild if she wanted to and that she had been saving for quite a while now to do so. Without saying anything she peered into his mother's eyes for a long moment, as if she were trying to burn her daughter's face into her soul's memory. At last she said:

"You have good boys."

The boy's mother looked down at the ground, and the boy knew that this was the best compliment his grandmother could give his mother. She said:

"You have very good boys."

A Feast for Lambs

His mother nodded without looking up at her. But his grandmother placed her dry, wrinkled finger under her chin and forced her to look at her.

"I'm trying to say something."

His mother nodded.

"I know you are…I know…but why are you are acting like this?"

"Like what?"

"So different."

"It's okay to be different sometimes."

"But why?"

His grandmother didn't answer. She smiled affectionately and shrugged. The boy supposed she really didn't know why she was acting this way and that she truly didn't have an answer. Then, all of a sudden, she did something he had never seen her do to his mother before. With quick, veteran hands, she reached out and pinched his mother's cheeks. She gave them a good twist and tug and seemed to want to pinch them forever as she peered deep into her and said good-bye with her eyes.

୧

It was his favorite dessert, his favorite smell. Sweet milk fudge cooking slowly over a portable, kerosene stove. As he stirred the thick mixture, he couldn't understand why burfee was only served after meals. He couldn't understand why it had been designated solely as a dessert. It made no sense. Burfee was a meal unto itself. He could have it for breakfast, for lunch, for dinner, for dessert and right before bed. Why not? Burfee, after all, was just butter, milk and sugar, and some flavor improvisation to make it personal. What, he wondered, could be healthier than butter, milk and sugar?

He couldn't think of anything.

At which point he had an inspiration.

He thought a bowl of buttermilk sugar would definitely go well with butter, milk and sugar. There was no such thing, of course. But he could make it up. He didn't see why not. He would have to find the right time and place to propose the experiment to his mother; she would probably correct him and tell him that he meant buttermilk with a little sugar.

Sweetened buttermilk.

Of course, that was not the idea at all; and he would have to correct her and explain it was just the opposite. Sugar with a little bit of buttermilk.

Buttermilk sugar.

The boy had been stirring the gooey, swirling golden mix over the stove for some time now. He had done everything under his mother's careful guidance and supervision. He had crushed the cardamom pods and the cinnamon stick and he had slivered the almonds. He had poured the milk and the clarified butter into the steel pot. He had added some rose water and sugar, lots of sugar, and then, he had added his mother's secret ingredi-ent--a tablespoon of vanilla extract. He mixed and mixed the sugary sludge and watched it melt into edible gold as he breathed in the swirling scents that filled his home with something otherworldly. And he felt sure that if the smell of hot, cooking burfee was not the smell of heaven, there was no heaven.

The boy did this while he watched his mother prepare dinner with his father. They sat by a makeshift counter his father had fashioned out of planks of discarded wood he had found in the alley near the gully. His mother chopped onions, ginger and garlic and prepared a spicy base mix for mut-ton keema while his father chopped potatoes and hot green chili peppers.

His father had never really cooked any-thing before, but today was not like any other day; today was the last day to learn how to make keema before his mother left for months. His father's mother had passed away a year ago and he still swore she made the best keema. He would have asked his mother-in-law, but his brother-in-law forbade meat in his house, which was another point of contention between the two.

In fact, they argued about vegetarianism all the time, which made get-togethers long, uncomfortable and, for the most part, undesired. His uncle contended that full Sikhs and not half Sikhs or quarter Sikhs or anti-Sikhs were forbidden to eat meat. Half Sikhs and quarter Sikhs and anti-Sikhs could do whatever they wanted; he didn't care about those Sikhs; those Sikhs were inferior to full Sikhs; lesser Sikhs he esteemed as apostates and weren't worth consideration.

The boy's father had scoffed at his uncle's misinformation and claimed that the Guru, like the Buddha, ate meat whenever it was available and especially on special occasions. He also pointed out that at one time or another the Guru was considered an adroit hunter and that vegetarianism in Sikhism was a relatively new concept pushed down by radical Sikh vegetarians who perhaps sought to further divide Sikhs and create yet another caste slot in the newly created Sikh caste system. His father laughed and asked his brother-in-law what he was considered now. A three-quarter, non-vegetarian Sikh with a last name?

The joke didn't go over well with his uncle. His face tensed, his eyes darkened, three veins began to throb and push and crawl up his forehead. But he wasn't upset at the Sikh caste joke or the remarks that spawned from them. He was furious at the idea of being called a radical.

His father tried his best to calm him down so they could all eat in peace and he said that he didn't think his uncle was a radical and apologized for saying such a thing. Then he said that he had probably exaggerated and that he didn't really want to waste any more time or energy on the issue and that they should just eat in peace. He added that he thought that maybe, just maybe, his uncle had some valid points and that he would definitely look into the matter and see where this concept of full Sikhs being vegetarian originated.

But his uncle didn't believe or accept his father's feeble attempt to politely tiptoe out of the argument, not for a second, and he certainly wouldn't lose an argument in front of his family. His need to be right overwhelming him, he continued on and on like a stubborn silverback. At last he argued his strongest point and said that the mere fact that meat wasn't served at communal religious lungar meals was a testament to how right he was.

His father sighed and politely disagreed. He then reminded his uncle of the purpose of the communal meal, which he maintained was not only to feed the poor, misfortunate and destitute, but to break bread with followers of other religions and beliefs. Lungar epitomized the Sikh belief that all religions were manifestations of the same unknowable Truth, a Truth that transcended knowledge and reason and human understanding and lungar, he assured him, sought to include, not exclude.

To serve beef was to exclude followers of Hinduism. To serve pork was to exclude followers of Islam. To ensure Hindus and Muslims would always feel welcome for the weekly communal meal, meat was forbidden. Otherwise Sikhs ate meat and had done so ever since they had been forced to hide in the forests and jungles to avoid persecution from the Hill Rajas, who saw a clear and intolerable threat against their caste system in the Sikhs. It was a matter of reverence and respect shown to other religions and beliefs that meat was not served at lungar.

The boy instantly looked at his uncle's forehead and waited for a new vein. But the veins hardly showed as they faded with his changing thoughts. His uncle wasn't angry anymore. The veins soon disappeared and he went very quiet and pensive and seemed to be reminded of something that he had known long ago but had somehow forgotten.

That evening, walking home, his father seemed distant and heartbroken. When his mother inquired, he said that he felt that Sikhs were losing sight of the real issues, which he took to be ego, lust, hate, greed, inequality and intolerance. He sighed and said that he was discouraged because his religion had been inspired by all the right reasons and was now being divided for all the wrong ones, and he didn't speak again the whole night.

The boy thought of all this as he stirred the burfee that steadily became harder and harder to mix with every drop of water that puffed out of the thick, golden sludge and released a small cloud of vapor like smoke into the air. His mother surveyed him carefully. He needed to be careful so as not to burn the bottom. One slip and he could corrupt the entire mix with the taste of burnt sugar, and they didn't have the ingredients for another batch. She warned:

"Careful not to burn."

"I know."

"Keep stirring so you mix it good."

"I know."

"If you don't stir it properly it will burn and taste burnt everywhere."

"I know."

She also had another reason to keep her eye on him. She didn't want him spoiling his dinner by indulging in steaming hot burfee.

"Don't even try it."

"Try what?"

He smiled mischievously.

"I know," she said.

"Know what?"

"I saw."

"Saw what?"

He pretended he didn't understand.

"Don't!"

"Don't what?"

"You know!"

"Know what?"

He raised the wooden spoon. It dripped with wonderful, steaming heaven. "I just need to test to make sure," he said, bringing it closer to his greedy little mouth.

"I said don't!"

He brought the spoon closer.

"Maybe it's already burnt."

"It isn't burnt. You'd smell it."

"You never know."

"I know."

A Feast for Lambs

"To be sure..."

"I am sure!"

He brought it even closer. "It smells good, but I wonder if it tastes good." His mischievous eyes smiled and the spoon neared his lips. He much preferred burfee directly from the cooking pot than cooled down and sliced up into squares to be shared.

This time she said nothing. Instantly she stopped dicing onions and stared at him with smoking eyes that dared him to disobey her. Slowly, the spoon descended back into the pot and continued mixing without another word. He sighed, but he had hope for the future, knowing his grandmother and his father would let him eat directly from the pot in the coming weeks.

A sudden commotion outside in the distance caught his parent's attention.

A window of opportunity.

Instantly the spoon came up to his mouth. As he hoisted the steaming burfee near his lips and nose his mother swung her eyes back at him.

He froze suddenly, convinced she had eyes on the back of her head.

She didn't shake her head, she didn't say a word; she just stared at him, and dared him with her eyes. Another sigh. Then he slowly lowered the spoon back into the pot with a defeated plop.

A sudden roar of anger shook the street again.

His parents exchanged worried looks.

Then they came again and again. The boy couldn't make out the drunken words, but he somehow made out that someone was screaming that all Sikhs should get out of Hindustan.

His parents leapt from the cutting table and rushed outside.

Curious, the boy followed behind and squeezed between his parents to watch what was going on and saw Sikh families standing in doorways silhouetted by the warm light pouring out of their puccas.

His mother mumbled for him to return inside; but he barely registered her whispered words as he watched a three-man mob, boldly and fearlessly stagger through the streets, drinking from a bottle, pointing at all the Sikhs in the doorways, shouting and slurring random, incoherent and chaotic anti-Sikh sentiments. Sentiments that many Sikhs understood existed amongst the extremists but had never experienced in their neighborhoods.

"Throw the Sikhs out!"

"Throw them out!"

"Die, Sadars!"

"All of you!"

"Sikh dogs!"

"Hindustan shall be rid of you!"

"Enemies of Hindustan out with you!"

"Hindu! Hindi! Hindustan!"

"Let no Sikhs be spared!"

"Get out while you can!"

By Hindustan the boy knew this three-man mob meant India and that often the words were used interchangeably by extremists who refused to acknowledge minority communities or any group that denied their caste system. The mob staggered left, then right, and they slurred and stumbled and continued shouting their unrehearsed anti-Sikh sentiments.

"Get out!"

"Take our jobs! Our land! Our water!"

"Die, Sikhs!"

"All of you!"

"Hindi! Hindu!"

"Hindu! Hindi! Hindustan!"

"Hindi! Hindu! Hindustan!"

The boy had never seen such anger and angst in a people before--not to mention courage. Three men taunting and insulting and challenging what could have easily been three to four hundred Sikh families without fear of being attacked themselves. It didn't make any sense. The boy gazed at the bottle the mob shared and nursed like soma; he wondered if that bottle alone could give those men that kind of courage or if there was something else.

"Hindu! Hindustan!"

"Take our business!"

"Take our land!"

"Die, Sadars! All of you!"

"Hindu! Hindustan!"

One of them suddenly stumbled over his drunken feet and collapsed to the ground. His two friends rushed to his aid and helped him clamber back up. He seemed lost, dazed, confused and it took a moment for him to collect himself. He mumbled something incoherent about Hitler and patriotism and then he pointed randomly at the Sikhs lining both sides of the dark, narrow street. Then the drunkards began mumbling something as they staggered away--too tired and weak to continue with their three-man, anti-Sikh parade.

The boy watched them staggering in and out of pools of light until they disappeared down the lane and around the bend. A wave of anxiety went over the street as one by one the Sikhs shuffled back into their homes and shut their doors.

The boy's neighbor, a short, Sikh man in a blue turban and a beige kurta pajama, mentioned that they had heard news on the radio. The prime minister had passed away in the hospital. He said that these small, random, incoherent drunken outbursts were to be expected for the next few hours. And then, seeing the concern on the boy's mother's face, he said that there was nothing to worry about and that they were just a bunch of drunken fools. He added that they should only worry if the men began to wear masks to conceal their identities. That, he said, would signify an intention darker than a curse. But then again, he concluded, turning away from them, they were in the nation's capital and such a thing wasn't even conceivable with the army just a block away. Sikhs, he was sure, had nothing to worry about.

His mother smiled uneasily and agreed, though her eyes seemed uneasy and pensive. Their neighbor then wished them a good night and retired into his home.

The boy stood a long while with his parents staring at the street wondering what his parents were thinking. A sudden smell jarred him back to the moment.

A Feast for Lambs

When he turned, he saw smoke rolling toward him from the open door. His parents suddenly ordered him to stay put and instantly rushed inside with a great sense of urgency. A second later his father came out with a flaming pot of smoldering carbon burfee. He tossed it into the street and his mother, following inches behind, smothered it with a blanket.

"I'm sorry," the boy said.

"It's okay," his father said. "We can make burfee another time."

His mother removed the blanket and gazed down at the charred, molten mix. She looked at the boy as he stared deeply at the smoking carbon, scrutinizing the darkness to see if there was something, anything, that he could salvage for himself and his brother. His mother seemed to read his thoughts, his guilt and his palpable disappointment. "I haven't given up yet," she said. "Have you?"

He looked up and saw unfaltering determination in his mother's eyes; staring into her eyes he somehow felt that everything was going to be fine and that he hadn't ruined the night and that his brother would have his burfee, and perhaps so would he. She hadn't given up and so he certainly wouldn't. He shook his head and his eyes gleamed with hope.

"Maybe we should leave earlier," she suggested. "Maybe we could buy some rotis and burfee near the airport. That's a possibility."

The boy considered this for a moment; dinner near the airport could be expensive and he knew his mother was on a tight budget. Then another worry suddenly replaced an old one and tugged at him. He asked:

"If we buy rotis…will you still have enough…?"

"Enough for what, bete?"

"To buy a glove?"

She smiled and laughed and pulled him closer. She then dusted his new kurta pajama and gazed at his delicate right hand, at his iron kara and breathed in the cool night air. "I think so," she said. "I should have just enough."

From a pocket in her dress she pulled out the sparkling white glove his grandmother had made him. "But you promised to wear this one, too." She extended it to him. She looked at the glove, then at him. After a moment she asked:

"Is it at least close?"

He stared at the glove for a moment, then shrugged. "It's a bit close," he said, trying to be as positive as he could be. This wasn't about his grandmother, it was about what he would have to wear in front of others, and he'd rather have no glove than a five-finger glove.

His mother scrutinized the glove.

"What do you feel it's missing?"

"I feel…" he hesitated, "…I feel it's missing a thumb."

"I see."

He held out the finger sleeve that should have been for his thumb. "Too long…too skinny…and too high up. It's hard for the thumb to feel comfortable." He looked up his mother, serious and concerned. "Real hard."

"But your thumb is like a finger."

"Yes. It's like a finger, but it's still a thumb."

"But it's good for now?"

"Yes. It's a bit good for now."

"Can I see?"

"Now?"

"Why not?"

He made a face, sighed inwardly, then commenced to squeeze his fingers and thumb into the glove. His thumb strained, choked, stretched, twisted and agonized. Finally he managed to force the glove on despite his twisted thumb. He held his hand out in a pool of light that poured out from the window of his smoking home.

His mother's eyes brightened.

"Looks like it."

He looked at her for a long moment with deep concern. How could she not see that this was unlike any glove that ever existed? A glove made for people with thumbs like fingers. Who was she trying to fool? But he knew she would do anything for his grandmother's heart. Still, he didn't know who she was trying to convince, but it wouldn't be him.

"It's important to show you appreciate it by wearing it."

"I know."

"She worked very hard."

"I know."

"You pinky promised to wear it."

"I know."

"Not everyone can sew a perfect glove."

The boy nodded that he understood just as his father returned outside for some fresh air. His mother turned to him. "Shall we eat near the airport?"

With a slight smile, his father nodded. "Good idea." He looked down at the boy. "Good idea?"

"Good idea!" the boy answered, trying desperately to pull off the glove. Succeeding, he tucked it away in an inner pocket his grandmother had sewn into his pajama.

Having decided on a plan, his parents then returned to their pucca, opened the smoky windows and fanned the smoke out the door with pillows. Then his father placed all the chopped vegetables on a plate and covered them with foil and promised he would use them the next morning and that there would be no waste. His mother nodded, tidied up the room, then, when she was satisfied, she grabbed her suitcase and hauled it out into the shadowy street.

As she hauled the suitcase into the street, the boy pleaded for her to let him carry it for her over to the main road where they would hail a taxi. His mother smiled, and the boy snatched the handle from her and commenced to haul his mother's cargo through the street.

Breathing hard and struggling, the boy pulled triple his weight and was fortunate the suitcase had freshly oiled wheels. Ahead his parents led the way through pools of light and darkness as they headed toward the main road, leading the way down one narrow street after another, stopping now and then to let the boy catch up to them.

As they walked he could hear his mother whispering about his grandmother; about how she had acted strangely before she had said good-bye; about how she was affectionate and teary-eyed and how she was never affectionate and teary-eyed; about how she had embraced her hard twice instead of just barely once; and about how she felt there was something her mother was not telling her. Something about her health or something she had sensed or dreamt about. She then lowered her voice and said that she was afraid she would never see her mother again and that she didn't want to leave. He told her to stop saying such prosperous things and that she was worrying for nothing.

After a silence, his mother agreed that she was making something out of nothing, but she still made his father promise to go see her every day. She also made him promise to take the boy with him and to make sure the boy was wearing the glove. He promised he would do so if she promised to stop being such a mother. They shared a brief laugh, and then they were silent as they exchanged their looks--looks that the boy knew would have been a song and a dance and an epic declaration in a movie.

Of all the looks his parents gave each other, these were the ones he cherished most.

When at last they reached the main road they signaled a taxi zigzagging toward them through the lawless chaos of the road. The taxi driver seemed to hesitate when he saw them; there was something about them he seemed to want to avoid, but then at the last moment he veered toward them and slowed to a stop.

The driver stepped out of the taxi. Without saying a word, he gestured to the boy that he would take over with his mother's cargo. The boy backed away from his mother's suitcase, smiling at the man, happy to be going on a taxi ride for the third time in his life.

But the driver didn't smile back or share the boy's happiness or enthusiasm. He silently grasped the handle, lifted the suitcase and popped it into the trunk. Then he slipped back into the taxi and slammed the door angrily as he waited for his passengers.

The boy's parents exchanged an uneasy look that troubled him. For a long moment his father's eyes seemed to be telling his mother that maybe they should hail another taxi, perhaps one with a Sikh driver. But then his mother's eyes reassured him and said everything would be fine and they would be okay. The boy's eyes, however, were beginning to panic. He just wanted to take a ride in a taxi; he watched them both and hoped his mother's eyes would win as they usually did.

At last his father opened the front door and eased into the passenger seat. The boy sighed his relief. Then he opened the back door and sank into the puffiest and most comfortable seat he had ever sunk into. He wondered if all taxi seats were this comfortable or if they had just been lucky with this taxi. One day, when he was older, he would save up all his money and ride different taxis all over Delhi in the day and night.

A Feast for Lambs

"Airport."

The driver stated the obvious.

"Airport."

His father confirmed.

"Airport..." the boy whispered to his mother, his voice filled with the promise of seeing massive planes landing and taking off with engines that roared like dragons in the sky.

The boy stared at the taxi driver's shiny bald head as he shifted into gear and headed toward the gate of the colony. Above his head the boy observed a blue-haired statue dangling from the rearview mirror and a picture of the driver and his two children on the dashboard. Then he turned to the back door window and watched all the lights zip by as he listened to the cacophony of the night. He turned to his mother and smiled, and she smiled back. Suddenly he noticed her hands suddenly tense as she stopped breathing and leaned forward and narrowed her gaze.

The boy leaned forward as well. He looked toward the gate and saw a clogged road of taxis and scooters and rickshaws and immediately sensed this was no ordinary traffic jam. This was something else. Something that made his mother intuitively shout out:

"Stop! Stop here!"

The taxi driver regarded the boy's father for confirmation.

"Just traffic," his father said.

"Stop here!" she demanded.

The boy's father nodded at the driver and the driver pulled to the side and came to stop several yards before the traffic began. Instantly, she bolted out of the taxi and stood silently, watching.

A moment later his father and the driver slipped outside and stood by the door and peered into the night at the traffic leading to the entrance of the colony. At first his parents seemed perplexed by what they were seeing.

Hundreds of men disembarked a truck while hundreds of other men bustled in and out of the headlights of a bus as they pulled tree branches and tree trunks and cement pipes over the road to create some sort of barricade.

The boy stared silently, but wasn't sure what he was staring at. He didn't understand any of it.

What are they doing? Why are they blocking the gate out of the colony?

These tall and thin men seemed to be creating some sort of a perimeter. For what, the boy didn't know, and he stepped outside and stood beside his mother. She barely noticed him. All she could see was the barricade and the men. Hundreds. Hundreds gathering at the entrance of their peaceful hive like deadly wasps.

In front of the bus a group of men gathered around a congressman the boy recognized from the posters on the walls and doors. The congressman seemed to hand out paper to designated leaders of the men who were slowly breaking up the men into smaller crews. He was also teaching them a slogan, something they could fill their heads with as they worked. A simple rehearsed slogan that unified their political campaign. One he could barely hear.

A Feast for Lambs

"Blood for blood," the congressman shouted, and the crews repeated. "Blood for blood."

Some of the men distributed tin containers of what the boy supposed could have been kerosene. Other men distributed long sticks and demolition tools. Had they been wearing masks the boy would have been sure they were a mob like in the movies. But they didn't wear masks and they weren't concerned about being identified so there was a good chance they weren't in danger.

The boy automatically assumed they were a working outfit, a massive demolition team for some structure the congressman needed destroyed. An army breaking up into crews with specific tasks while the safety perimeter and barricade was being established. But why would this congressman hire outsiders? There were plenty of men capable of demolition within the colony.

No one said a word.

Not a word.

And listening to the slogan the boy knew they weren't a working outfit here for demolition. This was something else.

They watched what was unraveling before them in silence, all of them trying to understand. The boy inched closer to his mother, and he stared at all the red and orange lights making a snake to the gate. In the gloom he noticed one crew of men searching the cars and asking the drivers if they were hiding Sikhs and that if they were they had better hand them over.

A sudden chill ran down the boy's spine.

The taxi driver stared at what was happening and didn't want to believe it. "Hai Ram," he whispered under his breath with wide eyes and his heart beating hard in his throat. The boy's mother suddenly yanked the boy and commanded:

"Get in the car."

"But I--"

A fierce look cut him off and instantly silenced any objection the boy might have had; a second later he was inside the taxi staring out the windshield.

There was a sudden commotion.

Ahead, the boy saw the silhouette of a turbaned man crisscrossing through the traffic, through light and darkness as he headed toward them with a crew of six or seven men in pursuit. For a moment the man seemed to have lost them in the darkness as he surged against traffic toward the colony. But when he took a moment to look back over his shoulder to see if he had lost his pursuers, it was a moment too long, and out of the darkness something lunged at him and snatched him and swallowed him whole like a formless creature from the very depths of oblivion.

All they saw were quick-moving shadows and silhouettes. All they heard were two savage thuds followed by a series or grunts and groans. When the groans subsided, the crew, seeing his father's turban, turned as one, and lumbered toward them, clanking their machetes and iron prods against the pavement.

At once his mother and father and the driver rushed back into the taxi.

But the crew was already on them.

A Feast for Lambs

One of the men slammed the hood with his open palms and stared at them through the windshield. He lifted one arm and pointed at the boy's father. Slowly, a vicious smile came to his face, revealing rotten teeth stained red with paan. He snickered at him and ran his finger across his neck like a villain would do in a movie, except looking like a perfect hero. Then the perfect hero spit red like blood on the windshield and laughed like a human jackal.

Without hesitation, his mother, in one fluid motion, lunged and locked all four doors. The driver looked at her through the rearview mirror with panicked eyes. "They won't let me leave if--"

"Start the car," the boy's mother said. "Start the car!"

Flicking his gaze from window to window, the boy watched the men circle the taxi, kicking and lashing and smashing it with melee weapons of every variety. For some reason none of this felt real to the boy as he watched and could not believe what he was seeing or what was happening to them. A jackal shrieked and the boy instantly grabbed his mother's arm and held her tight. The driver looked up in his rearview mirror and said:

"I can't take you."

A man suddenly kicked in the door and shouted for the driver to hand over their game.

"Sahib, please," the boy's father pleaded. "Please…"

The boy looked over the seat and could see the driver's hands shaking as they held the steering wheel. As the driver tried to calm down a man crept to the driver side, leaned down and stuck his face right up against the window. In a polite tone and manner he pleaded with the driver to open the door. The driver lowered his gaze and stared down at the steering wheel, transfixed. "Please...there is nothing I can do...please..."

"Bhaiji, please...start the car," the boy's mother said. She bit her lip and the boy could see that if the driver didn't start the car soon she'd lunge up and do whatever she needed to do to get her family out of this situation.

"Please..." The boy's father's voice trembled helplessly. "We can't get out...we won't..." His father stared at the men watching him through every window. "Please..."

The man at the driver's window suddenly exploded in anger and shook the car, telling the driver that he was growing impatient and that he should do his part for Hindustan and that to harbor and protect Sikhs was to be a traitor to their country and he would suffer the same fate as the Sikhs. Trembling, trying to convince himself more than anyone else, the driver muttered:

"I have no choice..."

"You have a choice!" his mother roared, realizing what he was trying to do, staring at him through the rearview mirror. "Don't say you have no choice. Start the car!"

The driver wouldn't look up at her. She took a moment to calm herself, then she added:

"Bhaiji...you have a choice..."

The taxi shook violently with the crew's anger.

A Feast for Lambs

The boy held his mother's hand tighter. She squeezed him tightly. He looked up at her and somehow the fire in her eyes made him feel like they were going to survive this and all would be well. She continued:

"Bhaiji...look...please look at me..."

He looked up at her and she held his gaze. Then, unable to take her eyes anymore, he looked down at the boy. He took in a deep, uneasy breath. "Start the car," she said in a whisper. "Just start the car."

The driver closed his eyes for a moment that seemed like forever. The taxi shook violently and the men screamed at him from outside, louder and louder. The boy felt like he was in another world with all the yelling and pounding and scratching against the taxi.

"Please..." his father said. It was all he could say. He seemed to be in shock, feeling the claws of death so close.

The driver sighed deeply, then mumbled a prayer.

At last he opened his eyes to find the boy's mother staring directly at him through the rearview mirror. Outside the crew attempted to kick in the windows and the boy felt as though he was in an earthquake and that the whole world was falling apart. Any moment now the ground would split open and they would be swallowed into oblivion, never to be heard from or seen again.

Gone.

Forever.

Suddenly, something snapped in the driver

and his eyes lit up. He had made his choice. Instantly, his hand made for the keys and he started the taxi. The crew outside cursed and screamed at him. He instantly shifted it into reverse and peeled backward, nearly crushing three raging men.

Bewildered, the crew backed away, screaming that he was a traitor to their country and that he was stealing money from their families. Then, as he shifted gears and spun the taxi around, one man rushed the taxi and cleaved through the front tire of the passenger's side with a machete.

At once the tire sighed and sagged. The driver shifted gears and the boy felt the engine kick and tremble under his seat. He bounced and jolted back as the driver gunned the engine, floored the pedal and thundered out of harm's way with one tire shaking and wobbling as it lost its tread.

Smoke and dust and sparks like fireflies spilled into the night as the rim cut and tore through pavement. Within moments they had gained twenty yards from the crew as the boy gazed at all the lights zooming by like he was in some crazy dream.

Spotting a cross street, the driver turned.

A measure too fast.

Within seconds he lost control, veered left, then right, then smashed directly into a parked car, bashing his head against the steering wheel.

Instinctively the boy's mother grabbed him and pulled him out of the crumpled taxi and into the gloom. Not far away he could hear the din of the crew careening toward them, their shouts intensifying with every second.

A Feast for Lambs

The boy was startled, but he quickly shook his head and snapped back to the moment and helped his mother haul his father out of the taxi. Then all three of them pulled out the injured driver.

The cries grew louder and louder as his parents quickly conducted the driver to a nearby alley and helped him sit down on some cement stairs.

It took a moment for the driver to remember what had happened. When he did, when he realized he wasn't asleep, that he wasn't in a nightmare, a sudden and profound shame washed over his shock.

"I should have done something sooner," he said. "I should have--"

"Never mind," the boy's mother interrupted. "You saved us. Don't think anything else."

The boy could hear the crew approaching them. His mother looked toward the street where the taxi leaked dark fluids into the gully.

"Don't go home," the driver warned. "Don't go home..." He looked up to the boy's father, then his mother. "You saw...lists..."

"I saw," the father said.

"You heard...blood for blood..."

"I heard..."

"Can't go home," the driver said. "Can't leave. There were hundreds, maybe more..."

"Let's go," the mother said and made a gesture to his father to lift the driver.

"No," he said. "Leave me. It's not me they've come for."

The boy's mother gave the driver a thankful

look. She gripped his hand and she seemed to wish upon him blessings for this life and the next. A moment later she grabbed the boy's wrist and conducted him out of the alley. As they moved noiselessly away from the driver, the boy could hear him whisper a deep and heartfelt prayer for them; for the Sikhs of Trilokpuri; for the Sikhs of Delhi; for the Sikhs of India; and he could sense his deep shame that he had not acted sooner and that such a thing could happen in his beloved country.

ः

His heart thundering in his chest, the boy followed
his parents through the early dark, listening and
watching for crews, avoiding light and hiding in
shadow. As they crept through the narrow street,
his mother, sensing danger, froze instantly and signaled for the boy and his father to stop. They froze.
The boy's heart stopped. A rush of fear and uncertainty surged through him as he tried to calm himself. He listened. Nothing. A dog barking in the distance. But a few seconds later he heard something
else. He heard laughs and whispers, men talking
casually about a Sikh they had pulled out of a bus
and beaten mercilessly in front of everyone. The
boy's mother led them into a nearby alley, then
stared out into the street. With silent, careful steps,
the boy approached his mother and peeked around
the corner to see who was whispering.

A five-man crew was searching for someone; maybe them, maybe other Sikhs, he wasn't
sure. What the boy knew for sure was that he had
heard nothing for the last hour or so. He supposed
that if all those men at the entrance of the colony
were planning an attack they would have attacked
by now. Or, at least, they should have attacked by
now.

In the movies it was always a quick attack

followed by a quick escape so as to avoid the police and the countless complications of the law. What these men were doing now, moving about the colony so casually, didn't make any sense from what the boy had seen and learned from the movies.

It made no sense that they would simply linger about in this way. It made no sense and seemed quite impossible to the boy that the congressman and his mercenary force could block off the main artery into the colony without knowledge or intervention by the police. The police would foil their plans any moment now.

The longer the crews waited the more risky their dark plans became. And what were they waiting for anyway? More trucks? More buses? More men? More weapons? More kerosene? Maybe they were waiting for the masks that would eventually cover their faces so that they could begin their dark work without fear of being recognized.

Or perhaps, like those cricket coaches on television, their coach, the congressman, was giving his hundred-man crew a pep talk and final instructions to fill their spirits with the motivation they would need to win the game.

Or perhaps it wasn't as he imagined it at all. Perhaps he had misunderstood the slogan the congressman had been teaching his team. Perhaps what had happened earlier in the night with the Sikh man was only a slight misunderstanding, a spontaneous eruption of emotion by a radical mob.

Perhaps the congressman wasn't preparing for the demolition of his colony or the extermina-

tion of Sikhs so that Hindus could take over their
land and homes as his parents had whispered earlier. Perhaps the congressman was teaching them a
political slogan so that they could sell a political
idea for some upcoming election.

The congressman was merely being polite.
He was preparing and waiting until morning so as
not to disturb the Sikhs of Trilokpuri in their sleep.
That's why the congressman hadn't sent out his
crew just yet. He was just a very considerate man.
He was preparing and prepping and making sure
his campaign was just perfect for the early morning.

The congressman had prepared lists and
set up a perimeter simply because he was feeling
very democratic and he wanted every Sikh to
weigh in on his proposed ideas whatever those
ideas might be. But still--

To barricade Sikhs inside a colony for a
political campaign seemed a little drastic. And why
the Sikhs of Trilokpuri?

If the congressman had done any research
before he had planned this campaign he would
have soon realized that the Sikhs of Trilokpuri were
the least political of India and that they would
probably shrug indifferently at any political agenda
he might present to them; unless of course the congressman wanted to relocate the Sikhs of Trilokpuri
and give their humble yet beautiful homes to those
who were now enthusiastically learning the con-
gressional mantra.

The congressman's actions made no sense
to the boy. But then again, when had politics ever

made sense to anyone? It was as his uncle had said: all smiles, lies and half-truths in white 'Neta' pajamas.

Perhaps that was why the Sikhs of Trilokpuri didn't involve themselves in politics. They couldn't bear all the scheming and abuses of the upper castes, who his uncle had told him made up one single political party but gave the semblance of many so that in the end the upper castes made up almost eighty percent of the Indian government, even though they represented less than two percent of India's population. A government of upper castes in a country of lower castes was not fair representation by any standard, his uncle would argue, even if they said they came from the same religion. Upper castes and lower castes had fundamentally different and directly opposing interests. It was like the slave masters ruling in the best interests of the slaves in the name of democracy. It could be possible, though it was highly unlikely.

The boy didn't really know what all this meant, and he didn't really care. But his uncle had said that the few had always ruled over the many for centuries now and that this had always been the case, even before the Persian word 'Hindu' had been penned down by the Mughals to describe the many societies of Sanatana Dharma and had later been used by Brahminical Society to define their society and to hide their rule and society under the veil of religion.

His uncle claimed that Brahminical Society had appropriated and established the word 'Hindu'

A Feast for Lambs

so that anyone who criticized or attacked the Brahminic hierarchical system of control or challenged the Brahmin birthright to rule attacked all Hindus--attacked all societies of the original Sanatana Dharma and not just those responsible for the unjust and dictatorial laws and treatment of minorities and lower castes. It was a clever trick to make the tyranny of the one the tyranny of the many. A trick Brahmin radicals had been using for centuries now and were still using as they attempted to strangle and choke and knead religions into their caste mold.

Anyone who criticized Brahmin extremism or Brahmin tyranny criticized all Hinduism. But this, his uncle swore passionately, was not the case. Brahmin tyranny, his uncle had warned the boy and his father, should never be mistaken with Hinduism. Never. Hindus were his brothers. Tyrants who oppressed and dehumanized an entire people weren't. And he said that it was important for all Sikhs to remember the true enemy, which was never the religion, never Sanatana Dharma, but always those extremists who used Sanatana Dharma to their political and economic ends. He then said that the untouchables were the most oppressed people in the world and that this Brahminical caste system was equal to or worse than something called Apartheid.

The boy didn't quite understand all of this or what Apartheid meant. His father had to explain to him that his uncle had basically meant that the ruling elite of India would often use religion as an excuse or as a tool to make the masses think, do, and believe whatever they wanted. The boy nodded that he understood, but didn't really.

His uncle went on to explain that Brahmin extremists believed Sanatana Dharma established an eternal and natural right for the pure to rule over the tainted. His uncle had said that this idea of a natural right to will over others who were considered lesser or impure had inspired one of the most depraved and immoral men in history so that this man would eventually adopt and disgrace one of the purest and most spiritual symbols of Sanatana Dharma. Had truth not prevailed, everyone in Europe would now be broken up and classified by color, occupation and blood in a hierarchical pyramid with the pure Nazis ruling at the top. He was glad truth prevailed in Europe and he wished it would prevail in India.

His uncle had told him that this was an issue that had bothered Gandhi deeply; it was something Gandhi had questioned since his experiences in South Africa; it was something he was even beginning to believe needed to be reformed or even abolished, and just has he had begun to discuss the complete and total emancipation of the low castes he was assassinated by a Brahmin radical.

Thinking about this, the boy angled his ear toward the crew. Deep down inside he knew he had not misinterpreted what he had seen at the entrance and he knew these men were here to hurt them. Deep down he knew that they weren't here to discuss politics or congress for an upcoming election. Deep down he knew his mind was trying to make things seem better than they were. He knew what he had seen and a sudden high-pitched buzzing filled his ears, a warning that something was amiss and all those melee weapons and cans of kerosene were part of a much darker and sophisticated, if not brutal, campaign.

The boy and his parents avoided his home because those crews had in their possession voting lists, and with those lists he could see they were now marking homes with chalk. He heard his mother say that the crews were waiting for all the Sikh homes to be properly marked before they attack. But his father believed that they were simply waiting for light and that they wanted to catch Trilokpuri by surprise. Either way, the Sikhs of Trilokpuri would wake up with their colony under siege. The only thing they could pray for was a quick military or police intervention.

The boy's mother had said that the police drove in and out of the colony almost on an hourly basis and that just as soon as they came upon the barricade and the trucks and buses they would call in for help.

Help, she was sure, was probably already on the way.

In the meantime they would have to find a place to hide just in case. When the boy asked her what she meant by 'just in case' she didn't have answer; or she didn't want to answer; but deep down inside the boy understood what she had meant by 'just in case'.

Just in case it was worse than she had imagined.

Just in case it was bigger than she had imagined.

Just in case her gorilla brother was right all these years and the police and the army were mere tools of upper caste tyranny with a long-term agenda to eradicate or destroy the message of Sikhism, a campaign that had begun centuries ago, ever since the Guru dropped his caste name and gave his Sikhs a uniform to symbolize the need to abolish injustice and inequality and fight tyranny wherever tyranny poked its ugly, demon head.

And why?

Simply because the first thing Sikhism ever did was challenge the upper caste's right to rule based on the contingency of birth; because the first thing Sikhism ever denied and rebelled against centuries ago was the oppressive Brahminical caste system where a few could rule over the many with complete and total impunity; where only the few could learn how to read and write and pray in the temples; where only a few could lay their eyes on the religious texts of Sanatana Dharma without fear of being beaten, humiliated or put to death.

His uncle had boldly assured his father that almost eighty percent of the Indian government saw a very real threat to their alleged birthright with the Sikhs and what their uniform stood for. Sikhs who did not and would not and could not by the very dictates of their Guru recognize or give respect to the ancient system of Brahminical control.

Sikhs who at one time in history had completely dropped their last name with baptism just like their Guru, who had gifted them with a name that represented strength, courage and equality.

One name, one family.

No more segregation based on color, race and gender.

No more caste.

This was why eighty percent of government would never accept Sikhism as a religion in India. Sikhism refused to acknowledge their right to rule above the law or with total impunity. This was why the upper castes humiliated the Sikhs by laying down a lie in the Indian constitution, as they had also done with Buddhism and Jainism, claiming that Sikhism was a mere degraded sect of Hinduism. This--the boy's uncle swore--was the same as classifying Christianity as a degraded sect of Judaism because most historians believed Jesus had been born a Jew. His uncle didn't believe in such nonsense. He saw Christianity and Judaism as fundamentally different and separate religions in their own right.

Yes, the first Sikh Guru had Hindu parents.

This was true.

This was undeniably true.

But that was undeniably it.

The Guru's parents believed in idols and demigods. The Guru rejected idols and demigods. The Guru's parents believed in the caste system as divine society. The Guru rejected the caste system as humiliating and degrading. The Guru's parents believed in the sacredness of sati. The Guru rejected sati as cruel and inhuman. The Guru's parents believed in animal sacrifices. The Guru rejected animal sacrifices, or any kind of sacrifice. The Guru's parents believed in the Brahminical spiritual monopoly of the religious texts. The Guru rejected any monopoly on spiritual texts or truths. The Guru's parents believed in the divine birthright of the Brahmins. The Guru recognized no such divine right and rejected their treatment of the low castes. The Guru's parents believed the untouchables were God's fallen outcastes and were born to serve the upper castes. The Guru believed the untouchables were God's children and were born to be free. The Guru's parents believed Sanskrit was a divine language and only uppers castes should be permitted to learn how to read and write and learn and recite the prayers. The Guru rejected the divinity of any language and believed all should be permitted the opportunity to learn how to read and write and learn and recite the prayers. The Guru's parents believed in the ritual of the thread ceremony to initiate the Guru into his upper caste birthright to be a sacred ceremony of the twice-born. The Guru rejected the ceremony, refused the sacred thread, and denied his so-called birthright, rejecting the idea of ever being considered an upper caste, or any caste.

The Guru's parents were Hindu.

The Guru was not.

Almost eighty percent of the Indian government saw a very real protest to their self-proclaimed birthright to rule with the Sikhs. This was why they refused to legally acknowledge them in the constitution. This was why Sikhs protested and disobeyed the upper-caste government. And this

A Feast for Lambs

was precisely why the Indian government was able
to attack the Sikh Vatican on Christmas Day. It was-
n't about a man; the man was a pretext; it was
about memory--the memory of Sikhs--a memory
and message that had been under attack by
Brahmin radicals for centuries now.

Times changed.

Methods changed.

But intention didn't.

The intention remained the same.

This was why the upper-caste politicians
were disappearing an entire generation of Sikhs.
And this was why they were using their ancient
technique of torture and torment to humiliate and
silence and break the spirit of their ancient protes-
tors. With patience and torture they would silence
them for good. And now--

Without a library and--

Without a strong and knowledgeable generation to pass on Sikh memory--

Sikhs were bound to forget what they once
stood for, what their Guru believed in, and why
they had almost been exterminated for their beliefs.

His uncle was sure the next generation was
bound to be lost and divided in a forest of lies and
half-truths fabricated by Brahmin radicals. And
perhaps the radicals would finally quash a powerful protest against their oppressive caste system
that had begun centuries ago with a uniform and a
name.

The boy's uncle even believed that the sudden resurgence of the last name with Sikhs and the
pride that went with caste was proof undeniable

that the Brahmin radicals had won a major battle in the silent war they had waged centuries ago. Their system of control would never be undermined. And this--with all the low-caste rebellions they had quashed over the centuries--history would prove.

The caste system would never be undermined. Never. Not by laws. Not by foreigners. Not by untouchables. Not by Hindus. Not by Buddhists. Not by Christians. And certainly not by the Sikhs or the Sikh Guru. And Sikhs would once again advertise their last names and their caste and they would, with great ego, say that they were so and so from such and such caste and their baptismal name would be relegated to a middle name. His uncle was sure that the Brahmin radicals would protect their system of control tooth and nail, even if it one day it came down to genocide.

But his uncle couldn't be right. He just couldn't be. And the boy certainly didn't want him to be right. But--

To barricade a colony unopposed and unhindered by the army or police in the nation's capital. This could only be a testament to the truth of every conspiracy theory and paranoia he had ever heard his gorilla uncle ramble on about in his anti-government tirades.

The boy never wanted his uncle to be right, even if sometimes, he suspected that he might be. He especially didn't want his uncle to be right this time, because this time he needed to believe the police and the military would be there to help Sikhs. And this time he hoped the police and the military would prove his uncle nuttier than an

A Feast for Lambs

almond tree.

But the more the boy thought about what he had seen at the entrance, the more something inside him insisted that the army wasn't coming any time soon and that they needed to find a way to escape Trilokpuri on their own. His mother said that they would try, but first they needed to reach his grandmother and his uncle and aunt to warn them about what they had seen; and then they would escape as a family.

God, please protect us and please help us escape. Please protect my family.

Praying inwardly and peering around the corner, the boy watched the crew quietly comb the streets, marking doors and searching for early morning stragglers that might spot them and possibly spoil their surprise.

The crew also seemed to be doing something else. They seemed to be accustoming themselves to the playing field as a cricket team or field hockey team might do before a match. All they were missing were t-shirts with their sponsor's logo. Considering all the cans of fuel he had seen, he supposed that the sponsor would be a kerosene company. For a second the boy thought of their coach, the congressman, and he attempted to recall his name from all the posters plastered over the walls of his colony. Then he thought of a few names he had overheard his uncle throw around his home as having already threatened Sikhs with extinction if they didn't stop complaining about being assimilated into the caste fold.

The boy mused with the names and imagined what their outfits might look like or the companies they might advertise. White and saffron, advertising--

Bhagat Kerosene & Company.

Saroj Kerosene & Company.

Ashok Kerosene & Company.

Bhagat Saroj Ashok & Company.

The boy couldn't possibly know who he had seen organizing the men at the gate or if he had remembered the names correctly; but he was sure it was one of those politicians who his uncle despised for having openly expressed respect and admiration for a man who had plunged the world into the dark recesses of war.

Now the boy watched the men as they read the lists and marked the doors and whispered inaudible jokes to one another.

Suddenly someone shrieked for help in the distance and the men went still and quiet as a few lights opened here and there, then quickly extinguished.

A random bludgeoning.

A reaction of drunks upset over the death of the prime minister.

The inhabitants of Trilokpuri probably told themselves that, like most random mob attacks, it was unpredictable and spontaneous and over before it even started. No need for alarm. Such random attacks were common, short, and to be expected.

The reason for the short duration of mob attacks, his uncle had once told the boy, was that it was hard for the human body to produce, support and sustain that kind of anger, hate and excitement for more than five or ten minutes; especially for those who weren't used to that kind of emotion coursing through their bodies. Boxers, he had said, trained for months before a fight, ran miles upon miles every day just to manage the emotion that would be surging through their veins for the hour or so they would spend dancing around a ring trying to survive or vanquish their opponent.

When the shrieks and cries faded to thumps and thuds against flesh and bone, the crew continued to creep down the street like jackals through the flickering light and darkness as they headed toward the boy and his parents.

The boy's father nudged him, calling him back into the depths of the alley. With careful steps the boy moved back, and so did his mother. Then, without realizing it, the boy stepped on a small, round stone, lost his footing, stumbled backward, and stepped on a crumpled can.

A faint crunch startled one of the jackals. He froze and stared toward the alley, silencing the others.

One by one the jackals went silent and looked toward the boy and his parents without seeing them in the gloom. The boy stopped breathing. The crew inched forward in small, careful, measured steps.

Each inch forward was a step back for the boy and his parents. They backed all the way toward a pucca where they could see the soft glow of a hurricane lantern pouring out of the small, dusty window. As the boy's mother led them toward a dead end, she took a chance and knocked gently against the door, staring the whole while at the glowing window.

No one answered. After a moment, she knocked again. And again. She waited. The boy stared at the window, then at the door with his breath caught in his throat, sensing the crew progressing slowly toward them.

Within moments the boy heard faint footsteps approaching the door. He breathed again and watched the door, waiting for it to open. They would be safe. They would be hidden from the crew.

Anxiously, his father stared at the mouth of the alley, then the door, then the alley, then the door, ready to bolt inside just as soon as it opened.

But the door didn't open, and the footsteps stopped suddenly at the door. There was a long, tense silence. All three of them stared at the door and waited for something that would never happen. Then, to their horror and disbelief, the light extinguished along with their hopes, plunging them into complete darkness. The boy's mother shook her head in disbelief, and with great urgency she whispered:

"No...please no...please..."

His mother gave his father a look, and his trembling hands instantly found his kirpan without unsheathing it. With a deep breath, he turned toward the mouth of the alley and prepared for the worst.

"Please," his mother continued. "Just my son. Please...just my son...just hide my son..."

A Feast for Lambs

The boy's father took a step toward the crew. He seemed to want to surprise them as he sucked in small nervous breathes and whispered God's name over and over again.

The boy, too, placed his hand on his kirpan, refusing to let his father fight alone. He would help him as best as he could, but he prayed inwardly that he would never in his life have to unsheathe his kirpan and that he would never have to hurt anyone to protect himself and that somehow they would be spared this deadly but seemingly inevitable confrontation.

The boy advanced on skinny, trembling legs behind his father.

But his mother would not let the boy unsheathe his kirpan or hurt anyone. She instantly grabbed him by the shoulder, stared at him with the eyes of a lioness, and she motioned for him to wait behind a small cement staircase; she then whispered that she would run and that she would lead the jackals as far away from him as she could and that he should hide until the police arrived.

At this the boy instantly shook his head. It was a request he could not obey. He wouldn't know what to do if she was hurt, and he couldn't possibly imagine a life without his mother or father.

But her eyes instantly told him that this was not a request, it was an order, and this order was not up for debate. This was a lioness protecting her cub and nothing--

Could stand in the way of a lioness protecting her cub.

The boy breathed hard and reluctantly took

a few steps back as he watched two lions stealthily prowl through the gloom, ready to pounce on a pack of jackals.

The boy's legs began to shake uncontrollably, his teeth chattered involuntarily and his heart thundered in a way he never knew it could. He felt that at any moment it would burst from his chest. He had never felt such fear and uncertainty in his life. Then, suddenly, he heard something.

Something faint, perhaps--

A trick of his frightened imagination.

But when he heard it again he turned and looked toward the source of the sound to see two white eyes staring at him through a slightly open door. A harsh, urgent whisper came again from a pucca directly in front of the pucca that had denied them refuge. The eyes widened urgently and a small hand signaled him inside. "You," she said. "Come…come quick…"

His mother and father heard the voice, too, and wasted no time. With impossible speed they shuffled back and his mother grabbed the boy by the arm and quickly pulled him through the open door.

A tiny, middle-aged woman in a dark Punjabi dress closed the door behind them and quickly moved toward the window and peered into the alley as the boy's mother frantically whispered her thanks and appreciation.

But the woman signaled for her to be quiet as she watched dark silhouettes search the alleyway, moving closer and closer to her home. The tiny woman then told the boy and his parents to hide with her two young daughters in the corner of the room. "They're coming," she warned. "Quickly."

Just as the boy and his parents sat in the corner beside the two trembling little girls, and just as the woman kneeled under the window frame, they suddenly saw a dark head fill the window, staring inside the pucca. His warm breath fogged up the glass as he scrutinized the dark, shadowy room. Then they heard a sound. A door opening followed by a man's voice whispering something to the jackals. A moment later the door closed, a bolt snapped, and there was a short, nervous silence. The woman stared at the boy and his parents and they stared back at her. Then the boy watched the door and prayed that the man who had not opened the door for them had not given them up. But his heart was telling him otherwise.

Suddenly there was a sudden abrasive knock at the door.

The boy held his breath. Time seemed to freeze as he watched the woman silently inch toward the door. She signaled for the boy's parents to come to her as though she already anticipated the crew's next move. A moment later the men outside pounded the door and demanded that the door be open so that they could check inside for Sikhs, swearing that any Hindu caught helping Sikhs would be treated as a traitor to Hindustan.

Then they fell silent.

Stopped knocking.

Stopped pounding.

Stopped trying to intimidate.

A moment later the boy could hear footsteps shuffling away from the home.

They were walking away. They had given up and were returning to their list, chalk and task. When the woman carefully rose to look out the window she didn't see anything in the alley. Turning to the boy and his parents, she breathed a sigh of relief and relaxed her taut face. Then, just as she was about to tell them that they were safe and that the jackals had disappeared, a dark head suddenly filled the window, startling her and sending her stumbling backward to her haunches. A second later someone tried to bash the door down with savage violence.

Instantly, all three adults rushed toward the door and pushed against it and the weight and force of the crew as they tried to force their way in. With every thud, every pound, every smash, the children let out silent screams and the boy could feel his breath frozen in his lungs and his heart pounding in his throat.

After a long minute, the jackals could see they were making no progress. Giving up, they announced that they would be back soon and with many more men. Then, when they were certain they were safe, the adults turned their backs against the door and slumped down with a collective sigh of momentary relief and stared hard at their children.

"They're gone," the woman said, catching her breath. "They may come back but by morning the police should have dealt with them."

His father and mother stared at the woman, then her children, then the woman again. She had

A Feast for Lambs

risked their lives for strangers. The boy could see his mother was preparing to say something, but this time, it was his father and not his mother who spoke first. He said:

"May the Guru protect and bless you and your family."

It was all he could say through quivering lips and emotion. The woman nodded and simply answered:

"May the Guru protect and bless all families tonight."

Then the boy watched his mother take the woman's hand and squeeze it. She looked her right in the eye for a long moment. At last she said:

"I shall never forget."

The woman nodded in answer but said nothing. A moment later she collected herself, stood and walked over to her daughters and told them to sleep under the only bed in the house in a small, adjoining room. The boy's mother told the boy to do the same. In a soft, weary voice she said:

"Try to sleep, bete. In the morning it will all be over."

The boy nodded, stood slowly and regarded his father as he stared out the window, watching over the alley. Not wanting to disturb him, the boy turned and followed the two girls into a room without a door, where he noticed a picture of a blue god on the wall. The picture was similar to the one he had seen at the sweetshop, and the thought of the sweetshop made him hungry so that he could feel his stomach turning against itself. But he knew it wasn't the time or the place to ask for food, so he eased his way under the bed, trying not to stare at the two pretty girls beside him and failing with every attempt.

Lying on their stomachs under the bed, the girls stared at the boy and he stared back at them and his eyes smiled involuntarily. Slowly, he grinned without understanding why. They grinned back and just stared without saying a word; then one girl reached into the shadows and pulled out a small pillow and handed it to him so he could rest his soaked head and close his eyes.

The boy took the small pillow and relaxed his head on it and closed his eyes and inwardly thanked God for sparing him and his family. He prayed that God would also spare his grandmother and his aunt and his uncle.

A few minutes later the boy slipped into unconsciousness and found himself trudging through a fog like smoke or a smoke like fog, slowly revealing a decimated jungle with trees burning all around him and the cries of mothers and children everywhere. The crying seemed to reverberate and come from everywhere and nowhere at the same time as he walked over ash and rubble and stone. Then, staring into the thick fog, a sudden wail jarred him awake.

He opened his drowsy eyes to see his father standing by the window in the early morning light. It all began to slowly come back to him. The barricade. The congressman. The car accident. The men marking Sikh homes with chalk. He wanted to return to his nightmare and stay there until they were safe. Then he turned and suddenly noticed that his mother was lying close by against the stone wall. When she saw the boy was awake she crawled toward him on her belly and held his hand. Then she looked up toward his father and asked:

"Is it okay?"

His father shook his head.

"No. Not yet."

"When?"

"When the police come," the woman answered, pouring the last of her clean water from a plastic jug into a blue, plastic cup. "When the police come it will be safe." She handed her daughter the cup of water and gestured toward the boy. With a faint smile, the little girl brought the cup over to the boy and his mother.

The boy pulled himself from under the bed and, sitting beside his mother, took the cup from the girl and tried his best not to smile, but couldn't help himself. There was something about her that he couldn't describe or understand that was just making him feel strange and confused and embarrassed without having done anything to be embarrassed about. And it was the same for the girl, who tried to restrain a smile as she stared at him for a long moment that felt to the boy like an eternity.

It was the strangest feeling the boy had ever felt in his entire life, and her smile was like a mysterious arrow in his heart that sent a wave of tingling warmth throughout his whole body. For a moment, just a moment, the boy forgot everything and it was just him and the girl and this mysterious feeling rushing up his neck to warm and color his cheeks and freeze his eyes and brain.

With a smile the girl turned from him and began to walk away. The feeling should have dissipated, but instead it seemed to intensify and take complete control of him as he unconsciously stood and watched the girl slowly return to her mother and sister, waiting. Waiting for what, he wasn't sure. He watched her walk through a shaft of sunlight and stop. Then she glanced back to flash him another smile and his heart stopped and his face burned and his eyes nearly popped as he suddenly realized that he was staring at the most beautiful girl he had ever seen in his entire life.

And he had seen many girls.

Caught in the moment, the boy couldn't even imagine a more beautiful girl. And now, staring at her in the golden light, if there was anything he was sure of in his life it was this: somehow he would see her again.

Somehow they would become friends.

Somehow, when the police came to help them, and when all this was over he'd return to her home and he would show her how to dance on air and he would tell her about the songs of fluff and the songs of truth he would one day sing to the world.

And maybe, just maybe, she would join him.

Maybe she would even sing with him.

Maybe they would travel around India inspiring others like the Guru had done with his Muslim friend Mardana.

But first he knew he had to do one thing, but that one thing now seemed to be an impossible thing. He had to talk to her and he needed to ask her--

Her name.

That would be tough. Maybe, he thought, he would talk to his father first to ask him how he had first asked his mother her name.

As he thought about this the girl returned to her mother and sister. A moment later she was giggling and whispering something in her sister's ears as they stared at the boy, who was growing hotter with every second, who stood without knowing why he was standing, and who enjoyed a daydream where he was singing and dancing with everyone in the colony just like the movies.

Suddenly the boy felt someone tug on his kurta.

He looked toward his mother, who smiled at him and teased him with her eyes. Pulling himself out of a perfectly choreographed daydream with his wife-to-be, the boy sat back down beside his mother and handed her the cup, saying he didn't want any water; but his mother instantly shook her head, told him she wasn't thirsty and that he needed to drink to replenish his muscles.

But the boy instantly knew what his mother was up to and he knew she wouldn't drink unless he drank first. So he took a few meager sips, nodded his satisfaction, then extended the cup back to his mother and told her that he wasn't thirsty any longer. She gave him a suspicious look and seemed to know exactly what he was up to.

With a sigh, she took the cup, stood carefully, and carried it to his father. But his father shook his head, told her he wasn't thirsty and proceeded to tell her to give the water to the boy. Within moments she was sitting beside him again and he was finishing the water, realizing that he was truly no match for his parents.

As the boy sipped the water he watched the tiny woman pull out some red and green chunnis and wondered what she had in mind. She unknowingly answered his question when she began to cover the windows with them so that no one could see who was inside her home, which was now shimmering and bouncing with red and green light.

The boy turned to the girl to see her in this new light and tried to imagine what her name could be. No sooner did he think of a name than his father suddenly started and shouted and unleashed a wave of panic throughout the room.

He had seen or heard something outside.

Instantly the boy's mother snapped to her feet and was by his side, asking questions, asking him what he had seen, and if men were still lurking about.

The boy listened but couldn't hear what they were saying as they stared out the window. Then suddenly spotting something outside, his mother turned to them and yelled incoherently. The last thing the boy remembered was her shouting for the children to hide under the bed as the adults moved away from the window.

As the children bolted under the bed the boy watched his father open the door slightly. He whispered something to someone outside. Then all at once his parents and the woman rushed straight out into the alley and left them alone. There was a long tense moment as the boy stared anxiously with wide eyes at the sunlight pouring through the open door.

Where had they gone?

What was going on?

What had they seen?

And just when the boy decided he was going to run out after his parents he heard a wheezing noise followed by a painful groan. He heard feet shuffling against pavement. He heard his mother barking whispered orders to his father. Then suddenly his parents emerged, blocking out the light, carrying a man with blood flowing out of a gash in his belly.

The boy stared at him, terrified. His head was all cut and warped and bruised. There were patches of hair missing here and there, as though demons had tried to savagely pull his hair out by the roots like weeds in a garden. He looked like a broken man, scared, bewildered, shocked to the marrow, staring at all of them with wide, disbelieving eyes, and he seemed surprised to be alive.

The boy couldn't believe what he was seeing. Couldn't believe he was staring at a dying person. And he couldn't understand what had happened to him. He had heard nothing outside, and he could still hear nothing outside. All he heard was a strange silence that didn't make any sense considering all the men he had seen preparing the night before. But then, as the adults carried the man to the bed, the boy suddenly heard a terrible roaring followed by whooping and hollering and the clattering of melee weapons. His eyes widened. He stopped breathing. He listened. They all did.

A terrible percussion of melee weapons against doors and pavement.

A yell here and there.

And then a terrible cacophony of agony. Women screaming and shrieking. Cries and wails so desperate, so profound, the boy thought he had never heard anything so terrible in his life. Not even in the movies. These cries a person could not pretend to make. Could not fake. Could not act. Not even actors as talented as Chuck Norrisji could recreate such a ghastly sound. These wails no human could ever even imagine.

Nothing could compare to this.

Nothing could have prepared him for this.

It was like a thousand mothers crying at once for the lives of their fathers and husbands and sons. It was like a thousand mothers screaming at eternity to spare the lives of their babies. It was a sound he never wanted to hear again. Not in a movie. Not in a dream. Not in his mind.

Every cry, every wail was like a curse--a promise to the killers hurting their families that if there was an afterlife they would be waiting for them and that these men would pay with their very souls.

And every cry, every wail was like a knife in the boy's heart; and with every cry, every wail near or far, he felt blood draining from his face, from his hands, from his heart. He looked up to his mother and she, too, was pale as a ghost.

A Feast for Lambs

The slaughter had begun.

Their worst nightmare--

Suddenly reality.

And the police had done nothing about the barricade.

His mother looked down at her son, then at the door and seemed to be saying a prayer in her head. Maybe they would be okay. Maybe they would be safe in this home. This home wasn't on the list. This home hadn't been marked with chalk.

Or had it?

Could be.

The crew from the night before might have marked them as they had been told that Sikhs were hiding in the woman's home. Her mother listened in disbelief to the killing and the dying outside. She just stared blankly at the red and green glowing window and seemed to want to pinch herself out of the nightmare.

Then, suddenly, she looked at the boy and snapped herself back to reality; not because she wanted to, but because she had to. A moment later she was all reason and action while his father remained mute and silent, staring at the door, listening, helpless.

The boy's mother instantly grabbed a few square pillows and moved toward the children. She kneeled down, approached them, handed them the pillows and ordered them to cover their ears.

She didn't have to repeat herself.

Within moments, the boy could only hear the muffled cries of agony coming from the streets. Then his mother rose and sat on the bed to talk to the broken man. "What's happening out there?" she asked. The boy uncovered his left ear and angled it to listen. Through the wails and cheers and hollers, he heard:

"What's happening out there?"

The man didn't answer.

"What's happening out there?"

He could hear his mother shaking him, trying to snap him back to the moment despite his wound.

"They're killing us...all of us..." the man's voice trembled at last.

"How could they have gathered in such a way? I don't understand."

"Nobody understands..."

"Where do they come from?" The boy heard his father ask in a soft, shocked voice.

"I don't know," the man said, and he coughed painfully. He took in a deep breath, then continued. "But there were too many...we couldn't stop them...my brothers are dead... my friends are dead...all of them..."

"You tried to stop them? What do you mean you tried to stop them?" his mother asked with rising anger. The boy understood this anger wasn't directed at the man but at the situation outside. The man continued to explain in a weak voice:

"We heard they were blocking the road with trees and pipes. My brother had seen them. He was trying to drive out to the city to see his friends. He nearly died trying to escape them...he ran back to tell us what he had seen. But I didn't believe him. Nobody believed him. I thought he was mistaken or that he was exaggerating. A mob of ten or twenty was believable. But he was saying there were hundreds and hundreds of men. I asked myself how such a thing could happen here. And the way he was describing it? I didn't want to believe it. But he was hysterical and I knew him to be the most honest man alive. So we gathered men all night. Maybe two hundred men. We were going to try and intimidate them. Push them away from us...free the road...."

He paused for a long moment, frozen in time. Then, with panic in his voice, he continued:

"It wasn't a mob! It was an army! They massacred us. All of us. There were ten for every one. Ten for every one! When I saw all those men, all those trucks....I ran...I did...I ran...I ran and I don't know why I ran but I did...I got so scared that I ran like a coward...but several caught me...I think I killed them but not before they did this to me..."

The boy's mother whispered God's name, and the man continued:

"They've been preparing all night. The homes are all marked. And now they're swarming in like wasps and there's nothing we can do! Nothing!"

There was a long, tense silence. The boy tried to comprehend what all this meant. But none of it made sense. How could thousands of men attack his colony without being stopped by the police? It was not possible. Not in the Delhi. Not in the nation's capital. Then, in a hushed, disbelieving voice, as though still trying to register what the broken man had just told her, his mother asked the question that was on the boy's mind:

"What about the police?"

"No police. I didn't see any police… not one…"

"Who brought these men here? Where did they come from?"

"I don't know…what does it matter…? They're here, that's all that matters now…they're here…"

The cries outside and the sound of melee weapons bludgeoning flesh and stone intensified and the boy squeezed the pillow hard against his ears. He didn't want to hear anything anymore. He had heard enough. He looked to the girls and they were smothered in pillows, sobbing terribly. Then he closed his eyes and squished the pillow even harder against his head.

He didn't know how much time had passed, but when he opened his eyes his mother was lying on the ground in front of him, staring at him. He released the pillow slowly and heard nothing.

No more cries.

No more screams.

No more racket.

Silence.

He stared at his mother and he prayed inwardly that his mother would never have to cry like those mothers and that she would be spared such a terrible fate. He couldn't bear the thought of hearing his mother cry like that. And as he thought this he felt a sudden lurch of pain in his heart.

A Feast for Lambs

Peering silently into her strong, dark eyes he realized something that was hard for him to understand. Peering into her eyes, he realized--

His mother didn't see a difference.

It was as though those cries had been her
cries. It was as though those mothers had been his
mother; those dying men--

Her son.

Her husband.

Her father.

And staring deep into her, the boy could
see that their agony was her agony and that she
could not and would not separate herself from
those mothers.

The boy thought about this, and he wasn't
quite sure what it all meant; but somehow he
understood that in the wails and the cries he had
heard there was more, much more, than a curse
and a promise of justice; somehow he understood
that there was a ferocious and unrestrained accusation to the unknown and the unknowable that such
a crime should have ever taken place; and somehow he understood that there was also a plea, a
desperate plea--a desperate plea that no mother
should ever again have to witness the savage butchery of her child or husband or father.

ଔ

"Bring out the Sikhs!"

A voice rang out somewhere in the colony.

The crews were scouring the Hindu and
Muslim areas of the colony. Somehow they had suspected that some Hindu and Muslim neighbors
would try to help the Sikhs survive their campaign
of murder and terror, which had now lasted
throughout the entire day. A jackal yelled:

"Do not deprive us!"

Another yelled:

"Do not steal from us!"

And still another yelled:

"We will find them, and you will pay for
hiding them!"

The children shook with every dark word
as they hid under the bed and the adults paced the
room and the broken man continued to ooze life
from the gash in his belly into the bed.

"Do not deprive us!"

"Do not steal from our families!"

"Bring out the Sikhs!"

The shouting grew distant and the cries and
wails and the wild percussion of melee weapons
had now all but faded away. The boy thought that
the crews must have been returning to the barricade
again. Throughout the day the boy had noticed that

the butchery would suddenly cease so that all he could hear were the sounds of the wounded and the dying.

When his mother inquired if the attack was over, if they were safe, the broken man shook his head, groaned in pain, and said that the crews would return after a small break. He said that they had returned to the barricade for some rest and that even murderers needed breaks to rekindle and rejuvenate their strength and energy.

They had been butchering since morning.

Now it was dusk.

Dinner time.

These butchers were some of the hardest working people the boy had ever known, and they were clearly in better shape than most boxers or soldiers who trained intensely for years so as to manage the intense emotion that came with combat. How was it that these men could kill longer than most boxers could fight? It didn't make much sense, and it was a strange observation.

According to his uncle, an untrained human being could not handle such intense emotional rushes for longer than two or three minutes without collapsing. Eight hours was virtually impossible for the common man. But, then again, maybe his uncle was wrong. Maybe it wasn't such a big deal to rage, scream, hate, slice, cut, kill, murder and burn for eight hours straight. Or maybe--

There was no emotion.

Maybe there was no fear or rage. Maybe this killing was the calm and indifferent killing of paid butchers in a butcher shop. No intense emotions there. Just the mundane chopping and cutting and slicing that could be sustained for hours on end with the right reward and motivation.

As the boy thought about this, someone suddenly pushed up against the door and shook it violently. Everyone started. The adults regarded one another and quickly rushed through the red and green light and slammed against the door with all their combined weight.

When the jackal on the other side realized the door was bolted shut, he knocked hard. Again. And again.

"Open! Open up!"

A terrible voice rang out.

"You can't fool me. There's blood on your steps!"

The boy's mother regarded the broken man, then her husband. She was scared, but she didn't say anything. The jackal knocked again.

"Don't you steal from us! I know you have Sadars in there!"

Listening to this, the tiny woman gently pushed the boy's parents away from the door. "I'll send them away," she whispered. "If not, they'll just keep coming back."

"They can't come in," his mother said, shaking her head. "They can't…"

"They won't come in," the woman assured her. "I won't let them."

For a moment it seemed that the boy's mother was concerned about the woman's intentions. Maybe she had realized she had made a mistake in helping them. Maybe she would hand them over to the butchers of Trilokpuri to save her own children. It was a possibility.

Reluctantly, the boy's parents moved out of her way. They quietly made their way toward the bed and hid beside the broken man.

The woman turned to them and looked at them for a long moment. She sucked in a deep breath and nodded that she was ready. Then she mustered her courage and turned back toward the door. With shaking hands, she unbolted the lock and prepared to open the door. She took in a deep breath and closed her eyes, as though visualizing or praying. Then, releasing her breath and opening her eyes, she opened the door slightly. There was a long silence as she stared into the dusk at the jackals standing before her.

Terrified, the boy came out from under the bed to sit with his parents. The two girls followed suit. His mother took the boy in her arms and held him close while his father held the two girls. In the soft red and green light the boy suddenly noticed a black and white picture of Sikh and Hindu and Muslim soldiers on some unknown tropical island.

The boy didn't know much about the wars, but his uncle had told him that the only country that had sustained more causalities and that had lost more soldiers than India was a country called Russia; he swore almost every day that these nameless Indians who had died on foreign soil fighting world tyranny--and not a few ivory--chair leaders--had earned India's freedom in blood.

His uncle claimed that these nameless soldiers were in fact the ones who Indians truly owed respect, homage and remembrance to; they, the anonymous soldiers who had spilled their blood for King and country, were the ones who deserved a national holiday for freeing India. They, the nameless soldiers who had fought and died to protect the civil rights and religious freedoms of the British, made it impossible for those same rights and freedoms to be denied to Indians.

His uncle also said that a lot of countries under British rule at the end of the First World War and the Second World War were given freedom and autonomous government because of their courage and honor on the battlefield. He talked with great passion about the Dominion of Canada and how their soldiers had fought incredible battles in both wars, and he always spoke about one battle whose strategy had stunned and amazed all the colonies. He had forgotten the name of the battle but his uncle had said it was one for the books and the Canadian equivalent to the Battle of Saragarhi.

The boy didn't know much about Saragarhi. But he knew that twenty-one Sikhs had died to the last protecting King and country against twenty thousand Afghan warriors. He also knew that all twenty-one Sikhs were honored with the highest medal the King could award any soldier, and that the King had said the kirpan and the turban would always be a symbol of strength, courage and honor in the British Empire.

But that was all he knew about the twenty-one Sikhs who had died at Saragarhi protecting the empire; though he dared not mention his ignorance to his gorilla uncle, who always seemed to pounce upon the younger generation for not knowing their stories. And as the boy thought about his uncle, he prayed inwardly that he and his aunt and his grandmother were safe. A sinister voice suddenly returned him to the moment:

"You know what we want!"

The boy stared at the tiny woman as she regarded the jackal outside and attempted to keep her composure. She leaned against the door, blocking the way, making it difficult for him to look inside. She seemed to consider her words carefully. "No one here," she said. "Just me and my children."

"There's blood on your doorstep!"

She looked down, then back at the man, and nodded.

"So there is."

"Step aside and everything will be okay for you. Believe me, you don't want any trouble from us."

The woman's gaze fell again. She stared at the ground. Then she raised her eyes back to the man. "Someone knocked," she said evenly. "I didn't open the door. They're gone now, though I think they might be in the house in front of us."

"Where's the blood?"

"I don't know. Ask them."

"Let us in."

"I'd rather not. I don't want you to drag blood into my house. Bad enough it's on my doorstep."

"Let us search. Then we'll be on our way."

"No need. It is as I said." The woman took in a deep breath and released it slowly, calming herself. "Where are you from?" she asked calmly. "I don't recognize you or your friends."

"Stop playing games and move!"

"It's interesting," she observed. "Most murderers cover their faces for fear of what comes after."

"Let us in!"

The boy watched her scrutinize the men at her door. "Let me guess," she said. "Thirty? Forty? How many karas do you have? That's quite a collection."

"Step aside!"

"Who are you bringing those karas to?"

"Bitch, let us in or we're coming in!"

"I told you I don't want your karma polluting my home!"

At this the jackals laughed outrageously. The boy couldn't understand how such courage could come from such a small woman, and he wondered how this stance against the men outside was going to prevent them from entering her home. They were coming in. He sensed it. Despite her courage, she would not be able to stop them.

All at once the jackals stopped laughing.

"Step aside or be moved aside!"

The tiny woman shook her head in disbelief and acted as though he hadn't said a word. "You do the deed," she said. "And he collects the barter. And he burns the evidence." She laughed. "You didn't think of that. You didn't come up with that. Sheep don't think that far ahead."

"What do you care?"

"Oh, I care...I care very much."

"Bitch, you're not worth anything to us, but you're making my life really difficult--"

With those words he suddenly and unexpectedly kicked the door open and the tiny woman went stumbling back. But before the man could take a step forward, she had regained her balance and had something dark and narrow pointed at the man's head; something that stopped him dead in his tracks. With a trembling arm and eyes wide with the intent to kill, she pushed the muzzle of the Luger against his forehead and forced him back outside in the near dark.

"You're not worth anything to me either," she retorted with a tremble in her voice. "I told you I don't want you polluting my home."

"We'll leave. We'll leave you be."

"I know you will."

"I don't understand why you would do this."

"You don't have to."

"We don't want to hurt you."

"You already have!"

The tiny woman took two smalls steps forward, and they took two hurried steps back. "Don't you have a wife?" she asked after a moment, trying to understand how these men could butcher families the way they did. "Children? How can you do this?"

The man didn't bother answering.

"How can you do this?"

"You can't protect every Sikh."

"No. You're right, I can't. Only the ones who stumble at my door. Now get!"

A Feast for Lambs

"We'll be back with more."

"Get lost before you turn me into a murder-er!"

There was a long silence as the woman watched the men hurry away. When they disappeared, she stumbled back inside, closed and locked the door, then staggered backward on weary legs and suddenly collapsed to the ground overcome by fear and anxiety. The boy and his parents and the little girls rushed to her aid as she trembled and retched on the floor, telling them over and over again that she didn't have any bullets, and that she had nearly gambled all their lives away.

"We won't stay," the boy's mother said to the woman, helping her up. "We can't stay. We can't endanger you or your family any longer."

"I wish I could help more."

His mother shook her head. "There's nothing more. We won't stay."

Suddenly the wounded man waved them over. When they gathered round the bed he told them that his cousin-brother lived close by and that his uncle had rifles that they could use to protect themselves.

The boy's parents thought it over, then nodded, agreeing that this would be the best place to hide until the police came. For a moment the boy could see his mother go silent and inward and he knew she was thinking about his uncle and grandmother.

"I'm so sorry," the tiny woman apologized for not being able to keep them in her home. "I don't know what else to do. I wish I could keep you here."

Her head fell hopelessly.

The boy's father approached her. "It could be over," he said. "The police must be coming."

The boy's mother shook her head fiercely. "We've been saying this all day. We can't count on the police. They've been killing since last night and where are the police? I hear no sirens, no gunshots. Where are the police? We can't and we won't count on them and we will act like they are not coming. We wait for dark--" She then turned to regard the broken man on the bed as he held his blood-soaked turban in his hands-- "Then we hurry to your cousin-brother's home."

The broken man nodded.

At this the boy's father nodded with troubled eyes. The boy could see that the absence of the police for the entire day profoundly disturbed him, and he seemed to be having a hard time accepting what he didn't want to accept and didn't want to believe.

Defeated, the tiny woman stared at the boy and her daughters. At the boy, then her daughters. Suddenly a light flashed in her eyes. She turned to the boy's mother and said:

"He can be my son…if he cuts his hair…if he looks like my son…he can stay. They will not know."

The boy blinked. Then his eyes widened in horror as he realized what the woman had just said. He turned to regard his mother and father as they considered this outrageous suggestion. At once a sense of foreboding seized the boy. He couldn't even begin to imagine himself without his hair. "No," he whispered to himself. "No." He looked up through the soft, red light at his father and watched his eyes begin to fill. His father looked down at the boy and tears streaked down his defeated and humiliated face and disappeared into his dark beard.

Instantly the boy turned to his mother. There were no tears, but he could see every sinew in her face tense and tighten as anger coursed through her and filled her eyes with a strange determination. Not to save his hair, but to save his life.

Now his parents turned and stared at each other and said nothing. They just stared. His father was the first to turn to the woman to indicate what he had already decided. He nodded without looking at the boy and then his head fell in defeat and resignation, unable to face his son. He would not let his son perish because of hair or religion. He just stared at the ground--

Defeated.

Humiliated.

Silent.

The boy's face went hard and he clenched his fist at his side. He watched his mother carefully, praying for her strength, praying for her courage. But he saw little or no strength or courage there. Not when it came to his life. All he saw was a mother who would do anything to ensure the safety of her child. She swallowed something thick and heavy in her throat and turned to the woman and nodded her agreement. It was the only way. She would cut his hair so that he would look like the woman's son and he would be safe and that would be that.

Seeing this, the boy stumbled backward, trying to understand. "No," he whispered, petrified that his parents would dare touch his hair. "No." Nothing else came out of his mouth. He stopped breathing, then sucked in rapid gulps of air trying to calm himself as he tried to make sense of what his parents were about to do to him.

His father never looked up; he just stared at the ground completely shattered inside as the boy watched his tears splash into a small, salty puddle on the floor. His mother pleaded:

"Bete, please. You can grow it back."

"No."

"You can grow it back."

"No."

"Bete…"

The boy took another step back, shaking his head, staring at his mother as though she were trying to kill everything inside him, everything he had ever believed in.

She was.

His breath grew shallow and anxious. His head spun and the floor wobbled beneath his feet. He took another step back and stumbled into the bed and found himself sitting by the broken man's legs. The tiny woman handed his mother scissors, and to the boy they looked like the executioner's ax.

"Mum, please...don't…"

She took a step forward.

"Bete, stop this. Don't make this hard for

A Feast for Lambs

me."

"I will! I promise I will!"

"Be reasonable…it must be done."

Her voice seemed very far away, as though she were speaking to him from another world. The boy waved his hand indicating that she was wrong and that she didn't have to cut his hair. "No!" he said again, desperately. "No!"

With trembling hands, as though unsure of what she was about to do to her son, as though waiting for some message or divine intervention to stop her, she approached the bed slowly. Within moments she towered over the boy and had his patka in her hand.

Two soft hands instantly grabbed her wrists, pleadingly, trying to prevent her from pulling off his patka.

But she was too strong, too determined, and she quickly overpowered the boy and within seconds the saffron patka was on the bed in a pool of coagulated blood. She held his topknot and stared at it, transfixed, suddenly uneasy and unsure about what she was about to do.

The boy's father didn't look up. He couldn't watch. He couldn't say anything. He could only cry for his son and hate the men who had driven them to such a crushing act.

"No," the boy sobbed. "Please…no…"

"It will grow back," his mother's voice trembled. "It will grow back…"

The boy knew it wasn't about whether his hair would grow back. He knew it wasn't about hair at all. Hair was the last thing this was about.

This was about something else. Something far more important than hair or a uniform. "No," his lips trembled, as helpless tears streaked down his face. "No..."

And just as his mother went to cut the top-knot, a bloodied hand grabbed her wrist and held it firm. His mother's eyes stared at the hand for a moment, then followed the arm to the broken man's steady gaze. He said nothing. He just stared at her. Then he shook his head and he said:

"No."

The boy took the sudden moment of distraction to kick and push himself free. Then he bolted into the main room where his father sobbed silently. "No! No! No!" He yelled and held his head high and he gritted his teeth and his eyes were feral and fierce and he challenged anyone to dare come and take his mane away.

The boy's mother just stared at the man, then the hand holding hers, then the man. "Why?" she asked.

As the man searched for an answer in his heart, his lips quivered and his eyes filled as he attempted to push the words out of his throat. For a long, somber moment it seemed as though he would never get them out. "Listen to him," he finally managed to say. "He knows...he knows..."

"What? What does he know? He's just a boy," his mother replied.

The man shook his head.

"He knows..."

"What does he know?"

The man released the boy's mother and her

hand fell to the side and she dropped the scissors. The boy's father turned to the man to understand. "I got scared," the man muttered to himself, lost in some dark memory that would haunt him for the rest of his life. "I got scared...and I...and I did this to myself..." He smashed his hand against his head, indicating his bruised and battered head.

They were the saddest words the boy had ever heard in his life.

"I did this to myself!"

The broken man smashed and struck his head with incredible force, then he began to yank and pull out patches of hair straight out of his skull as though he were losing his mind and needed to be put in an asylum that could help him restore his splintered and shattered spirit.

Now the boy looked to the man and saw that he was so ashamed of what he had done that he could hardly speak. He just mumbled the same thing over and over again:

"I got scared...and I did this to myself!"

The boy's mother grabbed the man's hand and attempted to console him. At her touch he instantly jerked his hand away, looked at her with wide eyes, and with rising anger he yelled:

"I got scared and I did this to myself!"

The boy's mother edged closer to him and tried to tell him that everything would be alright and that his hair would grow back and that nobody would think him a coward considering the circumstances. But the man just shook his head and made strange animal noises, as though playing the moment over and over again in his head.

Slowly, the boy approached the broken man, and the man turned to look at him. After a moment the man smiled as though the boy filled his eyes and heart with hope and he took his hand and said:

"No."

"No!"

The boy repeated firmly.

No.

And there was a profound understanding between them.

The boy turned to his mother, then his father, and he could see his parents believed his refusal to cut his hair came from his ignorance and his inexperience with what they always called real life.

But the boy understood. It was they who had not understood what he had meant by the only word he could say, and it was they who had not understood what was in his heart when he had said the word. But if they could know, they would know this--

They would know that he meant the word in the most sincere, the most pure, and the most final way the word could be used. That he used the word with the full knowledge that he was using the most powerful word a man or woman could use against injustice and oppression. A word that could smother tyrants before the fires of hate and oppression and intolerance ever had the chance to spread. And he used the word with the full knowledge that it wasn't about hair. It wasn't about an iron bracelet. It wasn't about a ceremonial dagger. It wasn't even about the uniform. It was about saying 'no' to those who would deny him or anyone else their religious rights and freedoms.

It was not about the uniform, it was about what the uniform represented, and what the uniform represented was everything, and what the uniform represented was and would forever be a real threat to one society that had decided centuries ago that it would rule over all the other societies. It was about one simple and fundamental truth.

The right to be.

Everyone's right to be.

The right to be with dignity. With honor. With respect. With equality. Without shame. Without guilt. And without having to justify or explain oneself. It was about the right to be without fear of physical or spiritual persecution.

The boy used the word and he used it with the full knowledge that he was once again saying 'no' to caste tyranny, a lie that destroyed a person's dreams and hopes even before they were born into the world. He was once again saying 'no' to the caste system. He was once again saying 'no' to the Raja armies and the Mughal armies who had nearly disappeared Sikhs from the very face of the earth because of their ability to say 'no' to the tyrant regardless of the consequences.

The boy used the word and he remembered his Guru and he remembered why he had been given his baptismal uniform.

The uniform had been gifted to the Sikhs to give them strength and courage in their cause--their cause to give women and lower castes equality and freedom and to forever break the invisible shackles of caste. To give Sikhs strength and unity and courage to face those who were trying to eradicate them from the very face of the world because Sikhs threatened a hierarchal system of control that had a few dominating the many.

The boy had his baptismal uniform because of the word, and he had his uniform because Sikhs hadn't always been able to say 'no'. Sikhs hadn't always had the strength and courage to face their persecutors. There was a time when Sikhs had once run to the hills and forests to escape and hide from tyrants who would exchange gold for Sikh heads.

And then came the Guru.

And then came the Guru who said--

No.

No--to hiding.

No--to fear and silence in the face of oppression.

No--to caste persecution.

No--to religious persecution.

No--gender inequality.

And then came the Guru who gave them--

Their uniform.

5 Ks.

And--

Their name.

Singh and Kaur.

Lion and lioness.

And everything changed.

For a long time the Sikhs had employed the ancient art of peaceful protest, and they had protested fiercely against caste slavery and gender inequality, saying all castes were equal, and that women were equal to men in every respect. And because they did this in a time when such indisputable truths were considered blasphemous, the rulers of the time, then and now, sought the extinction of the Sikh and Sikh memory.

And they had nearly succeeded.

They had nearly managed to break their spirit and message, and they had nearly managed to break their confidence and conviction through torture and torment that sought to humiliate and break and shatter souls--torture and torment that sought to inspire fear, cowardice and silence.

And the Sikhs had been tortured and humiliated and executed, and yet they had never struck back or lashed out in anger. And the ruling castes and the Mughals had chased the Sikhs, who had survived their death campaigns by going into the forests and hills like wild dogs with their tails between their legs.

And then came the Guru.

The Guru who had witnessed the indiscriminate extermination of his Sikhs. The Guru who, like his nine predecessors before, believed in the ancient art of peaceful protest and civil disobedience, but who soon realized that sometimes peaceful protest and civil disobedience proved ineffective in the face of a tyrant whose sole ambition was the annihilation of a people.

And then came a realization.

A realization that sometimes freedom and rights needed to be defended and protected with a sword.

The Guru would not let his Sikhs perish. He would not let them perish into oblivion without a fight. Enough was enough. The peaceful protests of the nine Gurus before him had not been enough, and after many years of studying and reading and reflecting, the Guru returned to his Sikhs with a new reflection.

A new truth.

A truth that could only be understood by a people who have faced extinction.

When all modes of redressing a wrong have failed, resorting to the sword is just and pious.

The Guru tells Sikhs they will not hide anymore, and he tells them that some truths are worth defending and some truths are worth dying for. He tells them that never again will they be ashamed of their beliefs or their cause to return equality back to the land. They will fear no more and they will courageously say the most powerful word in the world to any tyrant who would dare deny them or anyone else their right to be.

No more will they bow down or hide or turn their back on tyranny; he tells them that some truths are worth defending and some truths are worth dying for, especially when peaceful protest is mistaken for cowardice or weakness, or when peaceful protest leads to the complete and total annihilation of a people.

The Guru tells his Sikhs some truths are worth defending and some truths are worth dying for--

Human equality.

A Feast for Lambs

Gender equality.
Religious freedom.
Religious tolerance.
Not just for Sikhs.
For all.

And then came the Guru who, after watching the near extinction of his Sikhs to the Brahmin and Mughal rulers, said 'no' to Sikh persecution by giving them courage, unity and strength in the form of five Ks and one communal family name that confirmed equality and was the silent but official deathblow to the caste system for Sikhs.

And then came the Guru who gave his Sikhs the will and the confidence and the resolve they needed to face those who were trying to erase them from the world.

When all modes of redressing a wrong have failed, resorting to the sword is just and pious.

And this Truth stuns and shocks many Sikhs who are used to the peaceful protests and martyrdom of their predecessors--predecessors who died by the sword of tyranny, by refusing to fight back, but always saying 'no'.

And the Guru tells them that the key to this new truth is not the last part but the first part.

When all modes of redressing a wrong have failed...

All modes.

Only then is defense of freedoms and liberties justified. Only when every possible effort has been made to avoid conflict are his Sikhs permitted to resort to the sword to defend themselves, as any person, kingdom or country should be permitted when tyranny threatens at the door. But he warns them they must also remember this and this is crucial--

They are never fighting a religion.

Never.

They are fighting tyrants using religion to their political and economic ends. And that when they are fighting they must always show complete respect and reverence to the religion. He also tells them that along with reverence to the religion they must always show mercy and compassion to those trying to persecute them. He gives them this warning. He warns them to never put on the mask of the tyrant they are fighting against. Never torment. Never torture. Never humiliate. Always reverence--

Reverence and compassion for life.

And through the inspiration of one of his warriors the Guru creates a new type of warrior in his army, whose job is not to kill but to help and heal the wounded.

The Sewadar.

And the sole purpose of the Sewadar in the Sikh army is to help the wounded on the battlefield regardless of side. And the Guru does one more thing that the enemy and many who follow him cannot even begin to understand.

The Guru depletes his treasury.

Valuing life above wealth, the Guru tips his arrows with an ounce of gold so that if he does not kill his enemy, his enemy will have the means to seek out medical attention.

This is the new truth of a people facing extinction. Defense. Compassion. And the realization that the rebel may very soon become the tyrant if he is not wary of his thoughts and intentions.

And the frightened dogs who had escaped to the hills and forests with their tails between their legs returned to the kingdom--

Lions.

And lionesses.

With gold-tipped arrows.

Unified in name and uniform and purpose and ready to protect and serve truths universal to all.

And the boy knew the uniform was more than just a uniform. The uniform was the message, and each K symbolized a unique reflection of protest and a way to overcome the tyranny within and the tyranny without. Every K was a staunch reminder and symbol of everything the Sikh stood for the day they came out of hiding to face their persecutors.

Kirpan--

To remind the Sikh of the sin of silence, the danger of indifference, and the need to act boldly and fearlessly against injustice, inequality, and oppression. A ceremonial dagger to remind the boy that a Sikh never turns his back on abused humanity regardless of race, faith, color, caste or gender.

Kara--

To remind the Sikh to always do good in the world and for the world. A bracelet to remind the boy that he must not only celebrate Sikh holidays, but that he should also embrace the holidays and festivities of other religious communities and to feel and experience the divine in differences and collective happiness.

Khanga--

To remind the Sikh to always live a clean and orderly life in service of humanity. A comb to remind the boy of the destructiveness of sloth and disorder and chaos and to remind him to always walk with his back straight, head up and his heart open.

Kachera--

To remind the Sikh to always live a chaste life and to be wary of the five great enemies that seek to suffocate the soul. Lust. Greed. Rage. Attachment. Ego. Undergarments to remind the boy to always live a courageous life and to be wary of two great fears that could muzzle a lion forever.

Fear of death.

Fear of poverty.

Kes--

To remind the Sikh that he is a dedicated servant of the unknown and unknowable source of life. Unshorn hair to remind the boy that he does not believe in caste or make any references to caste and that to do so was to knowingly or unknowingly ridicule his ancestors, who died protecting the very idea of human dignity and equality.

And when the boy said 'no' he meant the word in the most sincere and the most final way the word could ever be used; and he knew it wasn't about a kirpan, a kara, a khanga, kachera, or kes. It wasn't about the Sikh uniform at all. It was about something else. It was about what the uniform symbolized. It was about what the uniform meant. It was about meaning and substance and years of

A Feast for Lambs

history that could not be erased from the Sikh consciousness, even if it had been erased from the Sikh
library. It was about history repeating itself, and it
was about so much more. And the boy knew this,
knew this with all his heart, and that is why,
regardless of his parents' fear, the boy still said--
No!

CB

Night descended as the boy's parents prepared to leave the tiny woman's small home. His father hefted the broken man on his back and carried him to the door while his mother kneeled before him and looked him in his eyes. Then she extended her pinky and asked him to shut his eyes and keep them shut until she said it was okay and that he could open them again. The boy nodded and promised her that he would do as she asked without question. He pinky shook on it and felt a rush of fear and uncertainly as his mother pulled him closer and did something she hadn't done since he was five years old.

Despite being smaller than the average seven-year-old, she took him in her arms, held him close, and carried him to the open door while he stared at his future wife-to-be standing next to her sister. There his mother thanked the tiny woman for her strength and courage and the boy flicked his eyes to gaze at this woman who had opened her door for them. A moment later his mother carried him through the threshold and out the door and his heart blessed her and wished her good luck and fortune in this life and the next hundred lives to come.

As the door closed softly and silently, his

eyes flicked back to the girl in the doorway, wishing he knew her name. The door closed, a bolt snapped, and they stepped into the gloom. His mother followed his father through the thickening warm air as the broken man whispered orders and directions to his cousin-brother's home.

Respecting his mother's wishes, the boy instantly closed his eyes; but he could feel his mother's heart pounding hard with every sob and whimper coming from the colony. Trying to shut the cries out of his mind by pushing his ear against his mother's chunni, the boy bobbed and bounced in his mother's arms and he could feel her fear in the strain of her shoulder and neck muscles. Then, all of sudden, she hesitated with her steps and the stench of kerosene and freshly burnt humanity assaulted the boy like a slap in the face.

A moment later his mother froze with a gasp of terror unlike any he had ever heard come from her lips, and he stopped bouncing.

He could feel her heart stop all of a sudden, then thunder all at once. Then stop. Then thunder. And then it froze for good. It was strange. It was as though her heart didn't want to believe or didn't know how to feel or respond to what her eyes were taking in. Then all at once he felt her heart pound harder and harder against her chest. And it seemed as though her heart were trying to push its way out of her chest. They all whispered God's name under their breath. His father instantly called out to the boy in a harsh whisper:

"Bete, close your eyes!"

The boy had never heard his father's voice

sound so firm and commanding before.

"They are."

"Keep them closed."

"What is it? What's happening?" the boy asked.

"Don't you open them!" his father commanded.

"What's happening?"

The boy wanted to know.

"Keep them shut," his mother whispered, slowly regaining herself. "Please...don't ask questions. You promised."

"What is it?"

"Keep them shut," she said in a voice so weak and chilling he didn't want to ask any more questions. "Keep them shut," she repeated. "Please...just listen..."

He did, and they began to move again. Only now they weren't running, they weren't jogging, they weren't even walking. They were inching their way toward safety, watching their every step, slipping and sliding and balancing themselves as though they were walking through a street covered with wet, decaying leaves. The boy also noticed that the air was unnaturally warm for the cool night and he sensed smoke rising and curling and spreading all around his face.

Not too far away the boy could hear a small fire burning and snapping and whipping the night. The burning and snapping and whipping grew louder and louder as his mother carried him toward it. Then, as his mother carried him away, the burning and snapping and whipping faded away along with the sobs and the cries and the wails.

Something powerful inside him wanted to open his eyes, wanted to know what his parents were seeing, wanted to know what they were walking through; something inside him wanted to know what that horrible stench was--that horrible, caustic stench that warmed and thickened and gave an unnatural weight and stickiness to the air. He had smelled the odor before; he had definitely smelled this odor before, and as he took it in, he suddenly remembered where he had smelled it.

His father had once burned the hair on his arms while trying to cook daal-rotis. The hairs sizzled and disappeared so fast he barely had time to process what was happening to his arm. Even when he smothered the small fire on his arm the entire pucca filled with such a retched smell that they all had to rush straight out of the pucca for fresh air. At that time he was sure that the smell of burnt hair was the worst odor in the world and that if death had a smell or scent or signature it was the smell of burnt hair.

Now he was sure of it, and the smell of death was everywhere. It completely impregnated the colony. It was like someone had made a massive Holi bonfire with only hair and nails to burn. Only that wasn't exactly true. This smell was a measure worse, as underneath the scent of burnt hair there were other smells he had never really taken in before. And then there was one that he did recognize.

The distinct and unmistakable smell of

blended urine and excrement.

Now as his mother took slow, calculated steps, the boy no longer felt the need to see what was happening. He already knew, even though his mind found it impossible to accept what the sounds and smells and smoky air were telling him.

The congressman had turned his colony into a living hell.

A living hell he didn't want to think about as the sobs coming from every direction in the dark void of his mind made him feel as though the entire world were suffering. Unable to accept what his senses were telling him, the boy did something he often did when things upset him.

He attempted to trick himself.

To trick his mind.

He told himself that his mother was hiking up a mountain after a heavy rain and that she was having a hard time carrying him with all the mud and wet leaves and rocks that covered the ground. This was easier to accept. Easier to imagine. Though his heart knew, it absolutely knew; it knew and could not or would not be fooled or tricked as easily as his mind.

And that was the thing about the heart.

His grandmother had always told him that the heart simply could not be fooled.

Could not be tricked.

It could be blocked.

It could be ignored.

But it could not be fooled.

And it very often knew things in advance and gave warnings and inspirations adults often ignored and blocked and much later regretted; but as you grew older you learned to trust your heart much more than your mind and you often did things that were inspired and irrational and considered foolish by many. But things you rarely regretted. And his grandmother had told him that it was better to live as a fool than to live with regret.

But now the boy didn't want to listen to his heart.

He wanted to block it, to shut it out and imagine something else, even though imagining something else grew more and more impossible with every breath he took.

The boy thought about his heart, and then he thought about his grandmother, about the way she had acted the last time he had seen her, and he prayed inwardly that she was safe and that she and his uncle had somehow found a way out of this living hell.

Suddenly the stench of kerosene and burnt hair intensified, and though the boy's eyes were closed, the smell alone filled his eyes with stinging tears. Desperately, the boy tried to filter the smell out through his mother's chunni and dress but it was useless.

It was everywhere and in everything.

It even seemed to stain his mother's clothes, hair and skin, and he suddenly wished his nose and ears had lids so that he could shut them, too. Deeply disturbed by the all-pervading stench of death, and his heart desperately wanting to reassure his mother that she didn't have to worry about him, the boy whispered in a quivering voice:

A Feast for Lambs

"My eyes are closed."
She whispered:
"I know they are."
The broken man said:
"We're close."
"My eyes are closed," the boy said again.
The smell was more than he could bear and he didn't know what else to say.

"I know they are," his mother said. "Think of something...good..."

The boy tried to think of something, anything good, but all he could think about were the thick, decaying, slimy leaves under his mother's feet.

"I can't..."
"Try."
"I can't."
"Try...bete...try..."

Suddenly he felt his mother begin to move faster and faster.

She had clearly passed through all the leaves and mud and was accelerating her pace. He bounced and bobbed and tried his best not to breathe. Odds were they were close now.

A sudden whooping and hollering and a terrible percussion of melee weapons clacked and thumped and pounded and thundered with the boy's heart.

The crews had officially returned from their break with renewed strength, energy and determination to finish the congressman's dark work.

Now the boy felt his mother charge through the night. Moments later he heard a new voice whispering out to them, telling them to hurry. He felt his mother's feet pound against the ground as she surged toward the voice. Then he heard a door slam, followed by the quick snap of a bolt. A second later his mother lowered him to the dusty cement floor and told him he could open his eyes.

When he opened his eyes, he saw an older man kneeling beside a bed, talking softly to the broken man. The older man had a white beard and a beige kurta pajama and he had a rifle slung across his shoulder. After a moment, he stood and motioned to the boy's father to follow him. The boy's father complied, left for a few minutes, then returned to them holding a rifle.

The boy stared at the rifle, then his father, then the rifle, and he wondered if his father knew how to use it; he wondered if perhaps it should have been entrusted to his mother. He didn't say anything, but he sensed his mother would do whatever needed to be done to survive. His father he wasn't so sure about. His father was perhaps one of the gentlest men he had ever known.

In reality his father couldn't even hurt an insect, let alone shoot a man. He remembered his father had once spent an entire morning trying to gently guide a bee out of an open window of their home while his mother went at it with her slippers. For a moment the boy smiled at the memory; then he looked to the broken man, who was soaked in blood and soiled in shame as he stared blankly at the plaster ceiling, lost in a moment he could never take back.

The old, grizzled man placed the rifle next to the bed for a moment, staring down at the broken man. He then raised his hands, fiddled with the back and side of his white turban. Then he patiently unraveled his turban to reveal a mass of white hair like his beard. When the turban was in his hands, he helped the broken man sit up slightly. He moved behind him and proceeded to gently wrap his turban around the man's blood-soaked stomach that was already covered with the boy's now crimson and brown patka.

Almost instantly the white turban blossomed red like a flower. Dark fluid seeped from under the makeshift bandage as the old man tied the turban tightly, then helped the broken man lie back down, saying that the crews outside would pay for what they had done to his hair. The broken man said nothing. He just stared vacantly into the dark void that had become his life.

Clearing his throat, the old man moved from the bed. "Stay with him," he said to the boy's mother, taking his rifle. Then, looking to the boy's father he said, "We'll guard the front." Saying this, he seemed to instantly notice the reluctance or fear in the boy's father's eyes. He looked to the rifle, then his father. He asked:

"You know how to use one of those?"

The boy's father hesitated, then nodded that he did.

"Good. Is it bad out there?"

His father nodded gravely.

"It is bad."

The old man considered this. "I need you to watch yourself," he cautioned. "Don't go shooting anything that moves. We have to be careful. My sons went out to help their sister and her family. They'll be back anytime now…they're probably stuck somewhere…"

The boy's father nodded, but the boy could see that his father didn't think the man's family was ever coming back. The old man seemed to read this, too, and his face suddenly grew grave and worried. He asked:

"Is it that bad out there?"

The boy knew he wasn't asking the question he really wanted to ask.

His father nodded silently, telling the old man with his eyes that he was sorry but that he didn't believe there were many survivors out there.

The old man's eyes watered slightly. Then he sniffed, wrinkled his nose and suddenly cleared his throat. "We've been through tough times before. My sons wouldn't let anything happen to their sister or my grandchildren. You just watch yourself with that rifle, you understand?"

The boy's father nodded.

"I will."

The old man turned to the boy's mother. "Take care of my nephew." He looked to the broken man, then turned with a sigh and walked toward the main room, where the boy could see two small windows on either side of the door. The boy noticed the home for the first time. It was bigger than most homes in the colony. It had three bedrooms and a storage room for cow pies, along with

A Feast for Lambs

a television and a radio.

The boy's mother moved toward the radio, which sat on a small, wooden desk. She turned it on to hear if there was anything on the news about what was happening to them, or if other Sikhs were being attacked in the nation, or the nation's capital.

But when she turned it on all the boy heard was peaceful Hindi music from the movies. With a soft sigh, his mother lowered the volume slightly so it couldn't be heard outside the bedroom. Then she and the boy sat near the broken man on the edge of the bed, listening.

Suddenly the music stopped.

There was a moment of silence.

Dead silence.

An instant later he heard something he couldn't believe. A man's voice he recognized from the movies was telling all of India to exact revenge on Sikhs. Even more strange and alarming was the fact that he was even regurgitating the congressman's practiced slogan, the congressman's mantra. Listening to the actor give the best performance of his career, the boy wondered how everyone could be chanting the same tune, and why that tune was being announced to the nation over the radio.

Blood for Blood.

The boy wanted to tell the actor that he was wrong, completely wrong, and that they weren't all Sikhs from the South with faces painted black with bloodshot red eyes like in his movies. He wanted to tell him that this was real life and that in real life Sikhs weren't all villains. But it was no use. The actor was giving his best performance; and the

219

actor, who had recently declared his interest in politics, continued to use his reputation, his influence and his words to spread the slogan and fuel the fires of mass murder.

How such a thing could even be permitted on the radio felt strange, and the boy wondered if those who controlled the radio would have allowed an actor to speak out for vengeance against the Brahmins when a Brahmin radical assassinated the father of their nation.

Thinking this, the actor's voice suddenly faded away and the announcer's voice rang out. He talked about the prime minister's funeral arrangements and then he declared that there were one or two mob outbursts in the country, but that for the most part there was peace.

Peace. What is he talking about? How can he say there is peace? How can he say that after such a performance?

The boy said nothing to his mother. There was nothing to say. She just stared at the radio as though she were staring at the executioner and listened to the music silently for a long time. Then, something snapped in the broken man. He turned toward the radio and gasped painfully:

"Turn it off...turn it off...I cannot hear the lies anymore...turn it off..."

His mother signaled a request to the boy with her eyes. He didn't need to be signaled twice. The boy snapped off the bed, took a few steps to the table and shut off the radio. Then he returned to his place beside his mother as the man continued:

A Feast for Lambs

"They say there is peace. One screams for vengeance while the other says there is peace. What are they doing? What are they saying? They've been butchering us for the last two days and they say there is peace."

"Save your strength," the boy's mother said, and grabbed his hand. "Don't let yourself be upset over them. There is nothing that can be--"

"I am upset! How can I not be?" The man shook his head incredulously. He swallowed his anger. He looked toward the radio. "I suppose the new word for murder is peace in India. Maybe that's why people think there is so much peace here."

"Save your strength, there is nothing we can do. This will all be over soon."

"Not if they keep saying there is peace."

"Save your strength...please..."

"You have hope," the broken man scoffed.

"I do."

"You have hope, even when they say such lies."

The boy saw his mother's face suddenly tense as she squeezed the man's hand--squeezed it so tightly as to be felt beyond the pain in his stomach. "I can only hope," she said in a firm voice. "I can only hope..."

The boy sensed she was giving the man her eyes.

"I can only hope and pray they have just made a mistake and they will soon report the truth. I can only hope and pray the police and military will be coming soon. I can only hope and pray, not for me but for others. Do you understand?" She squeezed a little harder. "Do you understand my meaning?"

The man looked to the boy, then to the boy's mother, and, after a hesitation, he nodded that he did. So did the boy. He understood her meaning and he knew his mother would do anything and everything she could to keep hope alive in the boy's heart, and that she would not let this man pollute their minds with fear and hopelessness, regardless of their situation or what they had just heard on the radio.

After a long silence, the broken man lifted his gaze to the boy. "Do you know the story of the Guru Tegh Bahadur and how he saved the Hindu people from religious persecution?" he asked.

The boy regarded the man for a moment and didn't know what to say. Of course he did. Of course he knew the story. But then, staring at the man, he thought that maybe he just needed to talk, and that talking would be good for him. Maybe this man was like his mother and he just liked telling the same stories over and over again, adding a new lesson with each rendition. And maybe, just maybe he would learn something new about the story. So he shook his head and said:

"I don't. I don't know."

His mother instantly threw him a searing look, but then, understanding, stopped herself from saying anything.

The broken man caught this silent discussion between the boy and his mother and he laughed out loud. "Of course you know!" he said.

A Feast for Lambs

He laughed and reached out and took the boy's hand and squeezed his small hands affectionately. "How could you not know? You probably know it better than me."

"I forgot."

"No, you didn't forget."

"I can't remember."

"That's the same as you forgot and you didn't forget. You remember." The man shook his head at the boy. He squeezed his hand tighter. "Only a boy who keeps his people's stories strong in his heart can say 'no' the way you say 'no'. I am sorry for even suggesting that you might be one of those boys who wears the uniform but doesn't know the meaning."

The boy nodded, then cleverly added:

"I know, but I don't know the story the way you know the story, or the way you say the story."

Now the man's eyes lit up and he smiled. He laughed some more, then calmed himself down. "The way I know it or say it," he repeated with genuine respect in his eyes for the boy. Amazed, he turned slightly to regard the boy's mother. "Kids have clever thoughts don't they? And good, clean, unspoiled hearts."

His mother nodded.

"They do."

His gaze returned to the boy. "So you want to hear my way of telling it, do you?"

The boy nodded sincerely. He did want to hear a new version of an old story he really loved and cherished.

"The way I used to tell it to my son."

The boy didn't even realize the man had a son, and he wondered if his son was his age, and if he was safe. The broken man was quiet for a moment, then he began:

"During the time of the emperor Aurangzeb--an emperor who had outlawed music and art and laughter, and who had poisoned his father and tortured and murdered his brothers to take the peacock throne--the Mughal army had strict orders to convert all the Kashmiri Hindus to Islam or slaughter them as infidels."

The man paused. His mother removed her hand from his shoulder and watched him carefully. The boy thought about Aurangzeb and how he had not known that he had killed his own family to take the throne, and he wondered what kind of a man would kill his own family for power. He liked all the information, but wondered if it was really necessary to the story. The man continued:

"Of course, this had nothing to do with religion but everything to do with ego and empire. In his need to be remembered as a great emperor he started a campaign to increase his empire in land and riches, using, as leaders often do, his religion to do so. If his enemies converted, the riches and land automatically became part of his empire. If they didn't convert, he killed them, and it amounted to the same thing."

The man paused for a moment to consider his words.

His mother looked to the boy to see if he was learning anything new. The boy thought about how leaders and extremists often used religion to do things that his grandmother had said not even animals would do to each other. Thinking this, the boy wondered for a moment what it would be like to live in such times, but then he thought about the crews hunting for Sikhs outside, and he understood that he was in fact living in such a time. The broken man continued:

"This is how the emperor ruled, and it proved to be a most efficient and effective method. Despite his cruelty, the emperor was also a very intelligent man. He was as intelligent as he was harsh. He realized that if he converted the Brahmins first, then he would have no problems whatsoever converting all the other Hindus. He instinctively knew that, at the time, the Brahmins ruled over the Hindus like kings. The Kashmiri Hindus would do whatever the Brahmins did. So these Kashmiri Brahmins, scared for their lives, sought out the Sikhs. They thought that maybe they could inspire the Sikhs to take their side, even though the Brahmins and Rajas had been killing the Sikhs for trying to abolish their caste system."

A shriek outside silenced him for a moment and the man closed his eyes sadly. His mother looked to the front of the house where his father and the old man stared out the window into the darkness.

The shrieks died down and then there was silence again. The man opened his eyes. He took in a deep breath and continued in an uneasy voice:

"I guess you can say it was a strange twist of fate. Even ironic. But when they found the Guru and spoke to the Guru, he told them he would not use his sword against the Mughals, but that he would help them. The Guru told them there was another way to defeat tyrants, and he told these Brahmins this without telling them how. They asked him. But he didn't tell them. He said nothing. He merely told them he would discuss their plight with the emperor himself, and they, of course, thought he was mad, as they knew no one discussed anything with the emperor."

The man paused to consider his words. His mother stared down at his stomach, which continued to ooze life. Ignoring his pain and his wounds, the man eased forward and continued:

"But the Guru would not take his sword. The Guru, like his predecessors, believed first and foremost in nonviolent resistance. Without anger and without malice he would show the emperor the error of his ways. Truth, he was sure, would prevail, and he would defeat this emperor with the force of his soul rather than the force of his sword. And so the Guru visits the emperor and he politely and respectfully requests that the emperor leave the Brahmins alone."

At this the boy wrinkled his face. He remembered a slightly different version of the story; he thought that the emperor had actually arrested the Guru, but he didn't interrupt the man's story. He listened intently.

"The emperor stares at the Guru--"the man feigned being the emperor staring at the Guru--"He laughs at the Guru. And then he mocks the Guru. The emperor even points out that the Guru is foolishly risking his life for those who sought his people's extinction long before he ever did. And the emperor is just about to insult the Guru when the Guru does something no one expects. He does what he had decided he would do long before he took the first step into the emperor's court to protect the rights of these Brahmins."

The man paused to let the words of his story sink in. The boy's mother stared down at his torn and shredded stomach. The boy was a little puzzled but didn't say anything. This wasn't exactly the way his mother or uncle told the story.

There were slight variances.

In his mother's story the emperor caught the Guru and brought him into his court, whereupon the Guru challenged the emperor for the Brahmins.

And this minor discrepancy, even though it was slight, caused a strange feeling in the boy's heart. He suddenly felt very sad and didn't quite know why. Then he realized what was pulling and tugging at his heart. Even though these were just minor discrepancies, the only texts and books and records and letters that could filter truth from fiction had been burned.

The boy's head fell and he swallowed something thick in his throat as he began to understand his uncle's frustration, and even, perhaps, his anger.

He then felt an even deeper pang of grief when he suddenly realized that fifty years from now the story would be slowly forgotten and possibly even denied by the upper-caste government, which had already begun to deny the Guru's act of

peaceful protest and martyrdom for the Kashmiri
Brahmins. As he thought about this he suddenly
imagined pictures being published with the first
Sikh Guru with caste marks, praying while holding
the sacred thread that he had outright rejected
when he denied the inequalities of the caste system.
The boy felt the anger churning within and didn't
want to think about it anymore. The man continued:

"The Guru would not draw his sword. He
would not swear or curse at the emperor. He would
challenge him. He would simply challenge him.
The Guru's Truth against the emperor's sword. And
there in front of his court, the Guru does just that.
He challenges the emperor. He promises him that if
the emperor can convert him, then all the Brahmins
will convert willingly and without fuss. But if he
cannot convert him, then he must let them go and
he must let them be free to practice their religion.
The emperor laughs at this and he quickly accepts
this ridiculous proposition. He thinks the Guru
doesn't know the extent of his cruelty. But what the
emperor doesn't know is the power of the Guru's
truth."

This part of the story was the same as his
mother's. But as the broken man told it, he seemed
to suddenly remember something and, unlike his
mother or uncle who grew excited and passionate
at this part, the man's voice became weak and wearied and distant.

"He thinks the Guru doesn't know his
methods. The Guru does. He knows about the torture. He knows about the boiling and cooking and

sawing. But what the emperor doesn't know is the Guru's will."

The boy began to sense the words were becoming more and more difficult for the man, and his eyes were now lost and in another world.

"The emperor tortured the Guru for days, and never once did the Guru submit or lash out in anger at his torturers or at their religion…"

The man paused for a long, pensive moment, his face distraught. The boy thought that something inside him was preventing him from finishing the story. He seemed to be growing weak and pale with every word. At last, the man finished in a slow, grave voice that sounded like he was speaking with a mouthful of stones.

"They eventually tired of their own anger and they decapitated him. His head was brought to his son, Gobind Rai, and the Kashmiri Brahmins remained Kashmiri Brahmins."

Gobind Rai, who would become the next Guru, and who would reject and remove his last name with every other Sikh on the day he blessed Sikhs with their baptismal uniform, had spent years reflecting on the ancient art of peaceful protest and meditating on the extermination of his people, which had erupted with the martyrdom of his father. A quote suddenly came to mind--

When all modes of redressing a wrong have failed, resorting to the sword is just and pious.

A reflection that many believed had saved the Sikhs from extinction. The boy thought about these quotes and he wondered how long they would live in the hearts of Sikhs before they would be denied or forgotten, or both denied and forgotten. Then he suddenly forgot his concerns when he saw the man's eyes slowly fill with deep remorse.

Tears ran down his face. He shook his head and stopped breathing for a long while and stared at the boy without seeing him. Then his lungs panicked and his throat and mouth suddenly gasped for air. "They tortured him for days and I cut my hair..." He closed his eyes and the tears continued to flow. Shame squeezed his voice to a harsh whisper. "They tortured him for days and I cut my hair."

The boy squeezed his hand as his mother placed a comforting hand on his shoulder. "You are not the Guru," she whispered. "You are not the Guru."

The man opened his eyes and looked up at her. She continued:

"It is one thing to talk and hear the story. It is one thing to say you wouldn't be scared and imagine you wouldn't be scared, but it is another thing to not be scared when it is real..."

The broken man nodded solemnly as he wiped away more silent tears. The boy understood what his mother was trying to tell him. He could see that the man understood too. But he could also see that the shame of what he had done to himself haunted him and it was slowly extinguishing the light in his eyes. There was a long silence. The man stared at the boy, then he reflected:

"We say children are fearless because they don't know any better."

He laughed at the absurdity of what he had just said. His voice grew stern and serious and he

A Feast for Lambs

continued:

"I say bullshit!"

The boy smiled and waited for his mother's reaction. But she just stared at the man, listening.

"I think that this is what we need to tell ourselves to feel better about our own cowardice. We need to tell ourselves this to forget what we've lost with age."

He laughed at himself.

"I say children are fearless because they know better. I say children know better than us and I think this is why they are so fearless. That's what I say. That's what I think. I think if I am ever given another chance...I will never let this--" he indicated his head with his free hand--"overpower this." And he placed his hand on his heart.

The man closed his eyes again and seemed to lose himself in a memory. "Thinking about it," he said with a little laugh. "My son taught me more than I ever taught him...and he didn't even know it...and he didn't even know..." He opened his eyes wearily.

"Tell him," the boy said. "You'll still be able to tell him."

At this the man closed his eyes. After a reflective moment he opened them and said:

"I haven't seen or heard from my son in two years."

"I'm sorry," the boy's mother said.

"He had courage," he said, opening his eyes. "He protested against the constitution and the government and the media always. And I always told him to leave it be. Just leave it be and live your

231

life. I just didn't want anything to happen to him. I just wanted him to be okay."

He closed his again with the memory and went silent.

"Disappeared?" his mother asked.

The man's eyes sprang open with sudden anger. "Please don't say that," he said. "Not disappeared. Don't say that..." His eyes closed again as though he were struggling to keep them open. "Not disappeared. I imagine he smartened up and got out of here." He smiled faintly. "He just left everything behind and took off. Took off to see the world I could never see."

He paused, breathed deeply, then continued:

"I imagine he's in Nairobi now. He always, always talked about the Sikhs in Nairobi and what they had accomplished there with great pride."

He nodded as if to convince himself more than anyone else.

"Yes. He's in Nairobi, teaching chess and English. He loved chess. In fact, the night before he left for Nairobi we went to a tea stall to play. Somehow I think he knew he wasn't going to see me again because he decided that he didn't want to play."

He cleared his throat as he recalled the night.

"Strangest thing. Not like him at all. He tells me he doesn't want to play because he just wants to talk. Just talk."

The boy looked up at his mother and he sensed that he knew who she was thinking about.

A Feast for Lambs

He turned back to the man as a sweet smile bloomed over his face.

"We never talked so much in our lives…and not like usual talk. It wasn't father-son talk. It was better. It was much better. It was like…it was like two long-lost friends who hadn't seen each other for years."

He breathed deeply.

"We talked all night. I don't know why we never talked like this before, but I'm so glad we did. We talked the whole night through. In the morning he went to the market and took off…and I haven't seen him since…"

He was silent for a long time. The boy looked at his mother and he could see her hugging someone tightly in her eyes. With a shallow breath, the man continued:

"He's doing everything I couldn't do but said that I would. He's living the life I never had the courage to live. One day's he's coming back home and he's going to explain everything to me. He's going to explain how he didn't want to break his father's heart and how he just couldn't bear to tell me he was going and that's why he left everything behind."

He paused, and with closed eyes he slowly raised his free hand. In his mind he was living a future moment he had created for himself and had probably played a thousand times. Tears streamed from his closed eyes. A long finger pointed at what the boy understood to be the man's imaginary son. He began to shake his finger as he went on:

"And I'm going to tell him to shut up and stop apologizing. Stop trying to say this or that; stop trying to explain what you had to do or why you had to go. No explanations necessary. No explanations necessary..."

His voiced faded and his hand fell to his side. The boy felt his other hand relax in his. A smile formed on his pale face and grew with the vision of his son. He opened his eyes and stared at the boy. But the boy understood the man was seeing someone else. He continued:

"I'm going to tell him he has nothing to explain. Absolutely nothing. Then I'm going to take him for tea. And this time he's the one who's going to want to play chess, but this time it's me who's going to tell him that I don't want to play. And I'm going to tell him I just want to talk. And we'll talk...and we'll talk...we'll talk all night long...like two long-lost friends..."

The man, smiling, froze suddenly with his eyes staring directly at the boy.

His mother sighed sadly. After a moment she took in a deep breath and reached out to the smiling man with her hand and gently shut his eyes for him. She turned to the boy. "Let him sleep," she said. "He's very tired."

The boy nodded sadly and saw in her eyes that the man would never open his eyes again. With another faint sigh, she rose slowly and walked toward the front of the house. The boy followed close behind, thinking about the man and his son drinking tea and talking--just talking--like two long-lost friends.

ॐ

The boy trudged through a fog-like smoke or a smoke-like fog, staring at all the burning trees around him, listening to the cries of mothers and children coming from everywhere and nowhere at the same time. With careful steps, he walked over the ash and rubble and rock toward the silhouettes of two tall and lanky men who stood at the edge of a precipice, grabbing shadowy things from a massive mountain of bags that wiggled and struggled to be free. One by one they hefted the body bags and hurled them down into the endless abyss before them.

As the boy approached the precipice, the silhouettes suddenly grabbed one sack from the mountain of bodies. The sack pushed and kicked and struggled violently to free itself. In a muffled voice that sounded familiar, it pleaded for its life and it screamed that it had to protect its family.

Too familiar.

Like his father.

Instantly the boy's heart lurched and he charged toward the precipice before these demons could hurl his father into the abyss. But as he charged forward the fog thickened like something wicked and conscious so that it was like running through an ocean of thick, white glue that stuck and pulled and tugged at him with every attempt he made to save his father from oblivion; and with every attempt forward the silent, glutinous, ethereal ocean grew thicker and thicker and pulled and tugged and seemed to enjoy the boy's desperate agony. Panting and struggling, the boy tried to scream through the fog for the men to stop, but it was like screaming through water with the weight of an ocean on top of his head, holding him back, suffocating and crushing him.

Helplessly, the boy watched the men through the living fog as they heartlessly released his father into the great, dark unknown. And just as they released him, the boy jolted awake with a terrible scream, sweating in his mother's embrace.

"It's okay," she said, placing a gentle hand on his wet forehead. "You were dreaming." His mother sat against the brick wall; his soaked, bare head rested in her lap. She ran her fingers through his hair.

Wearily, the boy looked up to see his father standing by the open window. The old man stood by the other window on the other side of the door.

It all came back to him.

The barricade. The congressman. The taxi. The car accident. The crews marking the doors. The tiny woman. The two girls. The broken man. The crying. The sobbing. The whimpering. The smell. Death.

The boy closed his eyes and wanted to return to the nightmare--the nightmare he could now barely remember. His mother looked up toward his father and asked:

"Do you see anything?"

"I don't see anything," the boy's father answered.

"If you do," the old man said, "you remember to be careful."

"I remember," the boy's father said. "I remember…"

"They're hiding somewhere," the old man said pensively, staring at a fire burning in the street with dark, tired eyes. "They'll be here soon." He took in a deep breath and sighed. "They should move now I think…they should come before the mobs return…"

No one said a word for a long while and it was quiet again outside. But then a sudden cry followed by a wail pierced the night and shattered the silence. The old man looked to the boy's father, letting him know that this was it. The killing had begun once again.

His father held the old man's gaze for a long moment, then he motioned with his eyes that he was ready to do whatever needed to be done to protect his family.

Both men raised their rifles and held them at the ready as they stared deep into the gloom, waiting. After a silence it came.

First, a clatter of sticks. Then, iron prods against the ground that created a cacophonous percussion of pure terror.

The boy's father breathed deeply. The percussion grew louder and louder as the crew approached them. Staring at his father, the boy could see that his hands were trembling and that he had difficulty holding the rifle steady. They watched outside. The boy's mother asked in a whisper:

"What's happening?"

The boy's father answered without looking down at her.

"They're searching."

"What do you see?"

"Just shadows."

"Are they close?"

He nodded.

"I think so."

"Will they find us?"

He hesitated.

"I think so."

"Will you shoot them?"

He didn't answer. His head lowered gravely and his trembling hands looked as though they were ready to drop the rifle at any moment.

The boy could see his father agonizing over what life was suddenly and unexpectedly forcing him to do, and he could clearly see that his father had never suspected that his life would have ever brought him to this moment, to this point where he would have to kill another man to protect his family.

God. Please make it so my father never has to hurt another man. Please make it so he doesn't have to pull that trigger. Please protect us. Please...

But just as the boy prayed for help, the crew approached the old man's home. His father and the old man started. "Watch it," the old man said, taking in a deep breath. "Here they come..."

A Feast for Lambs

The boy tensed in his mother's arms. She held him tight, staring up at the windows.

The old man turned to his father, looked at the rifle, then him. "We have to do this," he said, as the racket approached them. "You understand that don't you? They have brought us to this."

His father nodded, took in a deep breath and tried to calm his nerves. But the boy could see that that his efforts were in vain and that his hands continued to tremble.

The old man turned his gaze back to the street. "Let me shoot a warning," he said. "You do nothing unless they charge us. You understand?"

His father nodded, pale as a ghost.

"Let's hope they leave us be," the old man added.

His father nodded again.

A tremble of sticks and a sickly laugh announced the crew's arrival. The boy could now hear them right outside the house in the street.

"Okay...they're coming to search..." the old man observed, and suddenly pulled the trigger.

Gunfire cracked and echoed through the colony.

"Come closer and I will put the next one in your heart," the old man yelled out to the crew. "I'd leave this house alone if I was you, but you can come if you dare. We've got dozens of men here! Dozens of guns! Dozens!"

The boy's father looked to the old man incredulously. The old man returned his look and shrugged slightly. There was a long silence; then, at last someone yelled back at him. "We've got hundreds! Will you shoot us-?"

Crack!

The old man silenced the man without hesitation or remorse. It was what needed to be done. With his mouth and words alone one man could inspire the crew like the actor on the radio had inspired the nation.

The boy heard a gurgling sound outside; a desperate attempt to suck air through a mouthful of blood; a horrible wheezing sound followed and was punctuated by a heavy thud as the vacant body collapsed to the ground. "We can shoot a hundred more!"

From the open windows the sound of panicked feet scrambling away filled the boy's ears. They had bought the bluff. For a long while his father and the old man stared out at the street without saying a word.

"You killed him," his father said at last, breaking the silence. "Maybe you didn't have to kill him. Maybe you could have wounded him. Maybe you could have shot him in the leg."

The old man turned to face the boy's father. His eyes told the boy that he was both annoyed and frustrated but that he held back his words. With a sigh, he turned back toward the street. "He was trying to call a bluff," he explained. "He was trying to tell the others to attack. They would have charged us if I hadn't shot him to silence him. I had to shoot him. We're alive because I shot him."

"You did what you had to," the boy's mother said flatly. "I would have done the same."

The boy's father gave her a look, then

turned away.

"Do you think they'll be back?" she asked.

"They'll be back," the old man answered. "With more men. More force. Maybe with guns. But don't worry. By then my sons will be back and we'll make sure no one steps within two hundred yards of us." He searched the darkness carefully. "They should move now while no one is around..."

The boy's mother nodded, but the boy sensed that his sons were never coming back, and he sensed that his mother knew this too, but that she would keep her thoughts to herself.

The boy watched the old man as he scrutinized every movement, every sound and every shadow on the street for his sons.

A terrible shriek and wail startled them all. The boy trembled involuntarily in his mother's arms as a child cried out in agony and a mother cried for the men to spare her son. Then her cries turned to agonizing moans as the men did things to her he didn't want to think about. The old man cursed with great boiling passion as the boy's mother covered his ears. But the boy could still hear the woman agonizing and he asked:

"Why? Why?"

His mother shook her head, then put a finger over his mouth so that he wouldn't ask her a question she couldn't really answer.

The boy watched the old man kick the wall in anger. He cursed loudly and the boy's father told the old man to keep quiet. But the boy couldn't really hear what he was saying through his mother's hands. Then he saw the old man make a sudden attempt to charge outside to help the poor woman, who was dying somewhere in the darkness; but the boy's father blocked the door and seemed to tell him that there was nothing he could do and that it was already too late.

The old man looked as though he were about to break down and cry. He just stared at the boy's father and the door, wanting to act, wanting to do something, but realizing that the boy's father was right. There was nothing that he could do now except pray that her suffering would be over quickly. He then smashed the wooden door with his fist, turned away and returned to his post by the window.

When there was silence again, his mother uncovered the boy's ears and she held him close and tight. "How long do we have to wait for help?" the boy asked.

"I don't know," his mother said.

"Why can they still do this?"

"I don't know."

"What will happen if they catch us?"

"I won't let them catch you. I won't let them touch you."

She took his hand and wrapped her pinky around his and shook. Then she released his pinky and seemed to lose herself in a thought. The boy stared up at his mother and he could see that she was thinking about something that was worrying her and for a moment she forgot to breathe. After a silence she took in a shallow breath and whispered to herself:

"She knew."

"Who knew?"

"She knew."

"Who?"

"Nothing…it's nothing…"

But the boy knew who she was thinking about and what she was thinking about. She was thinking about the mysterious double hug. When he looked into her sad eyes, he could see his grandmother hugging her tightly, telling his mother that she felt sad and that she didn't know why.

A sudden twist and gurgle in his stomach returned him to the moment. He hadn't eaten for almost two days. He wanted to eat something, anything, but he didn't feel comfortable asking for food from the old man who refused to take his eyes off the street as he anxiously awaited his family.

There were more important things to worry about now. The boy could wait until help arrived. And just as he thought this the old man and his father started at something they had both seen outside. The boy wondered if it was the old man's family as they both seemed anxious and relieved.

A moment later the old man opened the door and three police constables slipped in. His mother instantly snapped to her feet, pulling the boy up with her.

The head constable looked at the men, then he turned to the boy's mother and his dark eyes smiled as he gave her an appraising look--a look that instantly made the boy tense and feel upset and uncomfortable. The head constable then turned to the old man and the boy's father.

"Is everything alright here?" he asked.

"No. Everything is not alright here!" the old man said and cursed. "Why would you ask such a thing?"

The head constable wrinkled his nose, regarded the old man, and narrowed his gaze. "Only because we are trying to establish peace, but how can we do so…how can we do our jobs if you're shooting people?" His voice hissed like a slithering cobra.

"Do your jobs?" The old man questioned incredulously. "Do your jobs?"

The boy's father yelled. "They're killing us all! What do you mean?"

The head constable twitched his nose. "We've established peace," he maintained, and he smiled, revealing yellow stained teeth. "You don't need to worry anymore. I, however, am worried about those." He lost his smile and indicated both rifles with a scrawny finger. "I will need you to hand those over to my men without delay."

The two constables stared at the old man and the boy's father and waited for them to hand over their rifles. But the old man and the boy's father held their rifles firm.

"You've established nothing!" the old man yelled.

A nearby whooping noise corroborated the old man's accusation.

"Doesn't sound like peace to me!" he continued. "What are you telling us?"

"We have men trying to establish peace," the head constable assured him. "And I cannot permit vigilantes to take justice into their own hands."

A Feast for Lambs

A gleam of malice flared in his eyes as though he were daring the old man to disobey his authority.

The old man scoffed at him. "We take justice in our own hands because we have to, because the law has failed us. Where were you yesterday?"

The head constable stepped up to the old man so that he was staring into his eyes. "Listen to me and please be reasonable," he hissed. "I have men working hard to maintain peace and I will not and I cannot allow you to jeopardize their efforts."

The boy noticed the two constables exchanging a strange look at these words. One was grinning slightly, the other bit his lip angrily, and found nothing amusing in the head constable's words.

"They're killing us out there," the old man tried to reason with the head constable.

"Not anymore. It's over."

"It's over?"

"Yes, it's over. I am asking for your weapons so I can do my job."

"We shouldn't...I can still hear them..."

The old man looked to the boy's mother. She shook her head slightly, not trusting the constable. The old man turned back to the head constable and shook his head, indicating that he refused to surrender his rifle.

At once the head constables signaled his men. "I'm not asking anymore." A second later the boy's father and the old man were staring at two black revolvers pointed directly at them.

The old man scoffed. "It's over?"

"You have my word," the head constable

promised.

    With a sigh, the boy's father surrendered his rifle. The old man watched them take it away with knowing eyes. Then the grinning constable walked up to him and pulled it out of the old man's hands. Reluctantly, the old man released the rifle. Then the old man looked into the head constable's eyes and waited for something. Something he sensed was coming.

    They stared at each other for a long while and it seemed to be a battle of wills. The head constable lost, and looked away, first at the boy's father, then his mother, then his men. A wail rang out, followed by a cry.

    "I think your men are needed outside," the old man said sarcastically.

    The head constable turned to him.

    "But there is still another matter."

    The old man shook his head in disbelief and resignation.

    "What other matter?" the boy's father asked. "What other matter do you mean?"

    The head constable answered without taking his eyes off the old man. "The matter, I'm afraid, of the man with the bullet in his neck. Since you both had rifles I unfortunately have no choice but to place you both under arrest."

    "No!" the boy's mother burst out. "You can't do this."

    "I'm afraid I can. It's a matter of justice."

    "A matter of justice," the old man repeated sarcastically, his eyes burning through the head constable.

A Feast for Lambs

"You can't. Please!" the boy's mother pleaded. "You can't!"

"There's a body outside and there are witnesses."

"Witnesses?" the boy's father questioned.
"Your witnesses"--his voice grew to a feverish
pitch--"have been killing Sikhs all day."

The boy stepped up to his father and held
his hand tight. His father calmed himself and
looked down to the boy with eyes filled with anger
and fear and uncertainty.

"Witnesses," the old man repeated, shaking
his head again and staring at the head constable as
though he were staring at a demon here to escort
them to oblivion. The old man laughed. And
laughed again as though he wasn't even surprised.
Then, after a silence he confessed:

"I shot the man. I confess. I shot him. Leave
him be. Let him stay with his family."

"I'm afraid I cannot do that until we are certain."

"Certain of what?"

"That you are the one."

"I am the one!"

The head constable shrugged. "We'll see."

The old man looked at him. After a tense
moment he said:

"There is justice you know."

"I know."

"No," the old man said firmly. "You don't
know."

The head constable looked to his men to
avoid the old man's eyes, and he laughed his anxi-

ety away. "Stop being so dramatic," he said. "You Sikhs are always so dramatic."

"Please," the boy's mother begged. "Please don't take my husband. Please…"

The head constable turned to her with his yellow teeth. "I'm sorry about this misunderstanding. I'm sure that considering the circumstances no one here will see the inside of a prison."

"I'm certain of that, too," the old man said sarcastically. "I'm very certain of that, too."

The head constable turned back to him with a smirk, but didn't say anything. "So dramatic, really."

"Please don't!" the boy's mother said. She grabbed his wrist and begged. "Please…"

He turned and seemed to love the power he exerted over her. "Don't you worry," he said with a twitch of his nose. "Nothing will happen to you. You will have very special treatment from the police. I will leave someone with you, and I will be back shortly."

She released him suddenly. With a terrible shudder, she stepped back as though she had just seen a ghost. The head constable seemed to want to laugh, and to the boy he looked worse than the all villains from the movies rolled into one, even though his face wasn't painted black and he wasn't wearing a kara. Then the head constable motioned to the grinning alligator to escort the men outside. But the boy instantly let go of his father's hand and wrapped his arms around his father's leg and held on like an anaconda. He cried:

"Please don't go! Please!"

A Feast for Lambs

The head constable sighed.

"So dramatic…"

The grinning constable went to pull the boy off, but the boy's father stopped him with a firm, fearless hand. He indicated that he would take care of the situation. The constable nodded and waited for him outside. The boy's father kneeled before boy. They stared at each other for a long moment. "Don't let them take you," the boy said at last. "I don't think you should go. It's not a good idea." The boy's heart pulled fiercely, telling him that he should not let his father go with these men.

"I don't have a choice," the boy's father said. "If I don't go, there may be trouble for you and your mother."

"That's okay," the boy said, and his heart pulled even harder.

"No, it's not okay." He shook his head and swallowed his grief. "One day you'll understand, bete."

"I can come!"

"No. No, you can't. I need you to stay here to protect your mother."

The boy's heart tugged painfully and his eyes instantly filled. "You're not coming back," he said, shaking his head. "You're not coming back…I know it…"

"I am coming back."

"It doesn't feel like that!"

"I will be with you soon."

It was like some dark creature suddenly took a bite out of his heart. He choked with the pain of those words without knowing why.

249

With these words, the head constable pulled the boy's father away. "Don't worry, Sadar," he said. "We will be back to take good care of your family."

Ignoring his words, the boy's father stood slowly, giving his mother a look--a look the boy immediately recognized. It was a look that said more than words could ever say and it was the look he loved to see his father give his mother. Then he flicked his eyes to the boy, then back at her. He was telling her something. He was warning her, and his mother nodded her understanding, and the look told him she would protect their son no matter what happened and that she would find a way out of this.

The head constable then looked to the stone-faced constable and gestured for him to remain in the house with the boy and his mother until they returned. Then he quit the house without bothering with handcuffs or other formalities, or even closing the door behind them. They would be back shortly. They clearly weren't going very far.

The boy stared helplessly out the door as his father disappeared into the night. His mother stared blankly beside him. When he could no longer see him, he turned to his mother to see if she was feeling what he was feeling. That maybe this was the last memory he would have of his father.

One look at her pale, stunned face and the boy knew without her having to say anything that she was feeling exactly as he was. She looked like someone had slapped her in the face and she was still trying to process how to respond or react.

A Feast for Lambs

After a silence, she looked down at the boy, then the darkness, then the boy, and she seemed to be waiting for something. She seemed to be waiting to wake up. To snap awake. But there would be no waking up, and this nightmare was for real and her husband was gone.

For a moment the boy thought that maybe he was wrong. Maybe the police officer was honest. Maybe his father would be okay. Maybe he would never see the inside of a prison. And maybe, just maybe, he was authentically trying to establish peace in the colony.

But his mother didn't seem to think so as she stared out the door where he had disappeared. She stared deeply and she mumbled a prayer and she prayed. Then she looked down at the boy and he could see that she wanted to tell him that everything was going to be okay, but that she couldn't bring herself to say the words. He looked up at her eyes and they were wet and distant. He pulled on her dress and said:

"He'll be with us soon."

"I know he will, bete. I know he will."

At these words his face began to prickle with pins and needles. A slight high-pitched buzzing filled his ears. He didn't understand why this was happening to him suddenly, but there was something in his mother's words that disturbed him and made him want to run outside after his father and pull him away from the alligators that had snatched him away.

After a minute or so, his mother snapped back to the moment and turned to the constable behind them. She marched up to him and stared at him for a long moment. The whole time he refused to meet her gaze. He looked like a man lost in the wilderness, unsure and uncomfortable in his skin, as his eyes sought every other place but the boy's mother's eyes.

She inched closer to him.

"Why are you doing this to us?"

She whispered so the boy couldn't hear. But he could hear everything.

The constable shrugged. "What do you mean? We're doing nothing."

"Yes. I know. Why? Why are you doing nothing?"

The constable couldn't answer. The air was hot and fetid, and the boy could see that something about his mother frightened the constable. He said:

"Please step away."

She answered:

"No. I will not step away."

"Everything will be fine. You need not worry, and you need to please step away."

Shaking her head, she inched closer to him.

He shuffled back.

"Everything won't be fine," she said in a firm, knowing voice. "And I am worried. I am very worried." She stared at him, but he still refused to meet her gaze. "Don't you have children?"

He looked to the boy, then her, then he shuffled back uncomfortably. "Please--"

"Look at me," she demanded. "Please...look at me..."

For a moment he looked at her, trying his

best not to see her. The boy could see he wasn't like the other constables and that he was struggling with something within. His mother continued in a pleading whisper:

"They're not taking them to the station."

He sighed uncomfortably, and she continued:

"We both know that. No need to pretend. We both know my husband's not coming back."

She stepped closer and her voice dropped an octave.

"And we both know what's going to happen when your superior returns."

His head fell with shame and he could not face her; he could only stare at his boots.

"You know what's going to happen...I know you do..."

"There's nothing I can do."

"There's much you can do."

He looked up at her.

A hideous laugh came from outside and then faded as though to mock her.

Silently, the boy stepped up beside her and took her hand. The constable looked down at the boy. He opened his mouth to speak, then stopped himself. He hesitated, reconsidered his words and in a tired and hurt voice he repeated:

"There's nothing I can do."

He glanced away uneasily. His mother sighed and her head fell in defeat. "Then I ask one thing," she said in a deathly whisper. "At least do one thing...just one thing..." She looked up at him. This time he met her gaze. "Promise me..."

She was silent for a long moment.

"Promise you?"

"Not in front of my son."

The constable gritted his teeth hard and looked away.

"Please...not in front of my son..."

The boy looked at her with wide frightened eyes and tried to understand what these words meant. He squeezed her hand tightly and didn't know why she would say such a thing but it was like something had just clenched his heart and wouldn't let go. What did she mean? What didn't she want done in front of him?

"Please..."

"Stop talking."

"I'm asking..."

"Stop."

The constable couldn't bear her voice anymore, but she wouldn't be silenced.

"No. I will not stop talking. Not until you promise me."

"Don't ask me! I can't do anything."

"I'm asking."

"Don't..."

"I am."

"I have no choice in the matter."

"You only have choice in the matter."

At these words he raised his gaze and peered directly at her. The boy didn't know if the constable was angry or scared. Maybe both. But the boy could clearly see that his mother wasn't about to let him convince himself of a lie. She continued after a silence:

A Feast for Lambs

"There is following an order from a man and facing God. There is doing what is true and then facing a man. You only have choice. Don't ever think otherwise."

He sighed deeply and his gaze fell to the boy.

"Just promise me...not in front of the boy."

The constable looked up at her. He sighed heavily and seemed to be struggling with something profound. He closed his eyes and his whole face tensed with the battle within. Then, when he opened his eyes, he lowered his voice and asked her:

"Is there a blanket in the house?"

ᘓ

The night shuddered with the endless cries and
wails of the dying, and the boy watched the constable as he stared out into the darkness while his
mother searched for a blanket. He seemed concerned, torn, unsure, scared even, wishing he
weren't in this situation. But he was. And perhaps
this was a test. His test. And perhaps invisible eyes
were watching and wondering what this constable
would do with this mother and her boy. When at
last his mother returned from the bedroom with a
blood-stained blanket, the constable started; he
looked her over as if she were from another world;
then he nodded thankfully, took the blanket and
wrapped it around his head and back so that he
looked like some sort of eccentric hermit who didn't
want to be seen by the outside world. He didn't.
Having properly concealed his face and uniform, he
signaled for the boy's mother to wait as he hurried
through the open door and froze.

He listened carefully for nearby crews.
Nothing.
No melee weapons clanking against pave-
ment.
Only the sobs.
After surveying the street, he turned to the
boy's mother and motioned for her to follow him.

Without hesitation, she nodded, grabbed the boy in her arms and she didn't have to tell him to close his eyes.

Instantly the boy plunged into the darkness of his inner kingdom and listened to the universe as it wept and cried all around him.

For a long while he was bobbing and bouncing in his mother's warm embrace as she swiftly charged through the thick, stinging, greasy air. Air laced with the unbearable stench of burnt flesh and kerosene that with every breath the boy tried not to take filled his entire being with hell. She slowed down here and there as she negotiated the mounds of wet leaves on the ground. Then she stopped all at once. The boy instantly took in the odor of mingled urine and excrement. His mother gasped. She whispered:

"Bete, keep your eyes closed."

"They're closed."

"I mean really, really closed. Closed tight."

"They are."

"Promise?"

"Promise."

He felt her swallow something thick like molasses in her throat. Then they were moving again, slowly, carefully, moving an inch a minute. As she picked her way over the slippery ground, he imagined leaves and tree branches. After a long while, they were moving fast again, and he could hear his mother breathing harder with her heart thundering against his chest.

"Stop!" the constable ordered.

They stopped suddenly. He heard his

mother whisper God's name. Then he heard another voice not too far away. He wanted to open his eyes to see what was happening. He wanted to know why they had stopped so suddenly. Then he heard the strange voice again. First a laugh, then an accusation. He could hear feet marching toward him, melee weapons clicking and clanging against the ground. His heart stopped. So did his mother's.

"Where are you going?"

A dark voice called out.

He heard them approach, surrounding them. His mother held him tightly and whispered God's name again.

"Leave us," the constable told the crew.

"I can't let you steal from us..." The voice sounded like it was trying to determine who was hidden under the blanket. "Police sub-inspector? Is it possible?"

The boy heard something click, a shuffle of feet, and a collective gasp.

"What are you doing! You greedy bastard!"

"Move away."

"Bastard!"

"Move away. If any of you follow, I will shoot."

"Okay. We'll move out of your way. No reason to die for one boy. There's more out there. You want him. Fine. He's yours, but I will remember your face."

There was a sudden crack.

The boy started. He desperately wanted to open his eyes and it was all he could do to keep them shut. And he only kept them shut because he didn't want his mother worrying about him along with everything else.

"Anyone else looking at my face?"

He heard the thud of a body collapsing, followed by the scared steps of men scattering away like cockroaches.

"He was going to leave us," his mother whispered.

"He saw my face."

"What does it matter?"

"I have a family to protect, too."

And with these words the boy instantly understood the constable's situation, and they continued moving noiselessly through the colony. They pressed on for some time, moving slower and slower with every step. His mother was now giving the constable directions. Turn here. There. Here. There. With every command, he wondered where she was leading him.

The air grew thicker and thicker with the nauseating odor of death. The boy pressed his nose up against his mother's shoulder, trying to use her dress as a filter. But there was no filtering out the smell that now impregnated the colony. It was everywhere and in all things. The boy suddenly felt his mother stop.

"What is it?" she asked the constable.

"Are you close?" he asked.

"We're close."

"I must return, then. I will say you escaped."

There was a silence. Then he felt something rise up in his mother's throat. A moment later she mustered the courage to ask in a trembling voice the boy wasn't used to hearing.

"My husband--"

She couldn't finish her sentence, as though she already knew the answer. The boy's eyes watered and his face tensed as he waited and listened for the constable's answer.

"Your husband," he said after a silence, "would want you to hide until the army comes, and he would want you to stay away from the police."

It wasn't the answer the boy, nor his mother, wanted to hear. He felt her heart lurch as she repeated:

"Stay away from the police...all..."

"Wait for the army. It should be safe then."

"Should?"

"I think so."

"Why isn't the army here now!"

"You know why... Don't make me say what you already know..."

"Why us? Why here?"

"It's not just you. It's not just here."

The boy felt his mother's heart lurch again with his words. He felt her breath catch in her throat. He felt her lose her balance, then regain her footing. The boy, too, could hardly believe his words, could not believe this unhindered and unopposed killing of Sikhs was taking place elsewhere.

"I'm sorry," the constable said. "There is nothing more to be said. You need to hide in the day and move only at night and only if you have to."

She gasped.

"How can this happen? Days? Nights? Here! Delhi! The capital!"

"There is no time for why. Take your son and go hide…and save your questions for another time."

At once he felt every muscle in his mother's body tense with sudden anger and determination. The constable was right. She needed to stop thinking and just act. She needed to save all her questions and anger for later. She needed to survive and not lose to despair. She cleared her throat and he could feel her determination in every small movement she made. She had not surrendered to the darkness, not yet, and she still had hope. And because she had not surrendered, he would not either. And because she had hope, he had hope. He would take his mother's strength and make it his own.

"Thank you," she said to the constable. The boy prayed hard that this man who had helped them should have much luck, fortune and opportunity in this life and the next hundred. Him and his family. Then, with a deep breath, his mother was moving again.

As they pressed on into the darkness the boy heard a soft, barely audible whisper behind him:

"May Allah be merciful…"

And he never heard the constable's voice again, though he was sure he would never forget it; nor would God.

With his eyes shut tight, he smothered his

A Feast for Lambs

face in his mother's neck as she carried him through the tangle of streets. A sudden scream of pure agony tore through the night, and the boy couldn't take it anymore. He had heard it all day and night and now he couldn't hear it anymore. Quickly, and desperately he covered his ears and began counting his mother's footsteps to distract his thoughts.

One.

Two.

Three.

He counted to a hundred and still had the sense that they hadn't moved very far. He counted another hundred and he thought that maybe his mother had moved about ten yards and he sensed the ground beneath her feet was thick with wet leaves and branches.

Something inside him wanted to look and see why walking was so difficult. Something else, something stronger, didn't want to see at all, didn't want to know--never wanted to know.

And so, in his mind he continued to visualize his mother carrying him through a soaking forest covered with grime and mud and mounds of decaying leaves with the wind howling and crying all around him. This was easier to imagine than the truth.

Easier to imagine.

Easier to accept.

Mud, leaves, rocks, and the wailing and howling wind--that was all he needed to know. All he wanted to know. In his mind's eye he and his mother would escape this burning forest and when they did they would be reunited with his father, his brother, his grandmother, his aunt and his uncle in a free jungle where lions could be lions without fear of persecution.

As the boy visualized this, he lost count, and before he knew it his mother had stopped and was setting him down. "It's okay," she said. "Open your eyes."

When the boy opened his eyes it was like he hadn't. All electricity in the colony had been cut, and now he could only see the glow of several small fires striking and snapping the night like Holi as crews combed the streets chanting rehearsed slogans of hate as they celebrated death's ultimate triumph over life.

In this fire no one walked out alive like the story of Holi.

This fire took all.

Consumed all.

Reduced all to ash and smoke so that nothing was spared; not even the souls of those paying homage to death with their sticks and prods and their limitless kerosene.

A greater fire would consume them, and theirs would be an ultimate death. The end of being. The end of consciousness. Pure and complete oblivion. Their souls, along with all their karma, would perish. And now staring into the darkness, the boy had a hard time situating himself, and it took him a moment before he realized he was standing in front of his grandmother's house. When he did, his mother took his hand and led him to the door. Then she released him and peered into the

A Feast for Lambs

window to see if she could see anything.
But it was too dark; he could barely see his mother
and she was only a few feet away. So his mother
moved toward the door and eased it open, and he
could see that she was relieved that it was not broken and that no one had barged into the house.
Before she entered, she regarded him and said:

"Wait here until I return. I just want to see
if--"

She didn't finish her sentence.
She didn't have to.
He understood.
"I won't move."

She crept inside calling out his uncle's
name, his grandmother's name.

The boy didn't need to be told why he
needed to wait outside. He didn't need an explanation. He knew why, and he waited patiently and
silently, and he prayed that his grandmother and
his uncle were okay.

The whole time his mother was inside his
grandmother's home the boy stared at a smoldering
mound at the end of the street and felt a strange
darkness growing in his heart.

Pins and needles tingled around his mouth
and spread to his cheeks. A high-pitched buzzing
filled his head until he couldn't look at the glowing
mound anymore.

He turned away and didn't want to think
about what his heart was suggesting. He didn't
want to know what was burning. He leveled his
eyes at the ground and started repeating God's
name in his head and the pins and needles and the

buzzing gradually dissipated.

Suddenly a hand grabbed his wrist and jarred him back to the moment. He looked up into his mother's eyes and saw for the first time in years unshed tears. She held his gaze for a moment, then gently pulled him inside.

The house was upside down, but there was no sign that anyone had been hurt. It seemed to him that someone had merely looted the place and that his grandmother and uncle had probably escaped the colony before the butchering had begun.

But that wasn't what his heart was telling him.

His heart was telling him something else.

Something he refused to believe or accept.

His mother closed the door gently behind them, and the boy took in the room sadly. Without realizing it his imagination started playing tricks on him and he started seeing images of his grandmother and uncle being dragged out of the house and into the street. Inwardly he repeated God's name and tried to stop his imaginings. But they wouldn't stop. Then he was screaming God's name in his head, trying with all his will to stop his mind from imagining the worst. When he cleared his thoughts of darkness, he turned to his mother and asked:

"Where is Bigi? Chachaji?"

His mother only stared blankly at a box on a table.

"Where?"

The boy continued to ask and he grabbed

his mother's arm and tugged. His mother looked down at him, took his hand, then returned her gaze to the box.

"Where...?"

"They escaped," his mother said at last. "They escaped..."

His eyes instantly filled with tears. Sadness beat his voice down to a thin whisper. "They escaped," he repeated, going along with his mother as his knowing heart pounded in his throat. He nodded and convinced himself it was so. "Chachaji is smart. I know they are safe." He didn't know what else to say, what else to do, what else to think. His mother nodded her agreement as she stared blankly at the box. The boy wiped his cheeks with his free hand, but the tears continued silently. "They escaped," he said again, doing a good job at convincing his mind, but not his heart, definitely not his heart.

His mother nodded without looking down at him. "She knew we were coming," she said with difficulty, then she indicated the box with her gaze.

The boy followed her gaze to the box. He approached the table, then reached out and gently lifted the lid. It was filled with ill-proportioned semi-squares of burfee.

With a sudden rush of mingled love and sadness, he couldn't believe what his eyes were telling him. And he knew that just as soon as they had left her home days ago she had charged to the stove to prepare him a batch of the most perfect burfee.

He stared at the burfee and took in a deep breath. He loved his grandmother. He loved everything about her. Loved her with all his heart. And he told himself that the first song he would ever write would be about his grandmother. He wrapped his tiny fingers around a piece of burfee and pulled it out and stared at it.

Just stared at it.

Transfixed.

His lips suddenly quivered at the thought of never seeing his grandmother again. His entire being ached and he felt something tug painfully in his heart. "She knew we'd be hungry," the boy said.

"She knew, bete…she knew…"

He placed the burfee back into the box, then reached out for the cauldron beside it. He pulled it down, held it and stared at the massive lump of cold burfee on the head of the wooden spoon. He withdrew the spoon and returned the cauldron to the table and he admired the burfee as though it were the last burfee in the world. He looked to his mother, offering.

"Of course not," she said with a faint smile. "Eat. It's yours."

He turned back to the spoon and just stared. How many spoons of hot burfee had he secretly shared with his grandmother behind his mother's back? He couldn't count. It had always been their secret, though he was sure his mother knew.

He brought the burfee to his mouth. He closed his eyes and tried to smell the sweetness and for a moment, just a moment, he forgot everything.

A Feast for Lambs

Inwardly, he thanked his grandmother for this moment of respite. He opened his eyes, then his mouth, and he took a small bite.

A sad smile grew on his face when he realized it was less sweet than usual. And then it suddenly dawned upon him. She had done it. She had truly made the most perfect burfee in the world. He closed his eyes and savored every flavor as he held back tears. He wanted to thank her for this. He wanted to tell her without hesitation that she made the best burfee in the world. He wanted her to know how much he loved her, and he wanted to hug her again.

He wanted to hear her voice again. He wanted to hear her sing. He wanted to hear her shout. He wanted his uncle and father to argue like gorillas at the table while she told them both to shut up and eat.

When at last he opened his eyes, his mother was staring down at him with a small piece of burfee in her hand. She nodded with every movement her mouth made. Her eyes lit up and they asked him if her senses were deceiving her. He nodded slightly, and his eyes answered that she was not mistaken and that she was in fact eating the most perfect burfee in the world. They then sat at the table and filled their empty bellies and hungry hearts with the most perfect burfee in the world, and the most perfect burfee in the world like Amrit gave his blood and muscles the strength and energy he would need for the next few hours. Finally the boy reached into the empty box and pulled out the last piece. "Last piece," he said with a sigh.

"Last piece..." His mother could barely say the words. "I don't want it. You eat."

"I don't want it either."

"Eat."

"Can we save it?"

"We can."

And his mother took the last piece of burfee and wrapped it in a piece of cloth she found on the table and then she handed it over to the boy. He smiled. "We'll share it later," he said. "When we're hungry."

"Yes, we'll share it later."

With these words the boy slipped the last piece of burfee into his secret pocket and suddenly felt something rough. Something he had forgotten. Something with five fingers. He suddenly remembered the glove and a great wave of shame crashed over him. His mother instantly sensed his sadness and asked:

"What's wrong?"

"Nothing."

A tear slipped and then another.

"Bete..."

"Nothing--"

But just as he answered tears rushed down his face and he shuddered and couldn't hold them back. His mother instantly grabbed him and held him close and said nothing. She just let him cry until he could manage words through his grief.

"I'm sorry...I'm sorry..." he said at last.

"Sorry...why are you sorry?"

He lost himself in a memory, hoping that he hadn't betrayed his disappointment to his grandmother. At last he cried:

"I don't want another glove. I don't need another glove."

His mother instantly held him strong and close to her heart.

"I know I said I wanted another, but I don't..."

"Okay, bete."

"And I want Bigi to see me wear it."

"She will see you...she will..."

And the boy closed his eyes hard and squeezed his lids angrily and he hated himself in a way he never thought possible. With all his soul he wished he could go back in time and react as he should have reacted when she had presented him with the most magical glove in the world.

Not the world!

The universe!

He didn't know what he was feeling but it felt like someone squeezing and choking his heart, and that someone or something just wouldn't let go; and for the first time he truly understood his mother's sadness when her sister had unexpectedly died after they had exchanged angry words.

For the first time in his life he felt regret.

Pure regret.

With his eyes closed and his head against his mother's chest, he prayed for a moment, just one moment, to tell his grandmother how much he loved and appreciated everything she had done for him. He wanted to tell her he loved his ill-proportioned kurtas and her hoarse voice and all her songs. Then, as though his mother could sense his regret, she broke the silence and said:

"Do you remember when aunty died?"

The boy nodded, listening.

"I was sad for a long time. A very long time. Do you remember that?"

He nodded.

"I was sad and angry and I prayed so much that she had not suffered."

He nodded again.

"I wasted months and could not do anything with anyone. Not even you. Not even your brother. It was the saddest time in my life. And do you know Bigi is the one who helped me? Do you know that she was the one who forced me out of bed?"

The boy shook his head. He didn't know that. He thought that his mother had decided on her own that she wasn't going to be sad anymore. His mother laughed at the memory. After a silence, she continued:

"One day she just barges into our house and she charges up to me and towers over the bed and shakes me hard. Shakes me until she sees life in my eyes. Then she yells at me like thunder because she's angrier than ten Chachaji's all rolled into one. And she says, 'What are you doing? What are you doing?' I pushed her and told her to get away. She says, 'No! I will not go! I lost one daughter and I refuse to let despair take my second one. Refuse!' You don't know this, but Bigi shook me some more and then she said one thing and that was what did it. One thing. Just one thing and it was like a message from Waheguru. Like Waheguru talking to me through her."

She laughed again.

"She said, 'Your sister gave you an ocean of good and beautiful memories, an ocean of jokes, laughs and silly moments, an ocean of pure goodness, and you focus and dwell and cry over one moment. Shame on you!' When she said this I realized how wrong I had been and how true her words were and how they really weren't her words. They were coming from somewhere else. Some other place...maybe...I thought...even aunty herself..."

His mother paused with the memory, then continued:

"She was right, you know. Not only was I dishonoring aunty by focusing on her death, but I was depriving my sons and my husband of the ocean--of the smiles, laughs and silly moments. Then Bigi stormed out of the house like a monsoon screaming that she was the worst mother in the world and that she should be punished for how bad she was. Of course, she didn't think that. She wanted me to rise out of bed, go to her house and tell her that she was the greatest mother that ever lived."

The boy hadn't realized that it was his grandmother who had returned his mother to him from the depths of despair. After a silence, she added:

"Listen to me, and listen to me carefully. You dishonor a life, and you lose your own life trying to imagine or understand or figure out one dark moment."

Gently, she pulled him away to look him in the eyes. She held out her pinky. "Only the smiles," she said. "That's how you honor people when they leave your life. We all make mistakes and we all say things we sometimes don't mean and that's just life. And that's not what you think about. That's not what you focus on. Only the smiles."

The boy stared at her pinky for a long moment, then he nodded, wrapped his pinky around hers and shook. "Only the smiles."

He attempted a feeble smile through his grief.

Suddenly gunfire cracked outside, and they both started. His mother stood and moved to the window and stared outside. The boy could hear men whooping and hollering and sticks click-clacking against the ground. His mother's whole body froze as a shadowy figure suddenly appeared and stopped before the window.

She stopped breathing.

The boy stopped breathing.

His mother kneeled slowly and hid in the darkness. Then the shadowy figure charged away. She breathed again. He breathed again. "We aren't safe here," she said, staring out the window. "We need to find a place where we can be safe."

"I know a place."

She turned to the boy and stared at him. The boy knew she didn't trust Major, but he was sure no one would find them in his attic. He also knew that their options were limited and that was the best and only place that came to mind. After a reflective silence, his mother asked:

"Do you trust him?"

"I do."

"You think we'll be safe?"

"I think so."

She turned to the window. "I can't carry you," she said after a pause. "Too dark."

"Too dark to see."

She turned to him. "I want you to keep your head up. I want you to always look up. Never down, never at the ground." She moved back toward him, then tapped his forehead. "There are things outside we need to keep out of here. Some things we can never forget once they go in. Some things change us. Do you understand what I'm saying?"

The boy nodded. "I understand."

How could he not? He already wanted to rip out of his mind the odors he had smelled and agonies he had heard for the last two days. He didn't need to add to the horror. He didn't need to see anything. He didn't want to. He never wanted to. And he prayed to God to spare his mind from ever seeing what the congressman and his crews had done to his colony.

CB

Holding his mother's hand, his eyes staring straight ahead of him, the boy took one small step at a time as his mother led him through the perfect darkness, feeling the wet leaves and branches underneath his shoes, never looking down. Slowly, carefully, they inched their way through the narrow street. Hearing something moving up ahead, his mother froze suddenly.

The boy stopped. He listened. He heard something panting moving toward him. He scrutinized the darkness. A moment later the shadowy figure of a dog passed before them carrying a thing like a branch in its jaws.

When the dog disappeared, his mother continued again, moving slowly, carefully with her hand feeling and swiping at the emptiness before her.

Slowly and carefully she led him closer and closer to Major's home, humming his grandmother's favorite hymn in a soft whisper, trying to fill her mind with good thoughts, or trying, at least, to distract the boy's mind from the odor that pervaded every fiber of his being.

The boy tried with difficulty to keep his gaze away from the ground. But now and then he couldn't help himself; though even when he failed, even when he stole a glance here or there, it didn't matter. He couldn't see past his knees.

All he saw were the vague shapes and shadows of a decimated world. It was better this way. Despite his involuntary looks, he didn't want to know what he was stepping on or what was making simple walking such an impossible task.

He pressed on, trusting his mother.

The song of death was everywhere. Wails and cries and names of fathers and sons being called out. But now the song seemed far away. Distant. Like they were coming from another colony. Another country. Another continent. Another world. A hellish world where these things happened. And even though they felt so far away, every dark note tugged and yanked at his soul, pulling him down into an endless pit of despair.

How could such a thing happen here?

How could such a thing happen anywhere?

How could people do such things to other people?

None of it made sense.

And maybe it wasn't supposed to.

Humming softly, his mother continued to find her way through the darkness, and he thought about his father, his grandmother, his aunt and his uncle. He felt their absence as an ache so profound he still refused to acknowledge or accept what his heart was telling him. He wanted to believe that they were safe and that he would see them again when this was all over.

He wanted to believe his father was at the police station and that his grandmother and his uncle were arguing with the police, telling them that they had the right to defend themselves and that anyone would have done the same in their situation. He could even see his father and uncle arguing over what was happening, and he could see his uncle telling his father:

"I told you it was so."

This is what the boy wanted to believe, but something in his heart, some dark thing, coiling and slithering, refused to let the boy lie to himself. And the boy knew they were gone.

He hated them.

He hated them all.

The congressman.

The crews.

The police.

He hated them and he could feel his heart fill with something foul and blistering like a sack of deadly poison. And inside his heart he could feel something else, something growing and pushing and thrashing as it attempted to burst out of his heart like larva in a dark, deadly cocoon.

It was an awful feeling. A feeling he knew the Guru had always resisted and renounced, even though everyone in his family had been tormented and tortured and executed. Never had the Guru unsheathed his kirpan in the name of anger or hate. Never. Always for the rights and freedoms of others.

The boy knew this about the Guru. He knew it well. But he also knew something else--

He was not the Guru.

And he hated.

And he hated deeply--hated in a way he never knew he could.

And he could feel the wicked slithering thing pushing against the wall of his heart, wanting to be free, needing to be free as the boy followed his mother through the darkness.

Now they took one small step every ten seconds as they felt the ground with their feet and scrambled over collected mounds of slimy leaves and branches.

For almost an hour they negotiated their way through a narrow alleyway that should have taken them less than five minutes to walk through. When they reached the mouth of the alley, his mother squeezed his hand in warning.

The boy froze in his tracks.

She had seen something.

Somewhere close by he suddenly heard a crew shouting their hatred for Sikhs. They were yelling something about having seen a woman and her child and how they would soon find them.

A chill went down his spine.

Had they seen them?

Were they searching for them?

How close were they?

He heard another shout.

Real close.

He stopped breathing, and all at once the crew went silent. Usually this meant they had their victim and were too busy bludgeoning to do anything else. This time, however, he didn't hear the melee weapons or the thuds of iron hitting flesh and shattering bone. Didn't hear the cries of agony.

A Feast for Lambs

Didn't hear the desperate pleas to God. This time
he heard nothing. Nothing but silence.

But somehow he could sense they were still
there, prowling, searching, hunting. After a long
moment his mother seemed uneasy about stepping
into the fire-lit street. Hesitantly, she took the boy's
hand and was just about to conduct him out of the
alley and into the street when she heard the hum of
a motor approaching.

Instantly, she held the boy back.

They waited.

Within moments two beams cut through
the darkness and stared at the boy like the eyes of
some dark, metallic beast that had crawled into this
world from another dimension.

What was this?

He watched it carefully.

The truck stopped every two yards so that
men could clear the street of waste. Suddenly it
dawned on him. This crew was no killing crew.
This was something else. This crew was a cleaning
crew and they were moving toward the alley as
they hurled smoldering bodies into the back of the
truck with patience, method and indifference.

His mother slowly pulled him back into the
depths of the alley. Reluctantly, she signaled for
him to lie behind a stairwell in the putrid muck
beneath their feet. He hesitated. He didn't want to,
but he knew that he had no other choice. If they
flashed a light into the alley they would be seen. So
he lowered to the ground and tried not to think of
what lay beneath his belly. At once he felt the odor
of death inches from his nose and began to feel

nauseous. A moment later he started to gag.

His mother instantly covered his mouth to calm him down, frightened that he would give away their position. The boy shook and gagged and when at last he was calm again, she removed her hand just as the truck kicked into gear and hummed toward them.

Staring out of the alley the boy could now see hundreds of mosquitoes and the flies buzzing in and out of the truck headlights. Mesmerized, trying not to think of what was beneath him, he watched the light intensify as the truck drove forward a few yards.

As much as he tried to ignore what was under his legs and belly he could actually feel his kurta pajama absorbing the wetness and the foulness all around him like a sponge. But he kept his composure and struggled to think only of leaves and mud and grime as he listened to the cleaning crew. He could hear them talking as they hurled bodies into the back of the truck like sacks of salt. He trembled as the voices grew louder and louder as they approached. Then he heard something scurry behind him. A creature. A moment later he felt something bristly brush up against his ankles. He instantly turned to his feet, but saw nothing.

Only darkness.

Perfect darkness.

Once again the truck kicked into gear, and he heard the crunch and crack and snap of branches under its wheel as it drove forward. Then--

He felt it again.

Nibbling at his ankle. Without thought, he

thrashed his leg to scare whatever it was away. His mother instantly squeezed his arm in warning to be quiet and still.

The men were close. Real close. Close enough to hear him thrashing around in the muck. He needed to compose himself. Their lives depended on it.

A moment later the thing was gone and he relaxed a bit. The boy then looked to the mouth of the alley where he could see the men moving in and out of the light with the flies and mosquitoes.

But the thing prowling through the darkness wasn't gone.

As he stared at the cleaning crew the thing quickly scurried across his leg and leaped off into the gloom as though to tease and test him--as though checking to see if the boy was still alive.

Every muscle in the boy's body tightened, but he stifled his fear and disgust and tried his best not to react. Not to scream. Not to give away their position.

Silently, he scrutinized the gloom all around him, searching for the thing without finding it. He looked back at the men. Two of them lifted a stiff black corpse and moved through the light and disappeared. Then two other men returned to the light, kneeled down, and rose with another black corpse. When the area was clear, one man suddenly stopped and turned toward the boy and seemed to be peering right at him.

The boy held his breath as the man stared into the alley. After a moment the man called out to one of his coworkers to see if they should clear the alley, too, or wait until morning. A voice soon answered and told him they had enough with the main lane and that they would leave the smaller streets and alleys for morning. The man agreed, saying it smelled worse than a latrine in there and that he didn't know Sikhs could smell that bad. A short, cruel laugh followed as the boy's jaw tensed and he tried not to listen to the man's words.

Within moments, the men disappeared. Then the truck kicked into gear and moved forward, crunching and snapping what the crew had overlooked or was too small and insignificant to be recognized. The truck then slowed to a stop directly in front of the alley so that the boy could see the silhouette of the driver.

Suddenly he felt something bristly brush by his hand. It sent a tingle through his body. He jerked and turned to watch a fat rat soaked in something wet and shiny waddle across his arm. His breath caught in his throat as he peered down at it and it boldly looked up at him and seemed to smile.

Breathing hard, he stared into its greedy yellow eyes and thought of the congressman. They stared at each other for a long while, then it looked away with its smiling, devilish eyes and proceeded to sniff a trail up his arm. The boy jerked his arm slightly to scare it away. But the repulsive little rodent didn't scare so easily. Unafraid, it continued up his arm with a smile in its eyes.

Only the promise of death kept the boy from speaking up, from screaming, from thrusting this creature into the abyss for feasting upon the blood of his people. He took in shallow breaths and calmed himself as the thing in his heart stretched and pushed and pounded and tried its very best to break free.

And as the boy struggled with the thing in his heart, he watched the fearless little rat waddle its way up his sleeve and stop at his shoulder. Then, from the darkness, three careful fingers emerged and pushed the rat straight off his arm. The fat rat rolled over helplessly and plopped into the sticky wetness below, then it scurried away and disappeared into the darkness from which it had come.

The boy thanked his mother with his eyes, then they both turned back to the crew and fixed their eyes on the men who were hard at work cleaning up the mess the other crews had made as they recounted things they had seen or done during the day.

One man stopped in front of the alley again and seemed to sense he was being observed by the boy. Again, he turned to stare into the alley as though he could see them. The truck driver called out to him to ask him if everything was okay or if he had seen anything. He answered that he wasn't exactly sure.

At once they stopped breathing. All the boy could hear now was the steady pounding of his heart against his chest and the sound of tired men working hard to clear the lane. All he could feel were the man's eyes staring right at him.

A long, tense silence followed. Then another man yelled out that he had found a body that still needed to be burned and asked if there was any more kerosene in the truck.

Without moving his steady gaze, the man staring down the alley yelled for him to leave the body alone, saying that they had used up all the kerosene. He added that they should leave the body for the next crew. A man they couldn't see instantly agreed; then he added that many of the men were stealing and hiding the cans of kerosene for their own personal use later on.

With disgust and anger, the man staring down the alley said that stealing kerosene was nothing less than treason against Hindustan. Then he added that they were living in dark times when people actually stole from their own country. Staring down the alley, he turned to face his coworkers and reminded them that every single corpse had to be burnt without exception, with or without fuel, saying:

"No body, no evidence. No evidence, no crime."

The boy listened to each word, then repeated the mantra in his head. He wondered if the silhouette before him was a lawyer or a judge or a politician; or if the man was the son of a lawyer or a judge or a politician.

It would make sense. The clarity of thinking. The voting lists. The method. The cleaning efforts. The incredible foresight. The equipment. The barricade. The trucks and buses. The endless supply of kerosene that was controlled and regulated by the government.

Only someone with connections could

access the amount of kerosene it took to burn down an entire colony and all its inhabitants. And then there was the mantra. The one the actor had so masterfully performed on the radio. The rehearsed mantras and slogans to help inspire these sheep from another colony to kill and collect karas.

The boy thought of the words.

No body, no evidence. No evidence, no crime. .

Kill. Burn. Clean.

Perfect.

The perfect recipe.

Who had taught them the recipe? Were they using the same dark recipe everywhere? The constable had said that Sikhs were being exterminated all over India. Who, he wondered, could afford all the ingredients? Who had the ability to access so much kerosene? Who could keep the fires of murder burning for so long? How much longer would the fires continue to burn while the radios claimed there was peace? How many of his people were reduced to smoke and ash? How many families? How many fathers? How many uncles? How many grandmothers?

The perfect recipe.

Suddenly the truck kicked into gear and shook the boy out of his thoughts; the wheels began to squish and turn and the truck moved several yards forward. The suspicious man followed behind, leaving the boy and his mother staring at the red and orange glow of the truck's tail lights.

His mother breathed again.

So did the boy as he angled his left ear toward the crew, trying to see if these men would somehow answer the questions he was asking himself, or betray the name of the congressman who had summoned them.

But for some reason or another all he could hear in his head was his uncle's voice, telling him that there was no justice for Sikhs in India and that there never would be. He had said that this was a fact and it would always be so. How could there be justice from those radical Brahmin politicians who had openly expressed their admiration for a man named Hitler, the only other soul in the world his uncle could think of that would dare attack the Vatican on Christmas day to incinerate the Vatican library?

The boy didn't really know who Hitler was and his mother didn't want to discuss the man with him, saying that he wasn't worth her time or energy. She had merely told him that if any man were the personification of evil, pure evil, it was Hitler. She then explained that Hitler was the reason why so many hundreds of thousands of Sikh soldiers had hurt themselves or died so far away in Asia and Europe defending a people's right to exist and practice the religion of their birth.

His uncle had said that this demon Hitler had tried to do to the Jewish people what his uncle believed the Indian government was doing to the Sikh people. The upper-caste radicals and the sheep they brainwashed were even taking inspiration from a book Hitler had written in prison and which he had soon discovered was a top seller in Indian bookstores. His uncle maintained that it was a real shame that such garbage was even being published

A Feast for Lambs

in India.

A real shame.

The widespread disappearances, the massacre at the Golden Temple, the systemic killing of a generation, and the total destruction of the Sikh library, his uncle had warned them all, was just the beginning with this upper-caste government, which used Hitler to inspire the masses to be more patriotic, as if killing and humiliating minorities was an act of patriotism.

Now hiding for his life in putrid gore, the boy suddenly wished he had listened more to his gorilla uncle, and he knew now that despite his uncle's anger and his temper he had been right all along. He even began to understand his anger and he could feel that very same anger growing inside him.

And as it grew and pushed and pounded against the wall of his heart, the boy had a sudden realization. Staring at the shapes and shadows all around him, breathing in nothing less than pure death, he, letting his guard down, suddenly realized that he was surrounded by the bits and pieces of people he had once known and loved.

People he had talked with.

Danced with.

Joked with.

Laughed with.

Wonderful people who had been and who would never be again.

An uncontrollable numbness began to spread from his lips down his neck, and the high-pitched buzzing was once again so loud in his head that he could hear nothing else and think of nothing else but those people. He wanted to wake up from this nightmare.

He needed to wake up.

But there was no waking up. He shifted and groaned in his mother's embrace and his mother, sensing his nerves, sensing this sudden attack and confrontation with truth, quickly covered his mouth to prevent him from screaming. He thrust and pushed in her arms and tried to break free but she wouldn't let him go.

She whispered something he couldn't make out through the high-pitched buzzing in his head. It was the first time his mind let him see truth and it was too much for his young heart to bear. Only when his mother jerked him hard and fierce did the buzzing and numbness fade away. She stared at him with pleading eyes. He froze and stared back at her, then he calmed himself down, swallowed and nodded that he was okay.

Cautiously, she uncovered his mouth and he breathed in the stained air with difficulty. Then he turned toward the alley and listened to one man talk about how in the morning they had covered a Sikh baby in sugar and syrup and fed it to a colony of ants. The man said that he had left it there in the sun all day and that when he returned with others in the night it was just a mess of pulp, flesh and bone. Then he laughed and said they all jumped ten feet back when it started to cry.

The boy covered his ears. He didn't want to hear any more. He couldn't. And only when he saw the red and orange lights disappear, he uncovered

A Feast for Lambs

his ears and said:

"I hate them. I hate them so much."

"Be strong, bete...be strong..."

He told himself that, despite his uncle's firm and unshakable belief that all politicians were above the law, he would dedicate his whole life to tracking down the filthy rat in white kurta pajamas and he would make him pay in blood for what he had done to the people he loved. And at the very thought of vengeance the thing in his heart jolted awake and seemed to laugh joyously as it slithered and hissed and thrashed around its cocoon, restless to break free.

But what if his uncle was right? What if he was truly right? What if the problem was bigger than just a few congressmen? What if the problem was bigger, much bigger than a few radical, upper-caste politicians trying to maintain their birthright and their caste system?

Thinking this, the boy suddenly remembered a very special evening he had with his family when his uncle had desperately wanted to treat the whole family to a dinner in celebration of his brother's scholarship and opportunity to live in a democratic country.

The boy remembered walking into an elegant and severely overpriced restaurant. He remembered walking by a table of politicians dressed in pristine white kurta pajamas arguing heatedly over something that probably meant nothing. As they were being seated, he remembered his uncle walking right up to the table, knowing that he was up to no good. His uncle said a few polite words to the politicians, then he boldly declared:

"My friends, let's be honest, Hitler would really love this place."

The restaurant owner had instantly taken offense and confronted his uncle; but his uncle had assured him that by 'this place' he wasn't talking about his restaurant but his country and the radical, pure Aryans that ran it. Contrary to his uncle's expectations, the politicians smiled, thanked him very kindly, thought over his declaration, and then finally agreed that yes, indeed, Hitler would quite possibly love this place.

Then the white kurtas broke out into separate discussions about Hitler's fascination with the Brahminical concept of pure blood, about Hitler's love for India, and about how people quite frankly didn't truly understand or appreciate Hitler for the disciplinary genius that he was.

His uncle staggered back in mute disbelief.

One politician continued on about how just because they appreciated his mind it didn't necessarily mean they condoned the actions he may have committed, which may have been construed by some as barbaric. He agreed that Hitler had killed a lot of people, but that didn't take away from the fact that he was disciplined, dedicated and patriotic, and that the Indian people needed his discipline, dedication and patriotism.

He uncle staggered some more.

Frozen.

Disgusted.

Another white kurta fully agreed and added that a Nazi memorabilia store had just opened in his neighborhood; he was happy to say that Hitler was drawing a much younger crowd who were actively buying Hitler books, T-shirts, keychains and even bandanas. Soon, he laughed, they would make a movie about him.

His uncle swallowed hard and was too terrified to say another word. How could these men say such things?

A few white kurtas nodded their heads and said that a movie actually wasn't such a bad idea and that maybe a movie could inspire discipline and patriotism in the masses; maybe a movie would make their lives a lot easier. At this point a few white kurtas began talking about Hitler's life and how he had been a superb artist before he had ever been a politician and that they, too, fancied themselves artists in their own right.

Defeated, his uncle returned to the table and sank in his chair. He had wanted an argument. He had wanted to cause some trouble with these white kurtas. He had wanted to upset them. He had wanted his moment with the white kurtas, one he could brag about at the temple.

Instead they had their moment with him. They weren't even offended. Not even slightly. Nothing he had said had upset them, and this disturbed his gorilla uncle beyond words.

His uncle didn't speak the rest of the night, which frightened everyone who had expected and were quite frankly hoping to count veins. He just mumbled once or twice to himself as he stared at the table of white kurtas with incredulous eyes. The situation was far worse than he had ever imagined.

He ate his daal-rotis and seemed very distant and concerned.

Later that evening a man from another table removed one of his chappals and unexpectedly hurled it at his uncle, almost knocking his turban off. His uncle instantly looked at the scrawny, yet courageous man glaring at him on trembling legs.

Everyone, even strangers, stopped chatting and all at once looked to his uncle for his reaction.

They all expected the angry gorilla, but instead he stood calmly, grabbed the chappal, walked over to the hurt man and gave it back to him, staring right at him with affection. The man trembled but didn't move away from his uncle and seemed ready for a fight. His uncle beamed at this man who had the passion and the decency to thrust a chappal at him for what he had said. He stared at the chappal, the man, the chappal, and then the man again. And then he smiled.

Not maliciously.

Not sarcastically.

Authentically.

Then he spoke a few words to calm the man, but the man kept on shaking his head at his uncle, asking him to take back what he said about Hitler and his country.

To everyone's surprise, his uncle nodded at the man with respect and took back his words. Something they had never seen his uncle do. He then apologized for having offended him, but was glad he had been offended. If he apologized it was because of him and not the white kurtas. They exchanged a few words, then his uncle embraced this tiny Hindu man like a true brother; then he returned to the table smiling, saying that Hitler wouldn't love this place, and that there was hope for India after all.

His mother asked him what he had said to the man. His uncle responded that he had not said anything the man didn't already know and that next time--though he was sorry for what he had said--he should aim his chappal at those men who had afforded him the opportunity to say such a thing about his country; those who supported and propagated Hitler memorabilia or paraphernalia; those who actively sought to inspire the masses with Hitler's good side; those were the men deserving of the chappal; those men who openly expressed admiration for evil manifested as discipline and patriotism and who--instead of looking for another example of discipline and patriotism-- had the nerve to consider making a movie glorifying a man who would resort to genocide in the name of patriotism. Those were the ones deserving of his chappal. Those were the ones who truly gave his country a bad name. He was just the messenger. He didn't make what he said true. The white kurtas did.

His mother nodded.

His grandmother, too.

And just as his father was about to say something to his uncle he was suddenly interrupted. Something like a grenade crested the air. At once the boy looked up to see the chappal soar across the room like the Chappal of Truth.

In his mind's eyes the boy watched the

Chappal of Truth in slow motion as it hit a politician right on the head, bounced into the air, and
then plopped dead into a plate of curry. The plate
exploded like a grenade and curry like blood splattered across their white kurtas and not one politician was spared. Not one.

Afraid of the police, afraid of their connections, afraid of disappearing without a trace, the
scrawny man bolted out of the restaurant while
dozens of waiters and waitresses and busboys
rushed to the politician's aid and tried their best to
wash the blood splatter off their kurtas.

But it was useless.

Futile.

Their kurtas were stained.

Stained for life.

Then, before anyone else could claim the
Chappal of Truth as their own, the boy's uncle
quickly rushed to their table, reached into the bowl
and retrieved the chappal. He proceeded to wipe it
down with a cloth, then he returned to their table,
saying he knew what he was doing was a measure
unhygienic but that he really wanted to show this
chappal, this Chappal of Truth, to others.

His uncle added that this was a very special
night for him and that this chappal represented
hope for his country and that not all the people
believed what the upper-caste radicals fed them
through the media and that his nephew should take
this chappal with him to America. His brother
refused with a laugh, and told his uncle to keep the
Chappal of Truth. His uncle smiled and said that he
would, but not as an idol, as a reminder that the

people of India still had a voice, even if they had to hide after they used it.

СВ

A sudden whooping snapped the boy back to reality. In the distance he heard one man call out that he thought he saw something moving inside a home. This man wasn't part of the cleaning crew. The cleaning crew was long gone now. This was another crew. Somewhere in the darkness a killing crew continued to comb the ruins for Sikhs. He listened. Other men cried out that they had lost the Sikhs they had been searching for, but that they would find them soon enough. They couldn't hide forever. Then they said nothing more.

When it was quiet again the boy's mother nudged him and signaled for him to stand. With difficulty, he rose slowly and felt twenty pounds heavier. He then wiped gore off of his hand and neck and proceeded to follow his mother to the mouth of the alley.

Carefully, the boy peered around the corner and stared at a dying fire in the distance. Near the flickering orange light he could see the silhouette of an arm sticking out of the gully like a tree branch.

"Eyes up," his mother whispered, as though she could sense them staring at the arm.

The boy nodded. Then, after a hesitation, she pulled the boy into the street and they hurried noiselessly toward Major's home.

But no sooner did they expose themselves in the street than a frantic yell startled them. They froze instantly. His mother turned to search the darkness behind them. The boy did the same. He saw nothing, but something told him they were coming, and they were coming fast.

His mother instantly looked to the charred skeleton of what had once been a car hidden in the shadows. In the faint fire light that spread through the street the boy could barely see the silhouette of a body in the driver's seat with the mouth agape, caught in a scream of agony. He stared at the silhouette for a moment, then his mother grabbed him and hurried him to the car.

"Under," she ordered. "Under…quickly…"

The boy slipped under the car. An instant later his mother squeezed beside him. Then they both stared at the darkness to see what would emerge.

It was quiet for a long time.

All they could hear was the faint crackling of the fire snapping carbon into the air. Just as the boy thought they were safe again, there was another scream, followed by the eerie cackles of cheerful men on the hunt. He stared hard but still saw nothing. Maybe they were searching somewhere else. Maybe these jackals were headed in another direction.

The cackles stopped suddenly.

Another silence.

They had probably lost the trail of their game. They were searching quietly, patiently. They had all the time in the world. After a moment, the boy nudged his mother to leave. She looked at him, uneasy. He motioned that they should press on and that they were safe now.

But his mother didn't seem to think so. She didn't budge. She shook her head and looked to the darkness, then back at him and shook her head again. She wasn't convinced that they were in the clear just yet. And just as she turned back to regard the darkness, they heard a man scream for his wife to run as fast as she could.

A woman shrieked. The jackals cackled and clanged their weapons. The song of the hunt grew louder and louder. The boy angled his left ear and listened carefully. After a moment of silence, a gunshot shook him and his mother and reverberated through the dead colony.

Then everything stopped suddenly.

Silence again.

A second later he heard the pounding of desperate feet and the panting of breath. He narrowed his gaze and waited. Nothing. The sound of hard, panicked breathing grew louder and louder as it approached them. Then, through the dancing firelight, a mother with something in her arms charged across the street.

She stopped for a second as a Sikh man with disheveled hair suddenly emerged from the abyss behind her. The boy saw that she was covered in grime and soot and he saw that she was holding a little girl. When she saw her husband was still with them, she continued on and disappeared round the corner.

But the man stopped suddenly. He raised

his revolver and fired a shot into the darkness. He turned to face the direction of his wife and child, then back to the darkness. The boy could see that he had suddenly decided to make a stand for them. He had decided to buy them some time. A chill ran down his spine and he prayed there weren't too many jackals and that he could hold them off with his gun.

Suddenly a jackal leapt out at him and he instinctively fired his weapon. With a crack, the jackal collapsed and fell to the ground with a thud.

Another jackal leapt with a cry.

Another crack.

Another thud.

The boy scrunched his fist and felt no remorse for the jackals; he wanted them to die, even though he knew he should feel remorse and compassion, even for his enemy.

Panicked, the man shot into the darkness until he had no more bullets. Even when he had emptied the revolver, he continued to pull the trigger as though he refused to accept that the gun was empty. A second later three jackals emerged and surrounded the lion who made a bold stand for his pride.

The boy's mother turned to the boy, held his chin, and tried to force his gaze away. But this time the boy refused to look away. He jerked his chin from her hold and watched the lion, praying for him with all his heart as the three jackals closed in on him.

God, please protect him. Please save him from these men. Please give him strength and courage.

A Feast for Lambs

With a roar, the man thrust his gun at one jackal and took a measured step backward, waiting for the attack, or preparing to attack, the boy wasn't sure.

The jackals crept forward in the dying fire-light, panting.

Now the boy stared at him like he was a warrior of old. He prayed deep and hard that God would spare him and his family. His entire face tensed with emotion, and he had never felt such an intense feeling before. Then, all of a sudden, faster than the thought that could perceive it, the lion withdrew his kirpan and the three men were almost instantly floored just as six jackals leapt out of the night to replace the ones that had fallen.

The laughing jackals surrounded the lion with their iron prods, machetes and sticks. The lion breathed hard and waited, waited patiently. A few other men suddenly emerged from the darkness, but ran right by them, searching--the boy was sure--for the lion's pride.

The boy observed that the lion had seen this too, and immediately understood that he couldn't wait for these killers to make the first move. Instantly he lashed out at them with all his force. He took blows to the back and shoulder and legs. But surging with more emotion than all of them combined, he leveled them one by one. And the boy felt the presence of his ancestors all around him, filling the lion with courage and strength and stubborn determination.

When there was only one jackal left standing, the coward began to beg for mercy. As the lion advanced, the jackal involuntary stepped backward until he disappeared into the darkness from which he had come.

The boy surged with indescribable emotion that God had answered his prayers and had spared this lion, this fierce warrior of old. He closed his eyes and thanked God with all his heart. But then as he opened his eyes a sudden and unexpected thing happened.

The lion stopped.

The lion no longer advanced.

No longer moved.

He just froze and stared into the darkness before him as though he were staring at death. Then he took small steps backward as the coward stepped back into the faint firelight with murder in his eyes and a whole new disposition. The boy didn't understand what was happening. Why was the lion backing away from the coward? Then he heard things in the darkness. Things he didn't want to hear or to accept. A second later three more jackals emerged. The lion involuntarily looked to where his pride had disappeared, then back at the jackals.

The boy scrunched his fist.

Please, God! Please!

Realizing what was about to happen, his mother tried to turn his eyes away again, but the boy refused. He stared up at the lion and prayed for him as the thing in his heart pushed and pulled and pounded and shrieked in his mind to be free.

Please, God! Please!

The four jackals surrounded him. The boy could see the lion was weak and wounded and that only one thing was keeping him up. His family.

One jackal attacked.

One jackal fell.

Thank you! Thank you!

Three jackals attacked.

Weapons clanged. Thuds and cries.

Then two jackals fell.

And only one remained.

Thank you! Thank you!

And just as the lion rushed the last jackal and raised his kirpan to deliver the deathblow, another jackal leapt straight out of the darkness and another and another. Soon ten or fifteen jackals pounced upon the lion at once and the boy didn't even have time to say God's name. He just watched in mute, stunned silence as the jackals ripped the lion apart, piece by piece.

This time his mother didn't have to try to turn his gaze. When she turned to him he was already staring at her with wet eyes and a heart full of hate listening to the thuds, not wanting to look anymore. The prods and machetes made their deathly music and the lion groaned and sighed painfully with every note. Then the lion made no more sounds and the bludgeoning and butchering stopped man by man, like dark musicians in an orchestra.

When it was all over the boy turned and gazed at the flickering shadows in the street and saw a man dousing the dead lion with kerosene. His eyes felt heavy and tired with defeat. He didn't think he had any more emotions in him left to feel. The only thing he felt was the thing in his heart, and the thing was clawing and biting and chewing its way out to be free. But then the thing growing in his heart froze--froze with the boy's heart when he heard a woman screaming.

No! Please, no!

Then the thing growing in heart fed off his sudden fear and anger and hate. It hissed and laughed at the boy as he heard a jackal call out that they had caught the lioness and that she was a bitch and that she had almost clawed his eyes out. He watched the darkness on the other side of the street and prayed it was the thing in his heart playing a mind trick on him.

Please, no. God. Please, no...

But as he prayed inwardly a man emerged into the faint firelight pulling and dragging the Sikh man's wife by the hair. Her empty hands swiped and hit and scratched and pounded the jackal's hands. But he had most of her long black hair in his hand and his grip was firm and tough and immoveable.

No! No! No! Please, no!

Laughing, the jackal dragged her to her husband's butchered corpse and said something about how it was only dutiful for a good wife to burn in her husband's funeral pyre so that in the next life she wouldn't be born a woman.

Heartlessly, the jackal then proceeded to lift her off the ground by the hair. A second later he thrust her against her husband's corpse and she fell into the flesh with a thud and splatter.

Trying to clamber to her feet, the poor woman instantly lost her breath when she realized she was soaking and slipping in her husband's blood.

Shocked and devastated, she stopped trying to get up and began to moan like a wounded animal. She crawled to what was left of his face and she touched her husband's broken cheek. She opened her mouth as far as it would open but nothing came out. It was as though her heart was caught in her throat and she was choking on it.

She fell back on her haunches and breathed quick, shallow breaths. She then tried to stand on quivering legs but failed with every attempt.

When she finally stood, she turned wearily to her husband's killers and instantly and unexpectedly received a mouthful of stinging kerosene.

The shock of the kerosene sent her stumbling back down beside her husband.

The boy stared in mute horror, caught in some surreal moment. His entire head began to tremble as he realized what dark intention they had in mind. They were going to burn her alive.

God. Please don't let them...please....

The woman spat and choked on kerosene as she tried to get up several times but was kicked back down with every attempt. A man then flicked a match to life.

A tiny flame flickered in the dark.

The boy's mother turned his face away from the scene and held it strong. The hand holding his chin shook terribly as she, too, realized what was about to happen.

The boy's chin trembled with his mother's hand as he waited. He stared at the two tiny specs of light in his mother's glassy eyes as they widened with each passing second. He watched the match reflected in her eyes like it was not happening, like he was in a movie theatre. Only in this movie the villains looked like the heroes and the heroes looked like the villains.

And then time froze as he watched the light of the match disappear for a moment. For a moment his mother's eyes went dark, completely dark, then all at once they lit up with spears of dancing flames and the night shook with a wail that chilled him to the marrow. The woman screamed in impossible agony:

"Waheguru!"

The numbness and the high-pitched buzzing began again; but not loud enough to silence the mother's bloodcurdling cries.

"Waheguru!"

The fresh scent of burnt hair and flesh assaulted his entire being, infiltrated his every pore, and the thing in his heart laughed and feasted on the poison filling his heart.

He had never experienced anything so horrible and disturbing in his life and thought he never would again. The woman's cries grew weaker and weaker with death.

"Waheguru."

She could barely speak.

"Waheguru…"

She wheezed.

"Wahe…guru…"

When the cries finally ceased, the jackals crept away as they continued their hunt for surviving Sikhs, and the boy wished he had never been born to have witnessed such a horror. He breathed in hard and thought that if there was such a thing as karma, and if there was such a thing as reincarnation, he wished to never be born as a creature as low and despicable as a human being. For the first time in his life the boy felt a shame so profound he could hardly make sense of it. A shame unlike any other.

Not of his country.
Not of his religion.
Not of his poverty.
Of his race.
Of his species.

The boy's eyes felt tired and heavy and he wanted to shut them forever. He closed his eyes and kept them closed for a long, long time. They might have been closed for one minute or an hour. He didn't know.

When at last he opened his eyes, it was almost like he hadn't. He could hear the crackling and the smoldering, but the light of the fires was extinguished. In the darkness he could barely see his mother; but he could tell she had not taken her eyes off the woman. Then, as he stared at his mother, a slight noise instantly seized his attention.

Please...no...

It came again, and again, and he looked to the source of the sound. He heard a whimper, and in that whimper he could barely make out a name.

Maybe a child's name.

His mother covered her mouth to keep from releasing a cry.

With a pounding heart, the boy prayed inward for God to please just end her suffering. He ground his teeth and couldn't take any more. The woman cried out the name again. And, before his mother could stop him, the boy forgot himself and crawled out from underneath the car. "We can't leave her," he said. "We can't..."

Trying to stop him, his mother quickly reached out and grabbed his ankle. "We can't do anything for her."

"She's in pain."

"How can you stop it?"

The boy had no answer. He didn't think he could. "She's alone." It's all he could say.

"She's making too much noise…"

The boy knew his mother was only thinking about his safety, and that if she didn't have him to think about she would help. But something inside him just didn't want the woman to be alone like that in the dark. "She's alone," he repeated. "She's alone…" And he kicked his leg free and ran into the thick darkness and followed the sounds issuing from her burnt mouth. He approached the groans and whimpers, then knelt down and felt around the dark for her. He froze when he touched a thing that was wet and sticky with chunks of crispy, charred skin peeling off.

A woman groaned with his touch. The boy breathed in deeply and gently found her burnt hand. He held it softly and soon felt the burnt fingers wrap around his small hands.

He knew she couldn't see him.

Couldn't smell.

A Feast for Lambs

She could only feel his small, soft hands
with what remained of hers. She whispered a name
again and again and the boy closed his eyes. He
whispered:
"Yes."
"You're okay…"
"Yes."
The boy didn't know why he lied to her. He
just did and thought that maybe she would hold on
to life until she knew her daughter was okay, and
he didn't want her holding on; he didn't want her
to suffer anymore than she already had.

At that moment his mother came up
behind him but didn't say anything. She merely
placed her hand on his shoulder and waited.

Again, the woman said her daughter's
name. But this time she said it differently. This time
the boy could hear relief, maybe even a smile in her
voice. Then he felt her life slowly drain away as her
hand weakened and she released him finger by finger. She whispered her daughter's name one last
time, then her voice faded into a lifeless sigh.
The boy stood slowly. He turned to face the shadow
that was his mother. He took in a deep breath and
said nothing. He wanted to tell her how much he
hated the people who had done this. But she
already knew how he felt and he knew no matter
what she said, no matter what lecture or lesson she
had given him in the past about anger and hate, she
felt the same.

How could anyone feel anything else?

But what she didn't know was this: that he
would trade in all the songs and magic gloves in

the world to do to the congressman what he had done to this woman. It was a strange feeling, but if he could, he would. He would trade in all his dreams for that one chance.

And he would make him pay.

He would make him pay for every cry, every sob, every agony.

And he would not feel the lesser for it.

And with his heart filling with poison, the boy stepped away from the charred remains of husband and wife and his mother took his wet hand and conducted him through the darkness toward Major's home.

CR

With exhausted, swollen eyes, the boy stared at Major's door in the flickering orange light. Several fires waved and danced down the street like Holi. The boy looked to his mother, then up to the attic. He didn't see anything or anyone through the chinks and fissures. Slowly, wearily, he lowered his gaze to the broken window, then to the shards of glass scattered across the ground reflecting specks of firelight like a hundred orange stars in the night. From behind him came a thick, suffocating air laced with death. Every breath burned his lungs. Every breath filled his heart with anger and rage--with a deadly poison that sickened his soul.

Breathing, the boy thought he could die by the stench alone. It was like breathing in pure arsenic, and he knew he would never forget this smell, even if he spent the rest of his life trying to. Breathing, the boy thought that if hell existed, and if hell wasn't just a state of mind as his mother had taught him, he was in a place far worse than hell. And if hell existed, and if hell had an odor, it could not even begin to compare to this odor.

At least if there was a hell, and if he were in hell, he could accept that demons had created this smell; at least then he could accept that demons had done this to his people for a being called the devil.

But to think, even for a second, that he wasn't in hell and that men had done this to his people for other men filled him with a hurt so deep he couldn't even begin to describe it.

A hurt that made him wish there was a hell.

Made him wish he were in hell.

Made him wish there was a place in eternity where all this would make sense and the dark opera of mothers agonizing in the night for their butchered families wouldn't torment his heart with every terrible note.

And if there was a hell, if there really was a hell, the boy wished that there would be a special place--a very special place--for politicians who wore pristine white kurtas to hide their blood-stained souls, who used religion to their economic and political ends and who defaced their country's good name.

Those few upper-caste politicians who controlled the many and who used the TV and the radio and popular actors to inspire men to be more patriotic and disciplined like the man his mother had said wasn't even worth mentioning and whose name she never wanted to hear in her home.

He wished these men a very special place in hell right beside their beloved mentor. And he wished that they would suffer every agony of every victim they were directly or indirectly responsible for upon their death. He wished this with all his heart and would give up all his dreams just so that the congressman, upon his death, would experience everything that mother experienced as she burned alive and prayed for her daughter's life in a bed of pulpy flesh and blood that had once been a loving husband.

He prayed that this congressman would suffer her agony and every other agony he had inspired in his dark, miserable life. He thought these things, and he had never experienced these thoughts or emotions before, and they were heavy on his soul.

The boy wished for justice and vengeance of a supreme and cosmic kind and he wished this with all his being; and as he thought this he felt the thing in his heart push and grow and pound against his chest as it fed greedily off the poison his heart produced with every dark thought.

Always, his parents had taught him to watch out for the true enemies. Ego. Hate. And fear. Always, he had done so. But this was something else. This was something he couldn't help.

This was hell.

True hell.

His hell.

Waking up two days ago, he would have never believed such cruelty and agony possible. And yet--

Men did this to his colony.

Men did this to other men. And though the boy remembered the stories and the lessons, he knew now more than ever that the words were easier preached than practiced. He knew more than ever that he was not the Guru, and if he had an arrow to aim at the congressman it would not be tipped in gold. There would be no mercy. No com-

passion. And if he didn't die, he wished the congressman to suffer and suffer long. And as he
thought this, the thing in his heart pushed to break
free--to turn dark thoughts into reality.

As the boy stood before Major's door, he
was now fully aware that he could do to those
politicians what they had done to that mother. And,
thinking this, he knew that when that mother had
died, so had a part of him. The good part. The com-
passionate part. The part that was like the Guru.
And deep down he knew he had died some sort of
a spiritual death, and that a spiritual death was the
worst kind of death for a servant of God.

For a Sikh.

And he didn't care. He knew that the mere
fact he was feeling this and thinking about
vengeance, he had given those upper-caste politicians what his mother had once called a 'double
victory'. They had killed his spirit and his heart.
They had caused his own mind to undermine the
uniform he so proudly wore. Yes, he had heard the
stories and the lectures a hundred times; about how
the warriors of old never permitted the enemy a
double victory by attacking out in vengeance;
always in defense. Always without hate or anger.

Yes, he had heard the stories and the lectures a hundred times; about how the warriors of
old never attacked a religion, but the men who
used religion to their political and economic ends,
though he hardly understood what that really
meant at the time.

Yes, he had heard the stories and the lectures a hundred times; but no, he could not under-

A Feast for Lambs

stand them or be like those warriors of old. His hate was overwhelming, all-consuming, and he didn't understand how it could be otherwise; and he wondered if those warriors of old had seen what he had seen; had felt what he had felt; had smelled what he had smelled.

To him it was impossible that they had seen the things he had seen, heard the things he had heard, smelled the things he had smelled and not felt anything other than pure hatred for the demons who could do such things in the name of the religion--a religion he now understood the radicals had taken control of and were using to do their dark deeds. It was impossible to feel anything else-- anything else other than what would give his persecutors their double victory.

And now, in a time when the stories and the lectures and the lessons mattered most, he knew they were easier preached than practiced. He barely heard his mother's words, his father's words, his brother's words, his grandmother's words, his uncle's words, the Guru's words in his head.

All he heard were those horrible screams.

All he heard was the dying whisper of a girl's name.

All he smelled was death.

And he hated those men.

And he hated that he hated them. And yet-

How could he not?

And he didn't care about this thing the warriors of old called a 'double victory'!

The boy didn't care about giving his enemy a double victory. They could have their double victory so long as he had his revenge and so long as they suffered and suffered dearly.

He hated; he hated in a way that he knew was unnatural for a boy his age to hate; and he hated his hate; but with every breath, hell filled his heart and mind and burned his inner kingdom until there was nothing left but smoke, ash, and smoldering embers where once goodness, imagination and dreams thrived.

Even if he survived this murderous campaign he understood that everything he was, everything that he had ever been, had burned away with the rest of his colony.

Even if he survived--

He hadn't.

Now the boy's mother grabbed the warm handle and slowly eased Major's door open. Cautiously, they stepped inside and picked their way through the shadows and light pouring into the home from the street. The room had been looted and overturned, and they soon found themselves picking their way toward the ladder hidden in the shadows.

As they reached the ladder, something suddenly moved behind them. They swiveled around. A crowbar reflected stars of orange light and fell fast and hard upon the boy's mother. Instantly, the boy screamed:

"Major!"

At once Major froze in mid-swing, the prod inches away from the boy's mother's head. He turned to the boy with his soot-covered faced. His good eye was wearied and bloodshot and he looked like he hadn't slept for days.

Panting, rage pumping through two visible veins at his temples, Major stared at the boy blankly, as though he thought his wearied mind was playing tricks on him. Then his good eye accepted the boy as reality and he smiled faintly. He stared at the boy in wonder and disbelief, as though he were staring at him for the first time in an eternity. His smile blossomed and spoke volumes. It told the boy someone else other than his mother was glad he was alive.

Was relieved that he was alive.

Was amazed that he was alive.

Major lowered the crowbar and his mother sighed and then tried to say something, tried to make some sort of an apology, but before she could speak the words, he silenced her with his free hand. "You'll be safe up there," he said, sparing her the apology, indicating the hole in the ceiling with his dusty glass eye. "I must check for something."

The boy's mother nodded her gratitude; Major nodded, regarded the boy again, then turned and carefully made his way into the burning street.

The boy watched him until he disappeared in the swirling smoke and darkness, then he turned to follow his mother up into the attic.

With difficulty, the boy hoisted himself up into the dancing firelight that poured through the chinks and fissures of the broken wall and that reflected off a broken mirror that scattered orange light in every direction. When he pulled himself up he saw that his mother was already sitting on the small bed with her back against the plaster wall, waiting for him.

Wearily, he dragged himself away from the hole and scrambled through the books, making his way to the bed where he sat against the wall next to his mother. After a long silence, she sighed and said:

"I think we're going to be safe now. They shouldn't be able to find us here."

The boy said nothing, but he knew she was right.

She went quiet, staring at the dancing shadows in the small, cramped attic. The boy looked up at her to see if she was okay. For the first time since the killing crews had begun their dark campaign he thought that she would break down and cry, and he thought that this would be the best thing for her.

She wasn't crying, but he could see her eyes were wet and far away. He stared at her for a long time and waited for the tears. Hoped for them. Prayed for them. But they never came. She never let herself cry. Deep down he wished she would, and he knew she was holding everything inside for him.

The boy stared at her eyes and he didn't understand her look, and her look made him want to grab her shoulders, shake her fiercely and force her to cry. To tell her to just let go and feel sad and helpless if only for a moment. He stared at her eyes and he didn't understand her look, but if he could, if he could know what she was thinking, he would know that she was feeling--

Like a fraud.

Like a counterfeit.

If he could know her look or what she was

feeling he would know that she could give advice but she couldn't follow it. He would know that she couldn't stop thinking about her husband, her mother, her brother and his wife. About what had become of them. He would know that she struggled desperately to remember the smiles, but couldn't stop thinking of what had become of them, hoping they were safe, but knowing that they weren't, knowing in her heart that they were gone and that she would never see them again, and that they had probably suffered, and suffered terribly.

And if the boy could know her thoughts he would know that she hated just as much as he did. Not a politician; not a people; but a thing.

Death.

She hated death.

She hated death with all her being and yet she could not say anything to the boy. It went against everything she had ever taught him about life and living. But she was a fraud and she knew it and she hated, she hated death, and she hated death with all her being.

And she hated death because no matter what anyone said, she knew this:

Death was final.

With death there were no second chances.

And she had hated death for a long time; she had hated death ever since death had robbed her of her sister and cheated her of any future moment to tell her sister how much she loved her and how much she appreciated her.

If the boy could know her look and if he could know her thoughts, he would know how much she wished she had given her mother a third hug.

A forth hug.

A fifth hug!

Horrible, despicable death!

And he would know her mind was consumed by one word and one word alone:

Gone.

She was gone. She would not see her mother again. And she felt as though at any moment she could go absolutely mad with the thought.

It wasn't possible.

It couldn't be possible.

In the entire world there was no woman like her mother, and in all of eternity there would never be another woman like her again. And she was--

Gone.

A woman who had given herself entirely to her family; a woman who had sacrificed everything for her children and her grandchildren; a woman whose voice and words had always been, in some incomprehensible way, the voice of God.

Gone.

A mother. A grandmother. She protected. She helped. She supported. She cared. She smiled. She sang. She laughed. She dreamed. She hoped--

She hoped and she dreamed for her family. She would have done anything for them. She tells them she loves them and everything will work out for the best. She tells her this all her life and suddenly her words, her hugs, her smiles, and all her hopes and dreams are--

A Feast for Lambs

Gone.

Never to be heard again. Never to be seen again. Never to hug again. Never to love again. Never to dream again.

Gone.

Not only from her family. Not only for a moment. Forever. And though millions upon millions of people will be born every minute of every day, there will never be another mother like her again.

Gone.

If the boy could know her thoughts he would know how close his mother was to losing her mind with the thought of all those people who would no longer bless and share their lives. Those who had been and would never be again.

But the boy could not know her thoughts, and so he just stared at her distant eyes and he wished she would cry; but he knew that she wouldn't because she was his confidence, his strength and his resolve, and that she would do anything to make him believe there was still hope. At last the boy took his mother's hand and said:

"It's okay…"

You can cry.

She looked down at him, and attempted a smile. "I know it is," she said. "I know it is…"

She had not understood.

Or maybe she had.

He wasn't sure.

She then spotted something dark on the boy's face in the flickering orange light. She took her chunni and wiped it off without looking at it.

"Bigi," she said after a silence, "believed strongly in the power of song...of words...you know that?"

The boy nodded.

He did.

"She couldn't sing," she grinned, and the boy laughed slightly, remembering her deep, hoarse voice, and for a moment they both fell silent with the memory. Something pinched the boy's heart as he realized he would never hear his grandmother's awful voice again, and all he wanted to do now was hear it. After a reflective silence, his mother cleared her throat and continued:

"She understood that words are more than words. Words can bring hope when all hope is lost. Words can fill you with love when it seems all love is gone. And love, love is everything. And where there is love, there is God."

The boy nodded; his grandmother had given him this talk before, had told him all this in a different way, in her way.

"Words can bring you closer to God when it seems there is no God. Or words can hurt you. They can really, really hurt you. They can make you despair when everything is good in your life. They can inspire hate and turn people into animals."

She looked down at the boy and became very serious.

"And they can enter your ears and creep down into your chest and eat everything that was ever good and pure in your heart--" She wiggled her fingers. "Like worms in an apple. Eat and eat until there is nothing left but an empty shell and a faint memory..."

A Feast for Lambs

It was like she knew his thoughts.

She paused, reached over and placed her hand on the boy's heart. It was like she could sense the foul thing growing there and that the love radiating from her palm would somehow kill it. She breathed in deeply, then went on:

"Words can inspire you in here and lift you to a place of dreams and imagination. To heaven. Or they can drag you down to a pit of anger, hate and despair."

She looked at him severely. "Songs. Words. Thoughts." She lifted her hand and tapped him gently on his head. "Watch what goes in here. Watch carefully. Words have the power of life and death."

The boy knew this, and he knew that through words and words alone a select few had long ago taken control of one of the oldest religions, going so far as to make it a sin punishable by death for anyone other than them to write and interpret the sacred words and stories. He knew by everything he had learned from his mother, Major and his uncle how powerful words were and how a few needed to control words to control the stories. And now, centuries later, the same few were doing the exact same thing to his stories in order to control and change the thoughts of his people. The boy's mother breathed in deeply and turned away. She looked toward the street. Her voice lowered to a sad whisper.

"With one word…this would have been over before it started."

She shook her head sadly.

"One word from one man and this would have never happened. One word from one man and the army would have saved thousands of lives. One word and--"

She couldn't finish the sentence. Her head fell and she closed her eyes. The boy could see she was thinking about his father, his grandmother, his aunt and his uncle.

One word and your father and your grand-mother and your aunt and uncle would still be with us.

There was a long silence, then the cries and the wails began again. His mother sighed deeply, and in her sigh he heard a question.

How long would the murdering continue?

The boy rested his head on his mother's lap and gazed at his mother's kara that reflected a star of white and orange light. He closed his eyes for a moment and thought about his father and said a silent prayer for him. He prayed that his heart was wrong and that he would see him again. He prayed that they would be reunited and that they would join his brother in another jungle far away, where minorities and low castes weren't persecuted or tor-tured or humiliated by the upper-caste politicians who would do anything and everything to protect their birthright that seemed to place them above the law. When he opened his eyes, he started at the sight of a glass eye staring down at him.

"It's just me," Major said. He held a radio in his hands. "I couldn't find batteries, and the power isn't coming back anytime soon." He placed the radio next to the bed on the floor, discouraged.

A Feast for Lambs

"Why does it matter?" his mother asked, wearily. "Don't you know? There is peace. There is peace everywhere. What more do you need to know?"

"We need to know what's happening out there."

She laughed despairingly.

"Peace...didn't you hear what I said? Peace..."

Major looked at her but said nothing. With a sigh, he walked over to a fissure in the wall and stared down into the street. After a long, pensive moment, he returned to the bed and sat beside the boy's mother. "When the radio begins to say there is trouble," he said. "Then we'll know that the killing has ended and the saving face has begun. Then the army will come."

"There will be nothing left," the boy said, staring up at Major. "Nothing..." The boy thought about the radio station he had heard hours ago. While the station played songs of peace, spirituality and love, his people were being beaten, butchered and burned alive. While they said there was peace in India the upper-caste radicals were slaughtering Sikhs like flies in a bakery.

Though Major seemed to understand his frustration he didn't respond to it. He was all business. "They cut the power," he said. "In a few days they will send in the army and they will begin relief camps for survivors. By this time they will have done exactly what they did in Amritsar: they will have cleared the streets of bodies, but they will leave a few left to be counted."

"How can you be sure?" his mother asked with a slight accusatory tone. When Major didn't answer, she added, "You seem to know a lot about how they work."

At this Major's head fell and the boy saw that he was struggling with something dark inside. After a silence, he turned to the boy's mother and said:

"The government knows it can get away with this. They succeeded once, and they will succeed again. They shut the whole world out for a week as they massacred women and children in Amritsar with tanks and machine guns and grenades. Then they cleaned up the scene so that you could practically eat off the roads. Only then did they permit the media into the perimeter. By then there was nothing left to report except the rehearsed rhetoric of a general who was willing to do what another wouldn't."

"No body, no evidence," the boy's mother said despairingly, repeating what she had heard in the alley. "No evidence, no crime."

Major nodded. He clearly knew the mantra well. He gave the boy's mother a severe look. "You survive this," he said. "And you take your boy and you get out of this fifth-world mess. It's only going to get worse for minorities... The world's silence to what they did in Amritsar showed this government that they can handle minorities the same way the Nazis handled the Jewish people. And this...this is just another test to see what they can get away with. And they will. They'll get away with it."

He laughed in disbelief that such a horror

could repeat itself.

"They have the same perimeter and they are using the same method. They want to maximize causalities in order to humiliate the Sikhs, in order to show them they can do whatever they want and the world won't do a damn thing. And, I assure you, just like Amritsar, they are not letting the media in. The killing has been going down for days and not a single journalist will be allowed through the perimeter. Right now no one knows this is happening. No one. And no one is getting through their barricade. Not until they have finished their job and the evidence is destroyed."

The boy's mother turned to regard him with deep concern. With a voice filled with sadness, Major continued:

"And what is happening here will be met with the same indifference as Amritsar. And so, it will happen again. And again...but not to Sikhs. In five years the Sikhs as a community will have been defeated. In five years the radicals will have squashed and silenced a protest against their caste system that began centuries ago. In five years--I assure you--Sikhs will be staunch supporters of the caste system, and they will have been properly divided, defeated and embraced into the caste fold that accepts Brahmin rule. And once the Sikhs are assimilated in the fold, they will be left alone."

Major sighed, and the boy's entire body tensed with the idea that the wizards could undermine the message and meaning of his religion in such a way. Sikhs would never embrace what their Gurus rejected and fought against. Never. It was impossible.

"All the extremists want is for Sikhs to accept their caste society in the same way the once-free societies of Sanatana Dharma were forced to do. The extremists want to bring the Sikhs into the hierarchal fold so that they can be controlled like the low castes and all the other religions that once upon a time tried to challenge and question their additions and their interpretations of the sacred stories that eventually supported and justified their divine rule."

Major was saying exactly what his uncle had said many times before about the extremists, only he was saying it differently, as if the Sikhs had no hope, as if they had already been defeated. The boy didn't want to hear or believe or accept any of this. Major continued:

"It's all they want. They want Brahmin Sikhs keeping Dalit Sikhs out of their Gurdwaras, even though caste was rejected and abolished centuries ago for Sikhs. And it will happen, and it will happen very soon, and once this happens, once Sikhs unconsciously embrace caste and bow before idols and Brahmins, once Sikhs are too busy fighting themselves over details the extremists erased and changed, they will leave Sikhs alone to their own undoing. Divide and rule was not invented by the British as many believe."

Major paused. The boy's uncle had once said that the wizards controlled more than eighty percent of government and industry and media. After everything he had heard on the radio, after seeing that endless supply of government-regulated kerosene, and after experiencing the indifference of the government-controlled police and army in the nation's capital, he knew without a doubt that his uncle wasn't as foolish as he once believed him to be. He knew his uncle's thoughts on the wizards were closer to truth than lies. The boy even had the sad feeling for a moment that, like the Golden Temple, not a single politician would ever have to answer for their crimes against humanity because extremists would always protect extremists in India. With an incredulous laugh, Major continued:

"Casteism is already returning to the Sikhs, I see it. I really do. Even though Sikhism from the first and last inspiration was a bold rebellion against caste, it is returning and the extremists have succeeded."

Major shook his head sadly.

"Long ago there were many protests against the Brahmin rulers by Hindus, but they were all quashed by the upper castes with extreme spiritual and physical violence. But Sikh baptism was something that couldn't be quashed so easily, and it took centuries. Sikh baptism is something to be studied before it's forgotten, something to be admired, something powerful, possibly the most powerful protest against Brahminical caste rule I have ever read about; and yet...and yet...when I hear some Sikhs speak, it is as if their Guru had never spoken a word against the evils of caste or those who changed the sacred texts."

He hesitated a moment or two before going on.

"I don't think Sikhs themselves understand

the sheer power of what Guru Gobind Singhji did on that faithful day when he denounced caste, dropped his surname, and declared all were equal. But I will tell you this: the Brahmin ruler understood. The Brahmin knew exactly what this meant to his rule and to his self-proclaimed birthright. And the Brahmin knew right away that here was another story they would have to change in order to maintain their control of the jungle."

The boy listened to all this and thought Major sounded very much like his uncle; he thought about what his uncle had said about last names and how he claimed that Sikhism had once been a very powerful movement against caste oppression and inequality, one to be admired and emulated, one considered by many British historians and scholars as the greatest blow against caste tyranny in the last five hundred years. The boy had heard his uncle talk about this many times, but he had hardly paid attention to him because of the way his uncle had presented his words; but now the boy listened to remember as Major continued:

"All they want is for Sikhs to accept and embrace their society and boast caste--to boast inequalities and superiority. That's all they want. To assimilate the Sikh into their system of oppression."

He sighed again and shook his head.

"Once the Sikhs are spiritually destroyed, once the message of baptism is undermined, the extremists will move on to the next big threat to their control--the Christians--and the Christians will be made to suffer just like the Sikhs for trying to convert their low castes into free men the way

A Feast for Lambs

Bhindranwala was doing by the thousands."

The boy listened to all this and he thought that if he did survive this dark campaign to erase his generation and its memory he would do as the warriors of old had done and he would drop his last name; he would do so just as his Guru had done so many centuries ago when Rai unquestionably became Singh.

And if his uncle was right and the wizards were using the Hindu religion as a tool to destroy the meaning of Sikhism, the meaning of forgoing the last name and taking on a communal last name that represented strength, courage and equality, if his uncle was right and the radicals were trying to protect the precious caste system, which the Sikh could not accept, could never accept--would always have to speak against--then the best way to honor all those who had died at the Golden Temple and in his colony was to speak fiercely and passionately against the caste system that enslaved more than two hundred million Indians. To protest not just for the protection of Sikh identity, but for what that identity meant, and to once again be a powerful voice against caste oppression and social injustice.

Suddenly a rush of emotion surged through the boy as he remembered things his uncle had said so many times at the dinner table that he could probably repeat his lectures word for word.

His uncle had said that long ago one society had corrupted the once free and interdependent societies of Sanatana Dharma with lies and half-truths that placed their society at the top of a pyramid of control. He had said that these lies and half-truths became laws and these laws became a system and this system had evolved to become one of the most evil forms of oppression known to man. His uncle had explained that this one society had turned these free and interdependent Hindu societies into grades of caste to serve and praise and revere them.

And ever since there had been countless protests and rebellions by the low-caste Hindus against the one society that now claimed dominance over all.

And after centuries of controlling the sacred stories, this one society had eventually silenced and defeated the countless Hindu rebellions against them by breaking their spirit of rebellion and protest through torture, humiliation and extreme violence. By destroying facts, obscuring truth and rewriting sacred stories.

And by doing something else.

By somehow changing the history of the rebellion and incorporating the rebels into their society to deflect the meaning and the purpose of the rebellion. By portraying their leaders as Brahmins or slaves of Brahmins engaged in Brahministic rituals. By taking a living member of the defeated rebellion or oppressed religion and making him a leader who would openly engage in Brahministic rituals to further muddle truth and obscure meaning to the younger generation. By using this puppet leader to conduct their dark campaigns against other rebellions that would dare threaten their rule.

The boy's uncle had called this

A Feast for Lambs

'Brahminization'.

He had said that 'Brahminization' was a form of religious terrorism that the radicals had mastered over the centuries, and it was by far the most efficient and effective act of silently taking over a religion or rebellion and diverting the cause away from its true purpose against ruling-caste oppression.

And there had been many minor rebellions against the ruling castes. Many minor rebellions and many major rebellions, much like the slave rebellions of ancient Rome. But Brahminical Society had managed to ostracize the most rebellious of the societies and turn all the other Hindu societies against them, using the other societies to their own political and economic ends.

Once the ruling caste had secured control of the original societies and stories of India, they used these very same methods to bring all the other religions under their control. And those religions that outright refused to be Brahminized, or those who protested against caste oppression, were sys-tematically erased or reduced to insignificance. Sikhs weren't being attacked or threatened by Hinduism. They never were. They were being attacked and threatened by extremists of one socie-ty. Those at the top of the caste pyramid who used Hinduism to their political and economic ends. And those at the top of the pyramid were not about to accept any protest against their birthright, nor did they want to stare at a uniform that reminded them and others of their oppression then and now.

And he remembered his uncle saying that, more than the Sikh baptismal uniform, the Brahmin radicals despised the Golden Temple and did so because of its very design. They despised the Golden Temple because its four entrances had been designed to welcome the four societies of Sanatana Dharma as equals. Because the Golden Temple did not ostracize the Shudra or create a special or opulent entrance for the Brahmin. All were equal in the Golden Temple. And this was unacceptable and incompatible with those who made up more than eighty percent of government and two percent of India's population.

The many free and interdependent societies of Sanatana Dharma, according to the boy's uncle, were the first religions to fall to Brahminical Society. Buddhism was second. Jainism third. Sikhism fourth. And the ruling society throughout history had been merciless in their attacks against those who would protest against their rule and hierarchy. And it was for this reason the Guru had taken such a hard and incontestable stance against the caste system.

And it was for this reason the ruling castes had chased Sikhs into the forests and jungles to exterminate these rebels against their society many centuries ago. And it was for this reason that any religion that began in protest against the one ruling society would not be recognized as a religion by the nation's constitution. It was for this reason the Golden Temple was attacked, destroyed, desecrated and the Sikh library incinerated. It was for this reason the radicals were using Hitler and the Nazis to inspire the masses to be more disciplined and patriotic when there were countless other good examples in the world of patriotism and discipline.

And it was for this reason his colony had been quarantined and his people exterminated by upper-caste patriots who sought to protect a system that afforded them a society of slaves. It was for this reason the radicals who dominated government were letting the patriots defend their nation's greatest resource with a seemingly endless supply of kerosene and weapons.

The Brahmin radicals were putting down one of the last major protests against the lie that placed one society as ruler of all societies. And if his uncle was right, then the best way, the very best way to honor all those who had died at the Golden Temple and in his colony was to never again give life through thoughts, words and actions to the caste system that enslaved so many Indians.

And to do this so that no people would ever have to suffer again at the hands of the radicals who would do anything to protect their ancient system of segregated oppression, and even--his uncle was sure and had said it many times--silence one of India's founding leaders.

And now, thinking of his uncle's words, thinking of the meaning of baptism, thinking of his Guru's words, the boy realized that his people were dying once again because of a bold protest his Guru had started centuries ago. Because his uniform, his very existence represented a very real and significant threat to a system of oppression that needed to be abolished in law and in mind.

And now, with all his soul, he vowed he would never in his life accept, support or give life to caste through his thoughts, words, or actions. Never. And he knew that to do so would be to disgrace all those warriors of old and all those who had to die so that a few radicals could silence the Guru's message of equality for all.

And then he had a sudden thought: Maybe he would dedicate his words and his songs to the complete and total abolishment of caste, and then he knew with a strange, mysterious clarity that his mother was right. She was absolutely right--

Life was too short for fluff.

He knew now that if he survived he would devote all his energies to change, and that one day he would write a song so powerful for the low castes that it would definitely inspire change. And he thought that maybe, just maybe, true victory against those who were trying to destroy his Guru's message was to remember the message, honor the message, reinforce the message, and to sing the message so loud that all of India would hear it just as all of India had heard their most beloved actor's message to kill all Sikhs.

All were one.

All were equal.

The Brahmin and the Shudra were equal-- both Brahmin and Shudra were worthy of integrity, freedom, respect and the right to hope and dream.

Caste was a lie.

Freedom is truth.

And truth would triumph.

Even if it took centuries.

A Feast for Lambs

And maybe, just maybe, his generation would not disappear as silently into the night as his persecutors would have liked or as they had cleverly planned.

Maybe, just maybe, his generation would be the generation to complete the rebellion and revolution his ancestors had started centuries ago. Maybe his generation would be the one to completely abolish from the Indian consciousness the now accepted control and tyranny of the ruling castes that allowed no lower caste the opportunity to learn or hope or dream--to live with dignity and integrity.

This would be victory.

This would be true victory.

And true victory was better, way better, than giving his persecutors their double victory. The boy thought all this in silence. After a moment Major sighed and continued talking about things the boy already knew about because of his uncle, who he longer saw as a gorilla.

"It's just a matter of time before other groups will be attacked. I'm not a prophet. I don't pretend to be. I'm just looking at history and what has happened in the past. What the Brahmin radicals did to the Golden Temple is nothing new. They did the exact same thing to the Buddhist temples long, long ago and all over India, and today you couldn't find a Buddhist temple if you tried."

He paused for a moment to regard all his scattered books as a wave of firelight shimmered over them, then he turned back to the boy's mother and continued.

"And this exact thing that is happening to the Sikhs today happened to them a hundred years ago, even though most Indians don't remember. But it isn't a new story. It is just a continuation of a very old one, with new weapons and ways to spread stories. A hundred years ago the Arya Samaj, led by Brahmins, persecuted the Muslims and the Christians and the Sikhs to protect their birthright. They even infiltrated their sacred places to push and promote idol worship and caste, and tried to weave these rituals into their religions. Their Mahants, disguised with turbans and beards, infiltrated Gurdwaras as puppet leaders, pretending to be Sikhs, and these Mahants made it so that only the upper castes could have lungar, when lungar was for all and had always been so. And very soon they did more, much more...they turned Gurdwaras into places of drug dealing and gambling and prostitution."

Major hesitated for a moment as if searching for something deep in his memory, then he continued:

"Sikhs resorted to peaceful protest against the Mahants to remove them from the Gurdwaras, but the Arya Samaj slaughtered hundreds of these protesters until finally the British stepped in with the law, and they enacted the Sikh Gurdwara Act, which purged the Gurdwaras of all these devious Mahants, who had been sent in by the radicals to deface and undermine the religion."

Major scoffed.

"But then the British left India and the Samaj took over-extremists took all positions of power and media, and the minorities were left to defend themselves, and what do we have now? Unrestrained murder and tyranny so that those at the top may remain at the top."

Major sighed gravely.

"If you look at history you will see that the Brahmin will never let his self-proclaimed birthright be challenged, and any religion or rebellion that does is cleverly and systematically undermined. It happened then, and it's happening now. And there is nothing to be done because their control of the government and industry and the nation's story is absolute."

Now the boy wondered how Major could know so much about Brahmin radicals and the Arya Samaj and the Mahants who had infiltrated and tried to destroy his religion more than a century ago. He thought about the Muslims and the Christians and the Buddhists and how they had been persecuted by the Arya Samaj, and then he thought about the Sikhs and the Golden Temple, and he wondered if a similar fate awaited them. Then he wondered something else. He suddenly wondered how Major knew so much about the Golden Temple, and he began to look at his face differently, and he suddenly thought that maybe, just maybe, a kirpan had made that scar, and that maybe he had killed Sikhs in Amritsar.

As though Major could feel the boy staring at his ripped face, he involuntarily touched his scar and ran his finger down its length. Pensively, he turned away from the boy and his mother and stared at the soft light flickering through the fissures. After a long reflective silence, he confessed:

"This is only happening now because the government knows the world doesn't care. For days we attacked Amritsar. For days we executed anyone who was Sikh. It didn't matter. Women. Children. The elderly. And for over a year we had been practicing the siege...over a year..."

He shook his head gravely and sighed with the memory.

"We could have cut electricity. We could have cut the water and power and starved the dissidents out in order to save lives...such a plan was proposed by a general...but Indira wanted to attack...she wanted to teach the Sikhs a lesson...break them...and the general...well, he retired because of it...he retired because he refused to attack the Golden Temple, refused to kill pilgrims when he knew there was another way."

The boy vaguely remembered hearing this from his uncle. Taking a deep breath, Major added:

"The general retired a year before the attack because he would not do what another would. He retired a full year before the attack because he outright refused to agree with Indira, who wanted a plan that would maximize, not minimize, Sikh casualties...to teach them a lesson..."

He laughed, but there was a profound sadness and regret in the laugh.

"To this day the world actually believes it was a last-minute decision. A general retires one year before the attack because he would not attack the Golden Temple and the world actually believes it was a last-minute decision. Isn't it a joke? It's

A Feast for Lambs

incredible what power can get away with in this country. Incredible. We could have listened to that general and taken an entire year to starve Bhindranwala out of the Golden Temple. Instead we took a year to practice on a mock temple in order to maximize damage and destroy what needed to be destroyed. History all over again..."

He shook his head.

"But we all knew it wasn't about Bhindranwala. It was about humiliation and it was about a show of strength. It was about showing the Sikhs all over the world what we could do to them without any consequences, and it was about something else--"

Outside they could hear a truck and a crew hard at work, clearing a lane not too far away. With a deep sigh, Major continued:

"For every dissident we killed, we killed ten families. We killed an entire generation of Sikhs and the world saw nothing, the world heard nothing, and the world did nothing."

The boy's eyes widened with blank disbelief and he clenched his teeth at Major's confession. Without realizing it he began to forget his thoughts of true victory against the radicals and his heart pounded furiously and felt ready to burst with rage; he felt as though at any moment he would attack Major for having been one of those jackals outside.

But he didn't.

He didn't, and he didn't know why he didn't, but he could see that somehow Major was in a hell of his own because of what he had done.

Suddenly he heard the truck shift gears. A moment later it rolled forward a few yards and screeched to a stop. The tired exertions of working men lifting and hauling and hefting could be heard over the cries of the dying. Major whispered almost to himself as if the guilt and shame of his whole country were laid upon him:

"We blocked out the media and journalists for a week and not a single person questioned what actually took place at the temple. Not one. Not even the date we chose. A perfect date. A date that attracted from all over the country the most devout and made it so that we could eliminate the most respectable and knowledgeable of the generation."

He sighed with the absurdity of what had taken place.

"The Sikhs wanted to protect their sacred temple and library; they wanted to be acknowledged in the constitution as a religion...they wanted to protect their language and identity...and...and we called them separatists so that we could kill them...and we killed them all...and the world bought it..."

Now the words seemed to come out without him wanting them to, as though he sensed his time coming and he needed to confess his dark deeds to the boy and his mother and empty his heart of its dark contents.

"We cleaned Amritsar and left only what we wanted them to see. All the bodies of the children gone...all the bodies of parents gone...disappeared along with everyone else who spoke against the injustices of this government." Major turned to the boy's mother. "No body, no evidence. No evidence, no crime."

Outside, the truck shifted gears and drove away. His mother seemed deeply disturbed by Major's words and appeared unsure how to react. She merely nodded and added:

"No crime, no justice."

"Justice," Major laughed cynically. "There's no justice in India. Not for minorities. And even if there were--" His voice rose with anger-- "Even if there were such a thing as justice in India there can never be enough justice. Not for this. Never."

He lowered his voice so that the boy couldn't hear him.

The boy angled his ear slightly and listened.

"A thousand lawyers working for a thousand years will never bring even an ounce of justice for that boy who hid behind a desk and had to watch his mother raped and beaten and burned alive by three Indian soldiers. What justice? There isn't enough justice for that poor boy."

Major suddenly broke and a silent tear slipped down his cheek. The boy's mother said:

"There is God."

Major scoffed at the mere mention of God but said nothing. He lowered his head and closed his eyes and tears of regret rolled down his face, glistening in the soft, flickering firelight. When his tears subsided, he cleared his throat and spoke in a strange, cryptic voice. "I have this dream," he said, opening his eyes and turning to her. "Always the same dream. I don't always remember my dreams but this one...this one I remember...this one is something else."

He paused to collect his thoughts, and the boy thought about his recurring dream. Then Major looked back toward the street and continued:

"It's a strange dream. I don't know how I get there, but I somehow find myself walking through an endless desert. Only when I look at the ground I realize I'm not walking through sand but something living. I mean...things are moving all around my feet, slimy things, wet things, really awful things. When I look closer I realize I'm walking through a desert of vermin, of maggots and crawlers and serpents. And as I walk through this desert I suddenly--and I'm not sure how I get there--find myself in this village. And this village is a ghost village way out in the middle of nowhere. And so now I'm wading up to my knees in vermin and I'm not sure why but I'm sinking and I'm sinking, deeper and deeper with every step."

Major stopped. He seemed to be seeing the dream in his mind now, and the boy wondered what it meant to be walking through a desert of vermin. He wondered if this had any symbolic significance to real life, or if walking through fog had similar significance. His grandmother would have said so. With a sigh, Major continued:

"Then I suddenly become aware that I'm thirsty. Not just thirsty. Thirstier than I've ever felt in my life. I look around for water and then I look at the homes, and for the first time I notice men in the doorways staring at me but not saying anything. They're people I recognize. People I hurt. Not with my hands, but with my silence. Not by what I did, but what I didn't do, and what I let happen. All of them looking like they did before they were incinerated. Tortured. Tormented. Faces frozen in agony, just staring at me. And as I walk by their homes their wives walk behind them and their eyes are black. Black like I have never seen. Black and empty...expressionless..."

He breathed in a deep breath. His voice lowered. His eyes dimmed.

"I try to run out of the village but now my legs won't budge, and when I look down, I suddenly realize I'm up to my waist in vermin and I can feel them crawling all around me, up and down my pants. I stop moving because I don't want to sink. But it's too late, and I'm already sinking in vermin like quicksand. I start screaming for help, but no one helps. They just stare at me with their black, expressionless eyes and they watch as the desert and the silence swallows me whole. That's when I wake up."

The boy and his mother sat silently. He could see that Major was now struggling to hold back more tears and that his lips trembled involuntarily. A sound of men shouting nearby startled them. When there was silence again, Major regarded the boy's mother. "I don't know about God," he said. "But I do know that they are waiting for me and I will be made to account for what I have done and for what I have not done."

He turned back toward the street. The boy thought he could hear men combing the street. "If there is justice," Major added solemnly, "each victim will have a turn with me...and I...I want them to..."

The boy understood now that Major was in hell and his guilt and remorse was more than impossible to bear.

"How many have they murdered?" Major asked himself. "Does it matter? One person killed for his beliefs is already too many. One. A thousand. A million. It's the same dark intention."

He turned to look at the boy's mother.

"This will only continue and the world won't say a word; not about this, not about the Golden Temple, not about the disappearances; and when the world does finally decide to act it will already be too late. And history will do as it does best."

The boy thought about this, and he wasn't exactly sure he knew what history did best. He waited for an explanation that never came. After a reflective silence, Major leaned forward to regard the boy and he said:

"You get out of this place and you live with your brother."

The boy nodded severely.

"And you remember this. You remember all of it. And you never forget."

The boy nodded. He would remember everything. Despite what Major had done, the boy sensed he was getting a message through him from somewhere else. Despite what Major had done, he felt he was staring at a warrior of old and that Major was being used as a tool to convey a very important message from the unknown and unknowable.

"And you never let fear enter your heart and turn you into a lamb like me."

The boy nodded.

"And when you get to that jungle, that free jungle, where lions can be lions, you have to do one thing, only one thing, and that thing is your responsibility, and it is a huge responsibility. It is the responsibility of all who live in free jungles."

The boy waited. Major just stared with his glass eye that seemed to see right through the boy and into the future. "What?" the boy asked at last when he thought Major had forgotten to tell him what his responsibility would be.

Major hadn't forgotten.

He answered simply:

"Roar."

"Roar?"

Major nodded. "Roar."

The boy grinned slightly. The first grin since the slaughter had begun. He thought that maybe this was a joke and that perhaps Major was taking his lion and lamb story a measure too seriously. But Major suddenly grabbed his wrist and shook him to let him know how serious he was. Then he touched his kara and with rising passion he said:

"Roar so loud the whole world trembles! Roar so loud that what happened here and at the Golden Temple is never forgotten. Roar so loud that all your ancestors who died for Truth hear you and know that they did not die in vain, and that without a shadow of a doubt that there still exists in the mortal realm a lion ready to meet the tyrant, no matter what the consequences. "

The boy felt something powerful and inde-scribable enter him, something like electricity, like pure energy, and he nodded with all his being and his nod was a promise to be that lion and tears came to his eyes as he thought about his ancestors.

And he promised God that if he could somehow survive this and if he could somehow find his way to a free jungle he would honor the duty and responsibility of all those living in a free jungle, and he would roar so loud the whole world would tremble. He would use his voice. He would use his voice and he would roar. And he would remember Major's words for as long as he lived. He closed his eyes and prayed inwardly.

Please give me one chance and I promise that everyone will know...everyone will know...give me the chance and I promise every song to be a golden arrow in the tyrant's heart. Spare me and my mother and I will do this.

For a long while the boy thought about Major's words while his mother closed her eyes and prayed softly. With a deep, difficult breath, Major stood slowly and made his way to the broken wall and stared out into the street where the small fires were now extinguishing one by one.

A sudden clanking noise below startled them.

Then another.

The boy's mother turned to Major. They exchanged worried looks, then Major placed a silencing finger by his lips and pointed downward

A Feast for Lambs

to the room below, indicating that there was someone searching his home for valuables. His mother
nodded, and the boy stared at the dark, wool blanket covering the hole, praying no one would find
them.

೮ಽ

A muffled shuffling noise came from below. Someone was picking their way through the over-turned chairs and furniture, rummaging through the mess. Stiff with fear, the boy strained his ears as Major crept noiselessly toward the hole. There he positioned himself behind the opening and waited in the faint light. Someone shuffled and cursed downstairs. The boy could hear the jackal kicking around furniture and cutlery and ornaments.

Major gazed down at the blanket, ready, but suddenly he realized he had forgotten his weapon. He looked up at the boy and motioned, indicating the crowbar, silently letting him know that it was leaning against the broken wall should he need it.

His mother saw this. She turned to regard the crowbar, then she turned back to Major and nodded; but she had misunderstood. He didn't want her moving or walking about. He didn't want her compromising their den.

When she made an effort to secure the crowbar, Major motioned her to stop at once, waving her still with his hand. Then he pointed down-ward and, placing a silencing finger by his mouth, shook his head, and motioned for her to stay put.

He didn't want to take any chances.

At this the boy's mother nodded her under-standing and stayed put while the man below continued to rummage through Major's belongings. Curious, the boy looked past the scattered books on the floor and leaned toward a hole in the floor to see who was lurking about. But his mother held him back, knowing that the slightest sound could give them away. Then, all of a sudden, to their collective relief, the rummaging and shuffling noises stopped.

They all stared at the blanket for a long while.

Nothing.

The man below must have silently left and moved on to another home. But just as the boy thought this he heard a barely audible sound which told him that the intruder was tiptoeing about the room. It sounded like he was investigating something he had found hidden in the shadows. Then it sounded like he was walking away. A long, tense silence followed. They waited, staring at the blanket. Then he heard it. A slight creaking.

The ladder.

Another creak.

And another.

Silence.

To everyone's horror the intruder had discovered the ladder.

The boy tensed. His eyes widened as he watched the blanket for the slightest movement. There was another soft creak, but no movement. He stared hard. Nothing. His mother also had her eyes fixed on the blanket. Major shifted slightly, adjusting his position, preparing.

The boy wasn't sure what he was planning to do, but he could see he had something in mind. He angled his left ear toward the ladder, straining to hear something, anything.

The intruder seemed to be right at the threshold of the attic, unsure about what he would discover above. The thought of capture sent chills down the boy's spine. He took in a deep breath and tried to keep his composure. He held his breath for a long moment, then released the warm, stinging air slowly.

His mother stared at the crowbar in the faint, flickering light, and the boy could tell that she was considering a quick dash for it, but she stayed put just in case he hadn't actually found the ladder; just in case all the creaks and subtle noises had come from an exhausted and overactive imagination.

There was a sudden noise. And then another creak as the intruder seemed to descend and walk away. They could hear steps walking toward the door. They heard the door creak open and shut. Then there was silence. They all stared at each other and exhaled a collective breath of relief. The boy looked up at Major and he thanked God for sparing them.

Soundlessly, the boy moved slowly to the edge of the bed, but his mother quickly held him back with an urgency that frightened him. She seemed to have sensed something or heard something. Then, just as Major was about to return to them, the blanket began to rise slightly like a ghost.

The bottom dropped out of the boy's stomach as he watched the rising ghost stop suddenly. A moment later he watched the blanket descend again. The intruder seemed to be uneasy; he seemed to be testing to see if anything else was covering the hole and blanket.

All eyes now watched the blanket and waited patiently for the inevitable.

Major widened his legs. He squatted slightly, fully concentrated on the moment, waiting like a panther in the dark. It was just a matter of time.

The boy listened hard. He had not heard anyone else downstairs. He was sure that this was a jackal that had purposely straggled away to secure loot he wouldn't have to share with the rest of the crew. The thought that he was alone made him feel that they might have a chance as long as he didn't posses a firearm.

With difficulty, the boy tried to stifle his panic, but fear clutched him by the throat as the blanket began to rise again. This time the blanket didn't stop; this time it didn't pause; this time it kept on rising until a dark face emerged and white eyes stared directly at the boy and his mother huddled on the bed.

The man didn't seem to see them at first.

He just stared blankly at the books, the bed, the crumbling wall and the mother and the boy trembling in the shimmering light and shadow. Then he seemed to see them for the first time as he framed them in his wicked, bloodshot eyes--eyes full of destruction and murder and dark intention.

A slow, menacing smile blossomed on the

man's face, revealing white, crooked teeth.
Time seemed to stop as the boy held the man's
dreadful gaze.

Then, when the man noticed the boy's eye
suddenly flicker to a towering shadow behind him,
he instantly realized his error and lost his smile.

In a move so fast the man had no time to
react, Major lunged downward, wrapped his arm
around the man's neck and lifted him straight off
the ladder into a fierce, deadly chokehold.

The man's legs pushed and kicked and
lashed at the empty air as Major squeezed the neck
harder and harder. Instinctively, the boy's mother
held the boy to her chest and attempted to turn his
head away without success. Even when his face
was smothered against her neck the boy could still
see everything through the corner of his eye.

He could see the man fighting for his life,
trying to slam and swipe Major with his hands. He
saw how he whipped his legs around and flopped
and thrashed like a fish in a net. He could hear him
choke and wheeze and sputter out life as he tried to
squirm out of Major's lock. And just when he
thought the man had breathed his last, he watched
him desperately sink his teeth into Major's arm and
bite through cloth, flesh and bone.
Major shrieked painfully, releasing the man so that
he fell through the hole, down the ladder and hit
the cement ground with a loud thud.

Staggering back against the wall, Major
breathed hard and seemed relieved it was over and
that they were safe.

But the boy had another feeling. A strange

feeling. He wasn't so sure. So he pushed away from his mother to see for himself. But when he reached the hole and looked to the ground he didn't see a corpse, he didn't see anything, but he heard the man struggling desperately toward the door.

The boy looked up to Major with panicked eyes that spoke more than words.

With instant understanding, Major flew down the ladder to make sure this man didn't escape to tell his crew about what he had found. As he rushed down, the boy hurried to a crack in the floor to observe the scene. Within seconds, his mother was beside him, staring through another small hole in the floor. When Major disappeared from his vision, the boy swiftly shuffled over the floor searching and scattering books everywhere to find another crack or fissure to watch what was happening below.

With a yell, Major charged the man and rammed him into the door. Then, with terrible violence, he grabbed his shoulders and yanked him back and thrust his head against the wall. Then he threw him to the ground, climbed over his stomach, held his arms down with the weight of his knees and wrapped his hands around his neck to finish the job his arm had started earlier.

The man spat and sputtered saliva and blood and his eyes bulged and nearly burst with pressure. But the man would not die. He refused to die. He struggled for small breaths of life any chance he could, and the boy could hear him desperately sucking air through a blocked throat.

Major squeezed harder and harder and

would not stop until he wrung out every last drop of this man's dark soul. With rising adrenalin, he pounded his head against the floor, as though trying to smash and shatter it like a mango. The boy watched him pound the man mercilessly in the living shadows as the man somehow managed to jerk one of his arms free.

With his breath caught in his throat, the boy watched as Major then took a second, just a second, to search the floor for something sharp to end the man's life.

It was just a second, but it was--

A second too long.

As Major reached over to grab a shard of glass, the man plunged a kirpan he had looted off a Sikh straight into Major's belly.

Major paused for a moment, incredulously. He gasped with the pain and his head sagged with the sudden loss of blood. He wheezed painfully as his fingers loosened around the shard. The man coughed and wheezed and cursed and swore he wouldn't be killed by a Sikh dog.

But then, to the boy's surprise, Major found strength again. With great difficulty, the hand squeezed the shard tightly. Slowly, he raised the glass blade over the man's head; but then, again, froze with pain shooting up his stomach and didn't seem capable of bringing the weapon down.

The man smiled.

The boy bit his lip, and his hand scrunched to an anxious fist.

The man's eyes flashed victory, and he cursed something inaudible at Major.

The boy looked to his mother, who stared through a smaller hole with disbelieving eyes. She seemed to have stopped breathing. The boy prayed that this would all be over soon, that Major could find the strength he needed to do what needed to be done.

After a moment that felt like forever the boy watched as Major suddenly found his will and strength and the shard fell viciously into the side of the man's head.

The man let out a terrible beast-like cry and they both shrieked in agony as Major pulled downward with the last of his strength and ripped the man's face open like a melon, cutting all the way to his mouth, doing what had clearly been done to him.

With a deep breath, Major then raised the dripping, crimson shard above his head. Thick, warm blood from a deep gash in his hand slipped down his arm and dripped onto the man's torn face. Ignoring his pain, he raised the shard again and prepared to deliver the deathblow.

But just when he went to plunge the shard into the man's neck, the man, filled with adrenalin and the will to live, instantly jerked forward, grabbed the hilt of the kirpan with both hands and pulled upward with all his might. Another scream shook the night. This time from Major, and it was more than he could bear.

The man released the kirpan, then covered his torn face with his hands as Major fell backward with a gasp. On his back, hardly able to move, he looked up at the ceiling and gazed at the boy.

A Feast for Lambs

Seeing the boy seemed to give him strength. He pushed himself to his side. He then attempted to clamber to his feet. He fell once, twice, thrice, then finally stood on quivering legs. He staggered left, right, then fell back against the closest wall. He had nothing left. He was finished despite his every attempt to continue. He sighed. A moment later he sank to the ground in the shadows where the boy could no longer see him.

The boy gasped in horror. He couldn't tell if Major was dead or alive. He wanted to do something but fear had paralyzed him as he watched the man stand with difficulty. Then he watched the man stagger wearily toward Major to finish the job, if it wasn't already finished.

The boy felt his heart pound.

The thing growing in his heart was now screaming for blood.

Everything in him wanted to rush down and help his friend. But his hands were trembling and fear had completely overwhelmed him. He had never hurt anyone in his life. He had never even argued with anyone other than his older brother.

But he knew he had to act.

He knew he needed to do something.

But he wasn't exactly sure what that something was.

Now the man approached Major, slowly, menacingly. He kneeled by him and the boy heard him whisper a few words that instantly told him that Major was alive. But he wouldn't be for very long unless he did something. He knew he had to act, and yet he couldn't move. He couldn't budge.

All he could do was watch.

Suddenly Major cried out in pain.

The man was playing with him. Toying with him. Making him suffer. Twisting and jerking the kirpan. The thing in the boy's heart cried out that it wanted to be free. To be free and to do its dark and beautiful work.

Major screamed again.

Now the boy couldn't see what the man was doing but he could hear Major begging the man for mercy, begging the man to stop, whispering and wheezing that he could take no more.

Another anguished cry and plea.

The man cursed at Major and promised he would prolong his suffering for as long as he could for what he had done to his face.

Another cry.

Major begged for death.

And another.

The man cursed.

The boy breathed fast and hard. He closed his eyes and prayed for strength, courage and protection. Then, as he prayed for help, in the darkness of his mind he heard something shift beside him. His eyes instantly sprang open and he turned to face his mother.

But she was gone.

She was nowhere to be found.

He quickly looked through the floor to see his mother, holding a crowbar, creep up toward the man as he tortured and tormented Major.

The boy held his breath as she approached. She was like a lioness prowling in the darkness. She would do it. She would kill this man because she knew that if she didn't they were next.

But as she neared the man, she stepped over glass and debris and the crack and crunch suddenly startled the jackal.

Without thought, he turned to evade a blow that would have cracked his head open but instead cracked the cement floor so hard that the boy thought he heard his mother's wrist snap in two.

The crowbar instantly bounced out of her hands and fell to the ground with a terrible, reverberating clang.

At this the man let out a laugh, rushed toward her, grabbed her by the shoulders and threw her against a chair, breaking it. Before she could scramble to her feet he was on her again. Without effort he lifted her to her feet by a fistful of hair and slammed her against the door. He pushed her head against the door as though trying to crush it. Then he stared into her eyes and whispered something foul in her ears.

No! No! No!

The boy couldn't believe what was happening. He felt like he was watching a movie. Everything felt surreal. He wanted to do something but didn't know what to do. And now he was shaking and moving but he was hardly conscious of his movements or what he was doing or what he was not doing to help his mother. And yet he couldn't take his eyes off her.

The man said a few more words and he went to smell her neck as though she were a rare flower. As he did, she suddenly jolted her head and chomped down on his torn face and shook and yanked like a beast and ripped a chunk of flesh straight off his shrieking face.

Instantly the boy saw black spots in his mind as fear, anger and rage surged through his body.

The man fell back screaming and cursing.

Without fear or hesitation she quickly tackled him to the ground and began smashing his head in a warm pool of Major's blood. The man struggled to breathe, to thrust her off. But she was all anger and adrenalin. A lioness protecting her cub.

With incredible rage she pounded his face and splattered and splashed blood in every direction. With two hands she pushed his nose into the dark pool and shrieked for him to die. To just die. His hands smashed and splashed blood everywhere as he tried to pull her off without success.

The boy was hardly conscious of all this. Even though his mother was okay, something inside pulled at him, and wanted that man to pay. It was a feeling beyond his control and everything started going black and he thought he was fainting as he shifted in and out of consciousness.

The man crawled desperately out of the blood. The boy's mother continued to ravage him, hitting and smashing him with everything she had.

But everything wasn't enough.

In a split second she accidentally slipped in the blood, lost her balance and fell right beside him. She rushed to regain her position, but as she stood he quickly lunged at her and grabbed her by the

A Feast for Lambs

wrists.

The boy struggled for every painful breath as he watched this and his heart felt ready to burst at any moment.

With the last of his strength, the man thrust himself forward and he savagely yanked the boy's mother downward, smashing the ridge of her nose with his forehead. The boy heard the crunch of bone and cartilage, and his mother fell back soundlessly.

She flopped around in the blood and attempted to crawl away.

But she was defeated.

Black clouded the boy's vision. He barely understood what was happening to him. Now and then he saw the man kicking his mother with full blows in the stomach. It was all happening in slow motion and hyper speed at the same time. He felt strange, like the thing in his heart was almost free and that with a few more efforts it would be born. Then, all at once, everything went black.

Completely black.

When the boy's vision returned, he didn't know how much time had passed but the man was now punching his mother with full blows in the face.

Exhausted, the man quit his savage assault and rose slowly.

He stood over her, gasping.

His hand touched his mangled and mutilated face and he cursed vengeance. Then he moved to the door. He opened it and filled the room with a soft, flickering orange light. A moment later he returned to the boy's mother, kneeled behind her and, with both hands, grabbed her firmly by the hair and dragged her, kicking and screaming into the street.

Everything after that happened in slow motion as the boy moved without realizing what he was doing. He rushed to the broken wall and stared down at his mother lying in the middle of the street. He searched for the man but couldn't find him. He could only see his mother lying on the ground, holding her nose as she drifted in and out of consciousness.

Get up! Get up!

A moment later the man returned with a tin can of kerosene.

No! Please no!

Fear, rage and hate filled the boy's heart at once, and as the man doused his mother with kerosene the thing pushed with all its might and burst free and all went black as the rage blood pounded through his veins and the dark thing rushed out of his heart and surged through him, turning fear into fury and fury into hate and hate into venom and venom into something else.

Outside, the man tossed the empty kerosene can to the ground and kicked it away. He felt his face again and swore that all Sikhs were dogs. Then he pulled out a pack of matches and gave the boy's mother one last look of disgust.

It was the last look he ever gave anyone in his dark murderous life.

With the most savage cry a child can make, the back of the man's head caved in and instantly froze his face in time. The man staggered forward, then back, then he turned to face the boy as his life slowly oozed out of his shattered skull.

The man stared at the boy for a moment, incredulous. He still didn't seem to realize that he was dead and that everything that would happen from this point on was a matter of minor details.

With another terrible cry, the boy, drunk with rage, raised the crowbar high above his head and let it crack against the man's forehead. The man crumpled before him as another blow came and he was stuck again and again.

Harder.

And harder.

And again.

With all his strength.

Slowly, his mother regained herself as the boy lost himself in his fury. She stood with difficulty and just watched as the boy turned muscle and bone to liquid and paste. She didn't even try to stop him. She just watched sadly as the boy lost himself with every blow he delivered.

In the burning street, with smoke and fire burning in the boy's eyes, he bludgeoned the head until he no longer saw the look on the man's face, until he was sure the man could no longer hurt his mother, until there was no head.

Just a pulpy paste of bone fragments and flesh.

Exhausted, the boy released the crowbar and stared at what he had done. The dead man's hands twitched and groped around, as if searching for his head, as if still not sure if he was dead or alive. And the boy stared at the headless, twitching body for a long while, letting the sweat, carbon and blood drip off his face. He looked back at his mother, then the corpse.

And then it hit him.

He had done this.

The blackness slowly dissipated and the rage blood slowly drained from his mind as the creature let the boy see his dark work. Shame, regret and disbelief washed over him.

He had killed a man.

He staggered backward and fell into his mother's arms. He looked up at her and she held his gaze and said nothing. There was nothing she could say. There was nothing to say.

After a long silence she took a deep breath and began to wipe her son's face with her chunni. As she did, she stared at the headless body, and she stared at Major's home.

When she wiped what she could from his face, she embraced him and held him tight with her eyes closed. Then, after a long silence with only the small fires burning and crackling around them, they heard a shout echo through the gloom.

And another.

Her eyes sprang open.

Men were calling out a name as they combed what was left of the colony for Sikhs.

She released her son with a terrible gasp.

They were close.

Real close.

She instantly took in the scene on the street. She turned in the direction of the sound. The boy,

A Feast for Lambs

too. He could see faint shadows. Flickering firelight. Men holding torches as they searched the
ruined puccas for their friend.

His mother looked at the body, then the
men, the body, then the men. Then the boy suddenly saw something flash in her eye as she decided.
But he wasn't sure what her eyes were telling him.

She kneeled to pick up the crowbar, then
she grabbed him by the arm. "Come quick!" she
said in a firm, commanding voice. "Come!" She
grabbed his wrist and rushed him back into Major's
home.

As they surged inside, the boy pulled away
from her and quickly rushed to his friend, but froze
when he saw that both of his eyes were lifeless. She
put her hand on his shoulder and ordered:

"Quick! Go up and hide!"

"No."

He turned from Major to face her.

"Bete, no time to discuss. Go up now."

He barely took in her words. A terrible cer-
tainty was darkening his kingdom. In a sudden
rush of understanding he vaulted toward her and
wrapped his arms around her waist and never
wanted to let go. And his heart was telling him that
he was right and that he should never let go. "No,"
he said. "No..."

He knew what she was about to do; what
she had decided when she realized there wasn't
enough time to clear the area. She was about to
make sure her son had the safest and most secure
hiding place in the colony.

"You need to hide."

"You need to hide, too."

"Please…"

"No…"

He knew, and she couldn't fool him. Not this time. Not his heart.

She didn't have to tell him anything. He had seen her gaze at the body and the crew. They would find the body and they would search until they had found the Sikh who had killed their friend. And he knew she would give them exactly what they wanted.

She pushed him gently away and kneeled before him. "Listen! Listen to me. It's okay. "

"No…it's not okay…it's not okay…" His head fell and his throat was thick with inexpressible fear, uncertainty and an impossible sadness.

She lifted his chin. "Don't do this to me now. Head up…"

"Back straight…" he finished for her and straightened his back.

"Yes, back straight," she said, and suddenly unmistakable tears filled her eyes. "Back straight, always…."

Tears slipped down her soot-covered face. No…God…no…

Now he knew with a hideous certainly that she was about to leave him and that there was nothing he could do to stop her and that he would never see her again. There was nothing he could say. She had decided and she would do whatever she had to do. His lips quivered beyond control. She cleared her throat, wiped her tears, and became

A Feast for Lambs

calm and militant.

"Listen! I haven't given up, have you?"

The boy shook his head slowly, staring at her tears that continued despite her every effort to restrain them or swipe them away. He stared at his mother, trying desperately to etch every last feature, every last detail in his memory. A tear dripped off her chin and fell on his kara and, clearing her throat, she suddenly said and sounded like a warrior of old:

"Son of Guru Gobind Singhji!"

The words entered his ears and his face instantly tensed with the power of the name--with the name of the Guru who had given Sikhs their uniform, the Guru who had prevented their extinction, the Guru who had refused to embrace or accept the injustices and oppression of caste, the Guru who had given them the confidence and resolve to face any tyrant who would dare infringe on the rights and liberties of a people. An unexplainable emotion surged through him and he suddenly looked at his mother as though she were truly a warrior of old. The kind he read about in the stories.

She grabbed his hands. "Listen to me. You need you to listen to me."

He nodded that he would, and he understood that she was right and he needed to listen to her, and that she was doing what she felt in her heart was best. He knew that she would die a thousand terrible deaths before she would ever let the jackals have him. And he knew he would do the same for her. Only she was the parent and she had the final say.

"I need you to go up and I need you to cover that hole."

"You too...please..."

He couldn't help himself.

Silent tears streamed from her eyes, and she couldn't answer. She nodded faintly, then firmly, but he wasn't convinced. He repeated:

"You too, please."

She nodded again, and she said:

"I'll be with you soon."

"You will?"

"I will."

At this promise he instantly held out his pinky. She looked at it and her eyes unwillingly filled again, and those tears told his heart that she was about to make a promise she couldn't keep. Slowly, she extended her pinky, wrapped it around his and shook it firmly.

"I'll be with you...soon...promise..."

The words were thick like dough in her mouth. She could hardly breathe. Tears dripped off her chin onto the floor. Men called out a name. A moment later she embraced him hard, then urgently conducted him to the ladder. She kneeled so that she could look at him in the eyes one last time, and he looked at her to remember her forever.

He didn't want her to go, and he instantly threw his arms around her again and his heart ached and felt very heavy and cold. He could feel her soundless tears slipping down against his face. Then, when another yell rang out from outside, she gently pushed the boy away and motioned for him to ascend the ladder.

He nodded, gave her a look that told her he loved her forever, then he rushed up the ladder as fast as he could. When he was safe, he stared down at her.

She gave him one last loving look, telling him she would be with him forever, then she forced her gaze away and, without looking at the boy, she lifted the crowbar--

And smashed the ladder down into bits and pieces so that it could never be put back together again. He wanted to shout for her to stop but it was already too late.

Outside the Jackals hollered.

They were close now.

The boy could hear them approaching. They were checking every corner, every crevice, every place a Sikh might hide. Then suddenly he heard one jackal yell that he had found their friend or someone who was wearing the same clothes as him.

As the man yelled that a Sikh dog had killed him, the boy watched his mother edge closer and closer to the door as she prepared to charge out and lead them as far away from her cub as she could.

With his heart in his mouth, the boy rushed to a hole in the floor and watched her as she eyed the men outside. He heard one man yell that they would find the Sikh that had killed their friend and that they were probably close by. His mother eased the door open. He watched her steady herself. He watched her tense. Then he watched as she turned toward the hole as though she knew he was watching. She looked at him to say good-bye and seemed to never want to look away. But a yell from the street snapped her back to reality, and she turned to face the jackals and she fearlessly bolted out into the burning street. At once the jackals started and shouted and rushed after her and a sorrow so profound filled the boy that he thought he would die of grief alone.

Without conscious thought, the boy snapped to his feet and rushed to the broken wall and watched as his mother rushed through the dark on weary legs--a battered and wounded lioness charging through the night, determined to lead these dreadful, bloodthirsty jackals as far away from her cub as she could.

Every muscle in the boy's face quivered uncontrollably. His mouth opened but no sound came out. He wanted to say something, anything, but there was nothing in him, and he watched his mother until she disappeared into the darkness. When she was gone, he listened and strained his ears with his mouth caught in a soundless scream as though frozen in eternity.

All the boy heard was a terrible, oppressive silence, and he wasn't sure if this silence came from the world or his heart.

Tears filled his eyes.

After a moment he smashed the broken wall with a clenched fist. His mouth quivered and began to close. Then it opened again, and closed, and opened, and closed, again and again, as though something were trying to escape. Then all at once his mouth jolted open and a sound so terrible, so painful suddenly erupted from the boy.

The sound of perfect agony to add a final note to the symphony of death that had begun days ago.

He screamed until there was nothing left in him to scream. He screamed until his throat ached and felt as though it were being torn to pieces. He screamed, and heard nothing but the great emptiness that replaced what had once been a boundless kingdom of love, joy and endless dreams.

And then he stopped.

And he stared vacantly into the street, barely able to process all that had just happened. All that he knew was that his mother was--

Gone.

❧

Through a smoke like fog or fog like smoke the boy trudged toward a voice--his mother's voice, singing and humming softly his grandmother's favorite hymn. He moved here and there searching for her, faster and faster, swiping the fog as he desperately called out for her. But every time he thought he might have found her, he lost her again, and he could hear her somewhere else. It was as though the fog was alive, taunting him, laughing at him, purposely playing games with him.

He called out for her.

But there was no answer.

Again.

Still no answer.

Only the darkness and the fog that surrounded him and swirled around his feet and legs and body and brought to his ears his mother's gentle song; it pained his heart with every note as the fog grew thicker and thicker so that he could barely see five inches in front of him.

The boy lumbered on. Slowly his mother's song faded away and was replaced by another sound. A harsh sound. A familiar sound. He peered through the fog but saw nothing, heard only the hard breathing and exertions of working men over the soft, crackling of fires he couldn't see and that seemed to burn all around him.

All he could see was the thick, stale fog as he walked on and on through the burning jungle, listening and searching, unsure of what he would find or what lay ahead of him.

Then, again, he heard his mother's voice.

Only she wasn't singing.

She was pleading, pleading for her life as the men continued to work hard to clean a jungle they were claiming as their own. His walk suddenly turned into a jog, then his jog turned to a run as she begged for her life and told the men that she had two boys that needed her and that she didn't want to die.

With impossible speed, the boy charged through the fog as it lifted and swirled away laughingly so as to reveal a precipice where two tall and lanky silhouettes held his mother by the ankles and wrists. They swung her back and forth like a sack of salt, building momentum as she begged and pleaded to be spared. But the demons just stared at a faceless man in a spotless white kurta who stood by a mound of bodies, surveying their work, holding in his hand the slave master's whip.

As the boy approached them he extended his hand out for them to stop; but they barely noticed him, and with cold indifference, the white kurta nodded, and the men suddenly released his mother into the abyss.

The boy screamed as loud as his lungs permitted, and the silhouettes turned slowly to regard him as he pounded the ground with his feet and rushed toward the precipice.

A Feast for Lambs

Rushing toward the slave master and his slaves, the boy gasped when he realized the men had no faces.

Just one slab of melted skin like the melted wax of a candle.

Then the faceless man in the white kurta pajama signaled for the men to ignore the boy and to continue their endless work for their jungle. The slaves nodded in unison, walked over to the mound and grabbed another body by the ankles and wrists and carried it to the edge of the precipice just as the boy surged past them.

Without looking at the slaves, without the slightest hesitation, the boy charged after his mother and leapt fearlessly off the precipice.

Screaming, the boy fell through the endless darkness and thought he would fall forever when suddenly he crashed into a mountain of bones with a loud, deafening crunch.

Groaning, the boy lay there covered in broken bones and the hideous smell of death in his lungs. He stared above at the pale, grey light. He could see unnatural vultures the size of cars circling above him, and he could hear millions of flies buzzing around as the bodies continued to crash like bombs one after another into the mountain of bones.

After a long while the boy collected himself and dug out of the bones and scrambled to his feet. It wasn't long before horror squeezed his heart and throat as he realized he was standing upon a massive burial ground.

When the boy looked closer, he realized he

was standing on an endless mountain of lion bones. Lions that had once been and who would never be again. Lions that had been erased from the jungle, from existence, never to be heard from or seen again.

Dead.

Forgotten.

Gone.

With a deep sigh he began to walk through this secret graveyard. He gasped as he took in the thousands upon thousands of bones, and he started every time a body crashed like a bomb close to him, sending a massive cloud of white dust and soot into the air.

One body fell so close to him that a shock-wave sent him stumbling back on his haunches. After that he didn't stand up for a long while. He couldn't stand up. He just sat in mute silence, staring blankly at the endless peaks and valleys of bones before him. Then, as he stared hopelessly into the nightmare, the living fog filled the endless graveyard once again and swirled all around him and brought to his ears his mother's song.

She sang gently as though trying to bring peace to his anxious heart. Hearing her words, the boy clambered to his feet and began to search for her.

He whispered for her.

And she continued to sing God's praises, filling his heart with strength, courage and truth, as though trying to kill that dark thing that had been born inside him.

And then in the distance he noticed a soft,

white light piercing the fog. He tumbled over the bones and charged toward the light, reaching out for it like a firefly just out of reach. With every stride it seemed to be moving farther and farther away from him.

Chasing the light desperately, he suddenly stopped as the singing voice began to whisper his name. He rushed again, this time with impossible speed, and when he was only inches away from the light he lunged out and grasped the thick fog and unwittingly tumbled down the side of the mountain, sending bones and clouds of dust in every direction.

When at last he slammed against the ground and found himself on his back, he felt the light hovering above him. Staring at the light, he heard his mother's voice and she whispered his name. He answered in a weak voice:

"I'm here ..."

Then she whispered a message that she had wanted him to remember and remember always. A message from one of the stories she had always shared with him. And the message was simple, and yet the message was everything. In a soft, fading whisper, she said:

"Fear not, frighten not."

And she said nothing more.

"No," he cried. "Don't go! No!"

But as he pleaded, the light faded away and plunged him into perfect darkness.

And his mother was gone.

Suddenly, a piercing wail jarred the boy awake with a desperate cry.

With puffy, dry eyes and a wet face he woke in a small, crammed attic filled with a pale grey, unnatural light that could barely pierce the thick carbon air that poured through the broken wall. It burned his nostrils, his mouth and his throat with every breath.

The boy didn't move for a long time. He just stared at the ceiling, wondering how long his wearied and exhausted mind had fallen asleep with his eyes wide open. He didn't know he could fall asleep with his eyes open, but he had, and now he didn't know what day it was. He didn't know how long he had been there. He didn't know if it was morning or afternoon or if he had fallen asleep for one or two or even three days. There was just the carbon fog, the smell of rotting humanity, and his dry, swollen eyes that felt like they had cried for an eternity and would never cry again.

The boy felt so weak and empty inside.

He didn't want to eat, but he knew he had to.

Wearily, he slowly reached into his pocket and searched for the last piece of perfect burfee. But when he pulled out the cloth along with his glove, he found it stained with something foul, dark and rotten. He let the burfee fall to his side along with a brown, fetid glove that would never reflect light again. Then he released a deep breath and stared vacantly at the ceiling, listening, listening carefully and hearing nothing.

Not a wail.
Not a sob.
Not a cry.

A Feast for Lambs

Nothing.

When at last he heard the sound of men marching, he rose slowly and moved to the wall and stared into a street obscured by a stagnant, putrid fog like a swamp. He scrutinized the fog but saw nothing as the faint footsteps gradually receded to silence.

The boy listened for a long time after that, forming in his mind countless scenarios and visions of his mother. In each one she outmaneuvered the crew and found her way back to the attic and helped him down, telling him that they were going to be okay now and that the army was here and that everyone was waiting for him at the police station.

The boy waited there a long while. When his mother never returned, he eventually decided that he needed to leave this attic before he suffocated. Then he thought that maybe suffocating wasn't such a bad thing. He wasn't sure how he felt about anything anymore.

Slowly, he made his way past the bed and to the hole. He removed the blanket and lowered his gaze and found the broken pieces of the ladder on the ground. He closed his eyes for a second and remembered. Then, opening his eyes, he kneeled and carefully lowered himself.

For a long, empty moment the boy dangled from the ceiling. Then he released his hold and tumbled over the sticky floor. When he gathered himself and turned on his belly to stand, he found himself staring at Major in the pale, grey sunlight. He stared right at him, right into his good eye, and he felt the coldness of death in his gaze.

Inwardly, the boy thanked him for all his stories and he prayed that he had somehow found peace in death, though he knew he probably hadn't. With a strange thickness in his throat, he stood and walked toward the door. He paused for a moment. He turned back to Major and stared. Then at last he whispered good-bye to the 'villain' of Trilokpuri and stepped into the thick grey.

Nothing could have prepared the boy for what he saw outside.

As he trudged wearily through the fog, he could see in the pale light the gutted and destroyed homes that had once shimmered with color and life. He could see all the rubble and broken glass and charred stones and bricks, and he couldn't believe this was his colony. He stopped for a moment in front of a home and remembered the mother and her three children. He remembered the laundry and the endless chasing and tickling. He remembered the laughter and the music and the colors.

Gone.

Now he was staring at an empty, smolder-ing shell. He could have been a spectator in a the-atre, watching a movie he wouldn't have been allowed to watch. It felt anything but real.

His eyes moved slowly across the street. Each shattered home the grey fog let him see was like a stab in the heart. After a long, oppressive moment, the boy turned, stared hard into the thick fog, and began a slow, staggering walk to the end of the street.

A Feast for Lambs

On weak, shaking legs, he trudged through a stagnant air heavy with the stench of putrefying flesh and blood. Unable to see five inches in front of him, everything felt surreal.

He would have believed himself in a nightmare if nightmares were this terrifying.
As he inched forward he felt his feet growing heavier and heavier; the soles of his feet were sticking to the ground as though he were walking through a strange mixture of mud and glue.

For a moment the grey fog seemed to come alive as it flowed away from his feet to reveal the thick, putrid, black mixture that carpeted the streets and alleys of the colony. Coagulated blood. Ash. Soot. Kerosene. Clumps of hair. Grime. Bone fragments. Here and there he saw morsels of rotting flesh that gave off a smell of a rotting, dead dog on the side of the road. Only worse--

Worse because he knew the flesh didn't belong to a dog.

The boy stood there staring at the carpet for what felt like forever. Then he began to move again with small, scared steps. He had only taken a few steps when his foot suddenly hit something round and heavy like a head.

He froze.

He didn't want to look down.

He didn't want to see.

But involuntarily his gaze lowered slowly.

When his eyes reached his foot, his stomach dropped as he found himself staring at a ball made out of turbans and chunnies and pieces of Punjabi dresses. Only now the improvised ball was a foul, turbid color as it had soaked in the fetid brown and black fluids carpeting the street.

The boy stared at the ball and remembered and wanted to cry but had no more tears to shed. He knelt slowly. He grabbed the ball despite the black, liquid coating. He even tried to lift it but found it was stuck to the ground in dry, gore like glue.

With a sudden prickling feeling in his lips, he pulled his hand away from the ball, feeling something wet in his palm. He turned his hand slowly and observed the black and sticky fluid. He stared at the wetness in his hand and his eyes suddenly widened with disbelief as he seemed to see his hand for the first time in two or three or four days. He wasn't sure.

It was caked in blood that had been impossible to see in the shadows. Mesmerized, he spread his hand so that this black, nameless fluid dripped slowly through the cracks and onto the dark, human carpet. Then his disbelieving eyes slowly followed up his arms. His sleeves were stained with indescribable colors, different shades of blood, grime, urine, and excrement.

He stopped breathing.

He didn't want to look at the rest of his kurta, but he had to.

He rose slowly in the pale light as his disbelieving eyes absorbed every inch of his kurta pajama. Not an inch had been spared. He was covered head to foot in the blood and gore of his people. He was covered head to foot in the destroyed hopes and dreams of an entire generation. He was covered head to foot in pure death.

He stared at one hand, then the other. He touched his face and felt the dry, caked blood and grime and knew his face was covered, too.

Suddenly he closed his eyes and felt the pins and needles.

After a long moment he opened his eyes and took small, hesitant steps into the living nightmare. With each step, the fog revealed a new horror. Row after row of charred limbs strewn over the ungodly carpet, some rotten, some burning, all silent. Piles of rubble and scalped heads and small, smoldering fires. Smoke curled, twisted and filled the dead colony. Flakes of ash fell from the sky like snow.

Step by step the boy moved through the thick, grey fog, stepping over things he couldn't see and didn't want to think about anymore. Then he suddenly stopped and scrutinized the grey. In the pale light he saw a burning limb sticking out of a pile of bodies that looked like a gnarled tree.

The pins and needles began to spread up his face and down his neck and into his limbs. Soon his entire soul vibrated in recognition of what his heart couldn't even begin to imagine or understand. His eyes widened and vibrated with what he could not even begin to control. It was as though his entire soul understood that it was in the presence of something incompressible.

Something very real.

Something very pure.

Something very evil.

Each detail suddenly magnified and the

high-pitched buzzing noise began in his head, and the boy attempted to block his ears without being able to block out the buzzing. The high-pitched buzzing just intensified with every attempt he made, as though it were coming from another place or dimension.

Now his entire body buzzed and vibrated as though his soul wanted to escape from his body. Every vibration multiplied level upon level a strange awareness of a presence only his soul recognized. Then all at once the buzzing stopped with a vision that the fog revealed for an instant. The vision could have been real or it could have been a hallucination. Through the fog the boy saw someone.

A little boy or girl standing in front of a burning body.

Maybe half his size.

Maybe half his age.

The fog suddenly thickened again as if to block his path, but the boy wanted to know if what he had seen was real. Was alive. With his whole body vibrating with the incomprehensible, he staggered forward.

With every inch the fog seemed to grow thicker and thicker, and gradually he became aware of something else, and that something else clutched his heart and began to squeeze and just wouldn't let go.

At last he reached the place where he had seen the silhouette. He swiped the fog away to gradually reveal a little girl staring hypnotically at a burning body.

A Feast for Lambs

After a moment she turned to regard the boy. Covered in ash and grime and soot, she didn't smile or react to his presence. She just stared at him with the same swollen, exhausted eyes. Then, at last, she broke the silence. In a barely audible, crackling whisper she said:

"I'm lost…"

The boy looked at her and nodded wearily.

He didn't know what to say, but he felt as she did. Very lost. Lost and alone. The little girl then approached him and wrapped her arms around his waist. With her touch, the pins and needles began to dissipate and feeling began to return to his heavy limbs, but something dark still clutched hard at his heart and refused to release him.

After a long moment, the little girl released the boy and took a small step back. She stared at his hand, stared past the blood and grime and she touched his kara. She looked up and her eyes spoke to him and the boy understood right away.

Without a word, he kneeled down and took her in his arms. He held her tight and stood slowly. She leaned her head against his neck. Then he turned toward the thickening grey and continued to walk into the unknown, feeling a terrible, unrelenting pain in his chest.

As he carried the little girl through the fog he suddenly understood what it was that had taken hold of his heart.

It was the very thing his ancestors had fought against every time they unsheathed their kirpans to protect the rights and freedoms of the oppressed.

It was the very thing that not only made oppression possible, but gave life, courage and strength to tyrants everywhere.

It was the very thing that fueled the machine and made the living nightmare reality.

And now this thing, this terrible and despicable thing, was all around him. Above him. Below him. Beside him. Inside him. It was perfect, and it was complete. It was unforgiving, and it was oppressive. And as the young lion and lioness disappeared into the thick grey jungle, a silence that had never known the song of life
swallowed them whole.